Bunny Mitchell lived                    ......ca for
several years before returning to England in
1998. She now lives in Sussex where she has
grown to love the South Downs and the history
of its people. Her novels encompass the
folklores of the region and the colourful Sussex
sayings that are in danger of dying out.

For many years Bunny Mitchell has
encouraged and helped many to write their
autobiographies. She now runs a successful
writing group.

with best wishes
Bunny Mitchell.

Also by Bunny Mitchell

The Farthing Mark

# A
# MAGPIE
# MOURNING

One for sorrow, two for joy,
Three for a girl, four for a boy,
Five for silver, six for gold,
Seven for a secret never to be told.
Eight for a wish, nine for a kiss,
Ten for a marriage never to be old.

(Old English rhyme for counting magpies)

**LP**
Luton Publications

Published in the United Kingdom
by Luton Publications

© 2010 Bunny Mitchell

A CIP record of this book is available from the
British Library

ISBN 9 7809545168 2 6

This novel is a work of fiction. Characters and
names are the product of the author's imagination.
Any resemblance to anybody, living or dead, is
entirely coincidental.

Cover Design by Rhett Thompson

Printed and bound in the United Kingdom
By 4edge Ltd, Hockley, Essex.

To Mark and Timea
With so much love

# CHAPTER ONE

Elizabeth was to remember that bright May morning when her father came down to breakfast with a gleam in his eye and an air of barely suppressed excitement. He looked, for all the world, like a small boy with a secret.

James Gilbert tucked a napkin into his high starched collar and rested his hands on his vast stomach. Elizabeth looked fondly into the shining, well-scrubbed face that beamed at her from across the table.

"You look happy this morning," she observed, pouring him a cup of tea from the silver teapot. "I'm surprised, considering you were called out in the middle of the night."

"Yes, it was young Crawley."

"Ah…. I heard someone bawling down the speaking tube but I couldn't make out who it was. What was the matter?"

"He came for his father. Old Crawley had been up with one of his heifers, tripped over

1

something in the dark and broke his leg. I had to set it, of course, and I don't mind telling you he made enough noise to wake the dead. Wanted to know then if I was expecting payment for inflicting pain on him!" He laughed as he spooned three lots of sugar in his tea.

"That accounts for the sack of potatoes and a dozen eggs that Aggie found on the doorstep this morning."

"The potatoes, yes, but I expect the eggs'll be from Mrs Norris. I called on her yesterday. She'll have a wretched existence when her husband's gone. He's only hanging on by his eyelids, you know, and her expecting an increase any day…. Be so good as to pass the butter, my dear."

James Gilbert was a busy doctor, genial and popular with the villagers, although how much his popularity could be credited to his bedside manner and how much to his willingness to accept a sack of potatoes, a joint of pork or a fowl or two in lieu of payment was a matter of speculation.

It was while he was attacking an ample portion of ham – payment for lancing a rather nasty boil – that he paused to point his fork at her and say, "I'm taking you out this morning, Elizabeth. I've got a surprise for you." He helped himself to another slice of wheaten loaf and buttered it thickly. "We'll go directly we've finished breakfast."

Fifteen minutes later he was bustling about her, his chin whiskers shaking as he urged her to fetch her bonnet.

"But where are we going?" she asked, not for the first time. "Will you not tell me or even drop a hint? What's the big secret?"

"You'll see. You'll see, all in good time. How goes the enemy?" He pulled a gold watch from his waistcoat pocket. "I have to see Bob Slater this morning. His insides are a fearful mess. There's another that's not long for this world. And then I want to call on Tom Potter, see how his feet are. So if you will finish titivating, we'll be off."

Elizabeth tucked stray tendrils of her honey-coloured hair under her bonnet and fastened it firmly under her chin. "Right, I'm ready. Where is this secret of yours?" she asked as she climbed up to sit beside her father in the high gig.

As they rode by the village green, Emily Waters, sweeping the path outside her stores, straightened her back to lift a hand in acknowledgement, and the women at the well paused in their gossip and turned to watch the gig's sedate progress. Her father waved to them all; he was in fine fettle today.

They crossed a stone bridge, humpty-backed, that straddled the river and turned left into a narrow lane, puddled by yesterday's rain.

From here they could see across the water to the back of the Scarlet Arms. Kegs were stacked against the wall and Wilfred Hoskins, the Innkeeper, was rolling one towards the door. His wife, in a vast white apron, watched, hands on hips, her head nodding at him as she directed operations. Elizabeth smiled. Poor Wilfred; it was obvious who ruled the roost in that establishment.

For a while they rode without speaking. The air was fresh after the recent rains and Elizabeth was content to enjoy the journey, the sun warm on her face and a breeze ruffling the curls that escaped her bonnet. A cuckoo called from the vivid green leaves of a chestnut tree and May flowers covered the countryside.

They passed the lane that led up to Marsden Hall, overlooking the valley and a landmark for miles. It was a handsome Georgian house and had been owned by the Marsdens for five generations; a dignified show of symmetry under a tiled roof, set in extensive landscaped grounds that were well tended by a small army of gardeners.

As the local doctor, Elizabeth's father had often been called up to the Hall and when younger she had accompanied him, so she knew the layout of the land well. To the right of the house were tranquil gardens leading down to the river, full of lavender and roses, herbaceous borders and apple trees. On the other side, close-trimmed lawns, where she had thrown grain to the peacocks, and an ancient chestnut tree. There, on sunny afternoons, tea was served from a silver tea service together with strawberries and scones and little sandwiches, all laid out on snowy white linen. Elizabeth had seen croquet played there and heard ladies fill the air with their genteel laughter while, in the house, kitchen maids with coarse work-reddened hands scoured greasy pans and dreamed their dreams.

Once, she had even been invited to a birthday party. It was all very grand, but she preferred the kitchens where she had waited for her father and where the cook, Mrs Tatlow, had fed her cherry buns and apple pie.

Elizabeth looked at her father. "So we are not going up to the Hall. There's nobody else along here to see apart from the Tulleys. How is Molly getting along these days? I don't know how they cope without a man about the place. It must be hard. Do you know when her baby is due?"

Mrs Tulley had been a widow for many years. Now her daughter was expecting and nothing would persuade Molly to divulge the father's identity. Mrs Tulley had annoyed the doctor for years with her herbal remedies that a lot of the villagers swore by. 'Well, she hadn't been able to cure Molly's problem,' he had caustically remarked when the girl's dilemma had become common knowledge.

"September, I think. That's only what I've heard. They wouldn't consider a doctor's opinion of course, more's the pity, for if they had, when Mr Tulley was taken ill, Mrs Tulley might not be a widow today. I can fight illness, Elizabeth, but I can't fight ignorance."

A mile upstream was a wooden bridge, precarious and creaking, but it had stood there for years, as long as Elizabeth could remember, and borne the weight of numerous carts going to and from market. Once anyone crossed over and set foot on the other side, they were on Matt Fuller's land. It was just a small farm that he had; sixty acres given over to wheat and pasture for his twenty-five cows. It had been his father's farm before him and his father's before that and no doubt would be handed down to the son his wife, Maisie, had just produced.

The thought of visiting the farm and seeing the new baby made Elizabeth smile, although she wondered why they had taken this roundabout route instead of the more direct way on the south side of the river. The lane, that had continued along the same level, now curved away from the river and started to climb. Elizabeth realised that her father didn't intend taking her to the farm either.

Plucking at his sleeve, she pressed him again. "It's not the Hall and not the Tulley's and not the Fuller's farm.    Come on, Papa, don't keep me in suspense. What's this surprise you have for me?"

James smiled too. He was enjoying his secret and happy to see Elizabeth's eager face. She had grown into a beautiful woman with her fine creamy skin and magnificent eyes, bright with intelligence and the colour of a summer sky. He loved her dearly.

"You'll see. You'll see right this minute. Whoa there, Jess. Whoa there!"

James pulled on the reins and the gig came to an abrupt stop alongside a dry-stone wall and a gate that had long parted company with its top hinge. It hung drunkenly across the path that led to an old cottage. Dun-coloured thatch fringed the upper windows like unkempt urchin's hair. Elizabeth thought it looked like a child's drawing with its central front door and four square windows.

"Why have we stopped here? Who are we visiting? I don't think I know...." She was speaking to his back as he climbed down from the gig.

"All in good time. Come now," he said, extending his hand to assist her.

She was curious about the people who lived here, so far out from the village, but further observation told her that the place must be empty. Weeds grew up between cracks in the path and the green paint on the front door

7

had peeled. The whole garden showed signs of neglect. It was completely overgrown. In places, the grasses were almost waist high and poppies nodded their scarlet heads in the breeze. A window to the right of the door had broken and shards of glass lay on the sill, catching the morning sunlight.

James opened the unlocked door and stood aside. She hesitated and he grinned. Her raised eyebrows asked of him a question; one that he would not answer.

Lifting her skirts, she stepped inside and found herself in a small hall facing a staircase, its wooden stairs steep and narrow with a handrail going up the wall. On either side was a closed door. She chose the one to the right and, lifting the thumb-latch, entered a small room. It had a fireplace with a high mantelpiece set into the wall opposite the window with the broken panes. Leaves had blown in and littered the stone-flagged floor. Unfurnished, there was little to see so she turned and went through the hall to the room on the other side.

She ducked under a low cross-beam and found herself in the kitchen; a room the same size as the first, smelling just as damp and musty. Bars of the sun's light lay across the floor from the front window. Another window, now in shadow, looked out to the back garden. Underneath this window, a broken chair lay on its side with a fly-spotted mirror in a mildewed frame propped against it.

On the floor, in the back corner, she discovered the body of a dead bird. It lay on its side with an oddly twisted wing and staring eyes. Elizabeth nudged it with her foot, not knowing why she did so. She knew it was dead and could now see that its body was full of maggots. She wrinkled her nose and turned away. Poor, silly bird, she thought. It must have come down the chimney and been unable to get out.

James hovered in the doorway waiting for her to say something. When she remained silent he asked, "Well? What do you think? It could be made very cosy couldn't it? We could have one of those cooking ranges put in." With a sweep of his hand he indicated the vast fireplace topped by a wooden mantel that was on a level with the crown of his head.

"And there are two bedrooms above; you haven't seen those yet. That's all we'd need... and there's an outhouse just here. We could make it into a scullery."

He opened a door next to the hearth to reveal a small room, a cramped, narrow place with a sink and a few shelves. A zinc bath hung on a hook from the wall and beside it a grubby rag, dry and stiff, suspended from a rusty nail.

"What are you trying to say, Papa?" She

couldn't believe what he was suggesting and yet she hadn't seen him as excited about anything since he had bought the gig three years earlier. "You can't be serious. Are you trying to tell me that you want us to come and live here? It must be two miles or more from the village. It... it needs so much work done on it. And we would be so isolated." She could think of a hundred reasons why it wouldn't be a good idea.

Her father's arms went about her shoulders as he steered her into the garden. "But that's the very reason why I've bought it, my dear."

At this, her head jerked round to his face, searching for some sign that he was joking. When she saw that he was in earnest her mouth fell open. She stared at him in surprise.

"For thirty years I've been at the beck and call of everybody in Barkwell. I want to spend the rest of my days quietly. I want to walk the downs and grow vegetables and... and just be away from... from things. I've had enough of people with their bad heads and bunions and everything in between." He raised his arms sideways and let them fall, and then he nodded his big floppy face at her. "And you know, if I stayed in the village I'd never be able to retire. Oh no, they'd still come asking.

"I know Doctor Rudd will be taking over the practice, but he's a young man, with new-fangled ideas, and folk prefer the old ways. They don't take kindly to change, indeed, they don't. I'm not saying there is anything wrong with progress and young Rudd seems a fine competent fellow, but it will take a while for them down there to take to him. And in the meantime, who will they be wanting to come to, eh? Eh? Good old Doctor Gilbert, that's who. You mark my words if they don't. Well, I'm telling you, I'm not as young as I was and I've had enough. I want to be... I want to be quiet."

He turned away, towards the front garden, and it came to her that she had never heard her father talk about... well, talk about feelings before. He had never given her any indication of what he wanted for himself in life and she, for her part, had never considered what his needs might be. She didn't know what to say to him; he had taken her by surprise. Well, he'd said he had a surprise for her this morning and he hadn't been wrong, had he?

For some moments she stood gazing at his broad back as he leant on the garden wall looking out to the river, but then she turned and picked her way down to the bottom of the garden.

There, in the fly-buzzing stillness, she found the privy, hidden discreetly behind a laurel bush. It had collapsed into a pile of rotting wood. Nearby, was an ancient apple tree, and in the long grass beneath, a dusty geranium struggled to survive in an overturned pot.

Elizabeth reaching up, rested her hand on the tree's gnarled bough, and looked about her. The idea of coming here was such a sudden one. Her father had sprung the news and left her with her mind racing in several directions all at the same time.

There would be a lot of work to do on both the house and the garden. The roof needed to be re-thatched and the gate mended. New panes of glass would have to be put in, the kitchen door replaced and here, where she stood, the stone wall had fallen down and was reduced to a mere heap of rubble.

They'd have to lay Aggie off. She wouldn't want to come all the way up here, especially with her feet the way they were. But there wouldn't be the work up here anyway, not with it only having the two bedrooms and the parlour and kitchen downstairs. She would miss the house in Barkwell with its elegant dining room and the sunny morning room where she liked to sew. Well, they wouldn't need all their furniture, that was for sure. They would have to get rid of a lot of it. And the piano? Would the piano fit into this tiny parlour? She didn't think she could live without her music.

And that was another thing. What were

they going to do with themselves out here? Papa had his plans, he'd worked it all out, but what about her? She would have her books. Oh yes, she would always make sure she had her books. But what else would she have?

She wouldn't even have Ruth for company. Ruth was the parson's daughter and the two of them had been educated together at the parsonage.

'Poor mites! Neither fish nor fowl nor good red herring,' she had heard the parsonage cook remark. And she had been quite right. Doctors and parsons stood in a class of their own within the hierarchy of the village. They were neither gentry nor were they village folk, so Ruth and Elizabeth were thrown together. Not only were they the best of friends, sharing the common bond of both being motherless, but they were each other's only friend.

Returning to the house, Elizabeth climbed the stairs, creaking under her weight, to find the two small bedrooms. Both had sloping ceilings with dark wooden beams. In one, among the dead flies accumulating on the sill of the diamond-paned window under the eaves, she found a blue ribbon, dusty and faded with age. From the way it was tied she supposed it must have fallen from a little girl's plait. Elizabeth picked it up, putting two fingers through the loop where the plait would have been. She gazed absently at the ribbon, wondering who had worn it, and tried to imagine that this cottage had once been alive with the sound of children.

She bent to look through the grimy window and saw that her father was as she had left him. With a sigh she dropped the ribbon and, dusting her hands, went to join him.

On the way home, James was full of his plans for the future. He was going to have a lean-to built for Jess and the gig and he told her that the field to the side, that was backed by a hazel coppice, came with the cottage and would be ideal for grazing the horse. In the back garden he would plant raspberry canes and roses, sunflowers and sweet peas.

Elizabeth scarcely listened. She was too full of her own thoughts. In her mind's eye she could still see the little bird on the kitchen floor. That is how I shall be, she thought with gathering alarm. Like that dead bird had been; trapped with no way of escape.

# CHAPTER TWO

The cottage was transformed during the weeks that followed. Although still full of misgivings, Elizabeth was pleased to witness her father's enthusiasm and tried to match it with positive thoughts. She told herself that two miles was no distance, no distance at all, that they had the gig and she would be able to enjoy the walk on fine days. The exercise would be good for her. She could visit Ruth and attend church on Sundays. It would be peaceful there and nobody would disturb that peace with frantic knockings at all hours of the day and night.

But underneath it all was the uncomfortable feeling that she was only trying to convince herself. She wanted to be pleased and happy for her father's sake, but for herself it was impossible and so, no matter how hard she tried, she could not shake the air of despondency that threatened to engulf her.

Most days they took the gig and spent a few hours sweeping and cleaning or measuring for curtains and furniture. James cleared weeds from the garden path and took delight in simple tasks about the place.

The new iron range came, one windy day, and it took three men to bring it from the cart and install it in the kitchen fireplace. There, resplendent in its newness, it dominated the small room.

James rushed about without his frock coat, his shirt sleeves rolled up and his gold watch chain gleaming across his straining waistcoat. He supervised those that needed no supervision and was untiring in his eagerness to get things done. Elizabeth had never seen him so animated; flapping his arms and joking with the men.

On the day that John Holland arrived to repair the roof, Elizabeth, in an old faded dress and with dirt under her fingernails, was in the garden trying to clear a patch of earth for pansies and forget-me-nots.

"Who is this coming, Papa?" she asked as a cart, piled high with straw, lurched to a halt by the garden gate.

James turned from oiling the latch of the front door. "Ah! Now he, my dear, is John Holland, the man who is going to repair the roof."

"I haven't seen him before. He's not from the village."

"No, he's from Chillingford. Matt Fuller recommended him. He's done quite a bit of work for Matt about the farm. Thatched his ricks last year so I'm told."

Together they watched the man jump from the cart and stride up the garden path; a tall man with a fine head of curling black hair. As he neared them Elizabeth could see that he had dark eyes set beneath heavy, dark brows, but what drew her attention was that while most of the young men she knew sported long drooping walrus moustaches – hoping, no doubt, that it made them look older – this man was clean shaven.

"Good mornin' sir... Miss," he greeted them, smiling broadly. "You be the doctor? Doctor Gilbert? If so, I've come to mend that roof of your'n."

James beamed at him. "Yes. Yes, you've come to the right place."

"I'd better get started then."

John Holland gave Elizabeth a cursory nod and went about his task of unloading the wheat straw, a ladder and various odd-looking tools that he took to the rear of the cottage.

Later, when Elizabeth had finished her work, she took a book and settled herself beneath the light-dappled leaves of the apple tree. She leaned against the trunk, feeling the rough bark through the thin material of her dress, enjoying the shade after the heat of the sun. But she didn't read her book. Instead, she watched the man who was up on the roof removing the rotten thatch. There was something about him; not just his good looks and ready smile. It was.... What was it? Perhaps it was his aliveness, she thought. He was certainly a man who gave the impression of extraordinary vitality.

John Holland was twenty-five and lived with his sister; just the two of them since their ma and pa and brother, Jed, had died of the fever twelve years earlier. Florrie had been fifteen at the time, working at the candle factory, and he had been taken on by old Tom Harris to help with the thatching, so they had been spared the hardships of the workhouse. They could manage the two shillings a week for the one-up-and-one-down cottage that had once housed the five of them.

He minded well the times when it had been hard though and many a day he'd nicked a cabbage or two from Barrett's fields. They'd scratched along somehow. Once, he'd done a bit of poaching but that was a mug's game. He would have got a month in quod if they'd caught him, and they nearly did once.

In recent years there had been no need

anyway. They managed well enough. There was always work a-plenty for a man who could turn his hand to most things. There was the thatching, and then he'd get taken on at harvest times, besides all the casual labouring jobs he could pick up.

Most men of his age were settled down and married by now, with a brood of children as well, but not him. No, he liked to be free. He had enough money for ale and baccy and a woman when he wanted. Not that he needed money for a woman. They always said he was such a charming bugger, said they couldn't resist him. It made him laugh, that, but he wasn't complaining. He'd be a fool if he did. No, he had no problem with women.

Unless you counted his sister, Florrie. Florrie was a problem. She had her good faults but he sometimes found it hard to believe that they had sprung from the same parents. As alike as chalk and cheese they were; in looks and in temperament.

Florrie was sharp-featured. And sharp-tongued when the mood was on her. What was more, she was a bit gridgen when it came to meals. It was a thing that allus lay cantankerous atween them. But, he'd certain sure found a way round that. He still hadn't told her that he's had a raise some time back, ever since he started going out on his own with the thatch. So when he brassed up on a

Saturday night he still gave her the same amount, and the difference he kept to supplement the meagre fare she gave him. A pie or a bun from the corner shop usually kept him going.

But he couldn't go on like this for ever. He knew that, in her own way, Florrie was fond of him, and he supposed she'd got into the habit of being a bit close with the money since those hard early days. No, he wanted more from life but at this moment he wasn't sure what form that 'more' would take.

He'd been working here for five days now and each day the doctor's lass had taken a book and sat under the apple tree. But she hadn't read the book. He would be an adle-headed fellow to think otherwise. No. she'd been watching him. He knew by the tilt of her head. The way she'd got her head pushed back and held her book so high, well, it wasn't natural. And she hadn't turned the page above once or twice. He knew that, for a fact, because he had been watching her.

All the while he had been removing the old thatch and as he gathered and sorted the soaked wheat-straw into yealms and assembled them in the yoke, she had been watching him. And while he had been putting on his leather knee pads, and the one that protected his leaning arm, and carried the yoke and cradle that contained his knives and shearing hooks up the ladder, he had been studying her.

She had a trim little figure and, by God, she had a way of moving that caught his attention! He had thought she was a bit prim and tip-tongued at first and hadn't taken much notice of her but there was something about her that interested him.

It was the way she looked at him with those purty blue eyes – the self-same colour of a Dunnock's eggs they were – and instead of lowering them modestly when he caught her looking, she would look straight back at him. Not in a suggestive way; not a bold look, as some of the lasses in Chillingford gave a man they fancied, but at the same time not what you'd expect from a doctor's daughter.

John pulled his shirt off and taking the cover from the well, let down the pail and drew up some water. The day had been dry and dusty. When he had slaked his thirst he scooped the water up with both hands and splashed his face.

And as he combed his wet fingers through his hair, he turned and saw a movement at the kitchen window. She was looking at him again. He wondered what she was thinking. Well, I'll give you something to think about, he thought, and smiled to himself as he strode towards the front door.

She knew. Somehow she knew it would only

be a matter of time and she questioned her sanity. What was it about this man that attracted her so strongly? She had been watching him at the well and had seen him removing his shirt, seen the sweat glistening on his sun-browned skin. He fascinated her and when he turned and saw her observing him, she knew she should have come away from the window. But she hadn't. She must have taken leave of her senses.

He stood in the doorway. She turned to him, wondering what he wanted, what he would say, but he remained, silently standing there, the low sun of afternoon silhouetting his muscular frame. A fly buzzed against a window pane. From the back garden she could hear the thud of mallet on stone as the wall was repaired.

John Holland, with drops of water still on his face, took a step forward. She looked up at him and the breath caught in her throat as he bent to kiss her half-opened lips. It was a soft kiss, a restrained kiss, but all the more disturbing for its gentleness.

And then, without a word, he turned and left the room.

Theirs was a strange courtship, she thought. John found ways of making himself useful to James. 'Would you like me to clear that long grass at the bottom of the garden, Doc? I could come over on my day off.' Or another time: 'I could give that door a lick of  paint on Saturday if you like.' James always agreed and John contrived, in this way, to prolong his employment for another six weeks.

And such was James enthusiasm to complete the renovations, and his thoughts in that direction so all encompassing, that he didn't notice if Elizabeth found work to do in the front garden when John was hanging the gate, or that the apple tree was a favourite spot to sit when John was clearing weeds there or painting the newly built privy . Nor did he notice the extra care she took with her hair or the flowers she pinned to the bodice of her dress.

On the Friday  that James spent with the new doctor, handing over his records and acquainting him with various aspects of the practice, Elizabeth found herself wandering about the house. She could neither settle with her books nor her sewing but sat at the piano, rifling  listlessly through her music. She started to play only to abandon the idea after just a few chords.

She had felt like this for days. Common sense told her that she would be more comfortable if she remained indoors but after lunch, although the heat was sweltering, she decided to walk up to the cottage with some curtains she wanted to hang.

But once there she couldn't be bothered so she left the package of curtains on the bottom step of the stairs and stepped outside again. She would hang them another day when it wasn't so hot.

After all the weeks of activity, of repairing and building, of men whistling and calling to each other and hammers banging, the place seemed strangely quiet. James had had a lean-to stable built. It was sited along the east side of the cottage so that it would receive the benefit of what sun was available and was divided into two sections. One part would be a stable for Jess, with a divided door that enabled the upper section to be hooked back, and the other part, much bigger with wide double doors, was to house the gig and all the stable and garden tools. It was considerably larger than originally intended but John had suggested to James that he have it made as big as space allowed. 'You never know what you might need to store,' he had said and James agreed.

"Good fellow that John Holland," he remarked to Elizabeth one day. "Full of ideas and always willing to work."

James had insisted that the stable be made of local stone so that it blended with the cottage walls and it looked well, thatched as it was, to match the main roof. It was pleasing to see the results of their labours; all the garden walls had been repaired, the weeds pulled from between the stones and the crazy paving that led up to the front door. The latter had been replaced, as had the garden gate, and both painted a primrose yellow. The new thatch gave the place a neat and cared for appearance and for the first time Elizabeth could imagine living there.

She latched the gate, crossed the lane and with her skirts held high, carefully picked her way through the long grass down to the river. On impulse, she gathered an armful of meadow sweet, softly humming to herself. There was no wind today and the sun shone brilliantly in a clear blue sky; the air heavy with the scents of summer. Perspiration beaded her upper lip and wisps of hair stuck damply to her forehead and to the back of her neck. Taking a handkerchief from the pocket of her skirt, she mopped her face and thought to rest a few minutes under a tree on the grassy bank. She could hear the water whispering its way downstream and watched a tortoiseshell butterfly, attracted by the strong sweet scent of a clump of ragwort, flit among the yellow flowers. How peaceful it was; she would rest here for five minutes before she walked home. She took off her bonnet and sat with the frothy bunches of cream flowers in her lap.

She must have dozed because when she

opened her eyes he was standing there. He towered over her, a red kerchief tied at his neck, his shirtsleeves rolled to the elbows and a wide grin spreading over his face.

As she scrambled to her feet the flowers scattered and fell in the rough grass where they lay unheeded. And like a startled fawn she stood poised for flight, wondering what she should do.

His voice was gentle when he spoke as if he sensed her indecision. "Don't go. I'm sorry if I startled you." He looked about him. "It's a middlin' fine day isn't it?"

"Yes. Yes, it is…. Was my father expecting you?"

"No. I just came up on the off-chance, like. Got a day or two to spare. Wondered if he had anything for me."

He threw himself down where she had a moment ago sat, and cheerfully selected a blade of grass to chew. Elizabeth watching him, liked the way his glossy dark hair curled at the nape of his neck.

With the grass between his teeth he looked up at her and smiled. "Sit down again. You don't have to go a-rushing off do you? I'm quite 'armless you know."

He patted the ground beside him and moved some of the strewn flowers aside. She hesitated a moment and then carefully sat some distance from him, her back straight and her hands clasped in her lap.

"How long do you think it will be before you move in?" he asked.

"Perhaps in two weeks. Most of the work has been done, as you know, but the furniture has to be brought up." In her nervousness her words gathered momentum like a stone rolling downhill. "I don't know quite how it will all fit in. I am sure my piano will take up all the space in the parlour; there will be little room for anything else. Papa has promised me I shall have it though...." Suddenly aware that she was prattling, her voice trailed away. She turned her head to look over the water, squinting her eyes against the glare of the sun.

"I didn't know you were musical. I like to play a bit meself. Not the piana. I've got a fiddle," he said. "Used to be me pa's. He used to give us a bit of a tune; played for his ale down at the Farmer's Arms. That's an ale house at the end of our street. Before he died that was. He could set all the folk's feet a-tapping when he played his old tunes. Taught me to play, he did. Me brother, Jed, he didn't care for learnin' it. Nor me, come to that. I didn't want to learn at first neither," he said and then added with a touch of pride and a nod of his head in her direction, "I can't read music but I've got a good ear."

She was watching him now, intrigued that this rough man with his hard-skinned hands could play a musical instrument. "I didn't want to learn to play at first either, but my mother insisted, and I'm glad that she did now. I couldn't imagine life without my music. It's a great comfort isn't it?"

"I don't know about that. It wasn't much comfort to me ma when I was doing the learnin'!" He laughed and she smiled at him.

"Does she like to listen to you now?"

He frowned and his voice was quiet when he replied. "Me ma's dead. She died along with me pa and me brother some time ago. Fever it was. Only got the one sister now."

"Oh, I'm sorry." Elizabeth tried to change the subject. "Does your sister play? What does she like to do?"

She marvelled at the situation. Here she sat making polite conversation as if she were in a drawing room and not, as she was, sitting unchaperoned on a river bank with this strangely disturbing man.

"What Florrie? No, she doesn't play. I don't rightly know what she do like really. She's one of those people that's up on the roof one minute and down the well the next. Not much good having a fiddle in either place, is there?" He laughed a great belly laugh at his own joke. He threw his head back, his eyes narrowed, the skin at their edges crinkling and his mouth opening wide to show his strong white teeth, bright against his sun-browned face.

She though he was a fine man. He made her feel alive and light-hearted and she wanted the afternoon to go on for ever.

Chewing all the while on his blade of grass, he told her about his family. He made her laugh telling of escapades he'd had with his brother and of how his ma had once been chased down the lane by a pig.

They sat at the water's edge watching a group of swifts flying to and fro, hurtling themselves across the sky. Yes. Yes, I like this man, she thought. More than like him. And she wondered what he was thinking behind the laughter and his easy manner.

She knew now what had lain behind her restlessness that morning. She had been hoping he would come. Had he come to see her father? Or had he, perhaps, come to see her? What was he really thinking?

He never kissed her again. Not once, since that day in the empty kitchen, had he tried to kiss her and he couldn't understand hisself because he was usually a man who took what advantage he could in any situation. But Elizabeth was different.

He wasn't quite sure of the exact moment when the idea had dawned on him, but the more he thought about it, the more it appealed to him. If he could get her to marry him then he'd be set up for life. The old boy couldn't live for ever and with no family to make a claim the cottage could one day be his.

And another thing; old Tom wasn't getting any younger and he'd hinted more than once that the business would go to him. There was hazel a-plenty to be found in the wood behind the cottage. It was all common land so he'd be able to help hisself to all he be a-needing for making spars and sways to hold down the thatch. Some thatchers used willow but he didn't think you could beat nut hazel. He could just picture hisself with his own cottage, working for hisself with the thatching, and all that hazel on his doorstep! Surely that was a good omen, all that hazel. Everything he could want in one fell swoop. He'd have to play his cards right though. Mustn't frighten her off.

And so he set about courting her. Without anything said, they were both aware that her father would be opposed to the friendship. Elizabeth slipped away when her father was busy, and when John was up at the cottage, putting the finishing touches to the place, they were careful to conceal their growing friendship.

How it happened, he hardly knew, but as the days passed John gradually became aware that it wasn't just the cottage he was after but Elizabeth, for herself. He realised that, for the first time in his life, he had met someone that he wanted. Really wanted. Not just for the night or a casual affair but for always. Good God! I'm in love, he thought and marvelled that he, John Holland, the womaniser, the man who prided himself for not being caught by a bit of skirt, had fallen.

The furniture was brought up one morning on a day that threatened rain. Elizabeth was fearful of the piano being damaged if it got wet, but a greater problem was to manoeuvre it into the parlour.

It wouldn't go through the front door and round the corner into the room because the hallway was too small. Eventually they brought it through the kitchen and straight across the hall into the parlour. Placed against the side wall, it dwarfed the room but Elizabeth was delighted to see it safely there.

The grandfather clock, made of walnut and parquetry, that James wouldn't part with because it had been in the family for generations, was too tall for the low-ceilinged room so the feet were removed. They stood it by the fireplace where it vied with the piano for attention.

By the end of the day everything had been installed and James, in a munificent mood, paid the men handsomely for all their work.

And as the sun was setting in a mackerel

sky, he waved them goodbye and turned to Elizabeth with a satisfied smile. "Well, it's been a lot of work but we've done it. I think we'll be very happy here, don't you? Very snug and cosy; just the two of us. What more could we want?".

Elizabeth didn't answer. She knew what she wanted but she had an uneasy feeling that it wouldn't be a straight furrow to hoe.

# CHAPTER THREE

James had had a visitor and he was furious.

"Over my dead body," he roared, "will you marry that… that good-for-nothing!" His fist came down on the table, the teacups rattled in their saucers and Elizabeth brought her head back with a jerk.

"He's nothing but a common labourer. What kind of life do you think you would have with him, my girl? He can't earn above ten shillings a week. How far do you think that will get you?"

Elizabeth opened her mouth to speak but her father didn't give her a chance. "And don't think you could come running to me to help you out. I'd… I'd wash my hands of you if you took up with the likes of him. He's got a nerve coming here, bold as brass, asking for your hand."

Outwardly composed, Elizabeth sat

with her back straight and her hands clasped firmly in her lap, but her heart was thumping.

"And what's come over you, girl, thinking you'd be happy with his kind? You, who have been educated and brought up for something better. Mark my words, no good would come of it. You'd regret it for the rest of your days."

He paused for breath and Elizabeth took the opportunity. "But Papa, he's a good man. You said so yourself when he was working here and I'm sure if you got to —"

"And where would you live? Have you thought of that? By all accounts he's living with his sister at the moment over Chillingford way, but there'd be no room for you there. And if there was it wouldn't be anything like that to which you have been accustomed…. And it's no good thinking he can move in here. He won't step over my doorstep again; I've made sure of that. I've sent him packing. Oh yes I have. My best advice to you, Elizabeth, is to forget about the scoundrel. He's all wrong for you."

"How can you say he's all wrong for me?" Her eyes narrowed as she pushed her chair away and took a step towards him. The normally meek Elizabeth, for once, was standing up to her father. "I suppose you'd like me to marry that insipid Arthur Maybury. Well, I'm telling you, if I can't marry John I'll never marry anybody else!"

"Then you'll die an old maid, Elizabeth Gilbert, for you won't get my permission to marry him!"

It occurred to her that maybe it was not only paternal solicitude that made her father take against John. She suspected that he wouldn't take kindly to her marrying Arthur, the son of his best friend, or any other man for that matter, but looked forward to her being a comfort to him in his old age.

The tears started in Elizabeth's eyes and her lip began to tremble. She turned away from her father and stood at the window seeing, but not seeing, the winter-bare garden, the river or the rolling downs beyond. She clenched her teeth and willed herself not to cry. Mama had impressed on her that tears were an indulgence that should be reserved for private moments. She wished that Mama was still alive. Mama would have understood, she was sure, and would have helped her to persuade Papa. But it was no good wishing for the impossible. She would have to cope with this herself.

But how could she tell him that the day John Holland had come whistling up the hill with his sun-browned skin and shining black hair, there had been born in her a wanting; a wanting such as she had never known before. No, not ever in her twenty years. It was his vitality, the laughter in his eyes, the swagger in his walk. He gave a fire to her being that she almost blushed to acknowledge.

His very presence gave a lightness to her step and a joy to her soul that was all the more miraculous at a time when she had been attempting to reconcile herself to the bleakness of the years that stretched before her. Endless years of loneliness, out here on the downs, looking after Papa till the end of his days. And what then?

The grandfather clock ticked monotonously. It sounded loud in the otherwise silent room. That is how my life will be, she thought. Like the clock; it will just go on and on… and on.

James saw the slump of her shoulders, the droop of her head and, in profile, her pinched white face. Conscious of the effect his words were having, he sighed, shook his head from side to side and, easing his bulk from the chair, came round the table to where she stood.

He patted her ineffectually on the shoulder and murmured, "It's for the best, my dear…. For the best."

He loved his daughter deeply and it pained him to see her so caught up with this young fellow. He had never denied her anything in all her young life but he couldn't, and wouldn't, stand by and see her throw herself away.

"I'm going out for a while," he said, going

into the hall and opening the door. Dark clouds scudded low across the November sky. "Looks like we're in for some rain. Still the fresh air will do me good. It is not my intention to be long."

Elizabeth didn't answer and he left the cottage, latching the door quietly behind him.

She watched him from the parlour window. With head down, hands clasped behind his back, he looked deep in thought as he made his way down the hill towards the river.

Most of the village turned out for the funeral. Doctor Gilbert had been a popular man and it was a pity, they said, that he had been called to his Maker just as he was set to retire.

At the cottage, after the funeral, his friends squeezed into the parlour, smiled at its quaintness and, with feigned concern, asked Elizabeth what she would do now that she was on her own. Would she return to the village? Did she have a relative with whom she could live?

They looked askance when she told them that she would remain at the cottage; that she had no intention of returning to the village or inflicting herself on some far distant relative. They clicked their tongues and shook their heads, horrified that she would live alone without companion or servant. And as to her reasoning, why, that was beyond their imagining.

Arthur Maybury suggested that he may call. She had always disliked Arthur. He had a washed-out look about him, a vapid face and a strut of pride that she found distasteful. She was polite but firm in her refusal and an affronted Arthur took his leave.

Elizabeth had conducted herself throughout with a grim composure, but the effort drained her and she was glad when they had all left. But what was left?

All that was left was an aching emptiness. Christmas came and went. Ruth invited Elizabeth to join her and her father for dinner but she refused saying she wouldn't be fit company. Ruth understood and didn't press her.

Elizabeth took care of the cottage, glad of her daily chores that helped to fill the long hours, but when they were done there was still endless time to fill. Her music brought her no solace and she wandered aimlessly from room to room, lost in thought.

And all the while she was haunted by the memory of a man with water droplets in his hair, who had stolen a kiss; a man who sat by the river on a fine summer's day and made her laugh. And she was haunted too by the memory of her father's words. 'Over my dead body,' he had said. The way was clear now but the man had gone. And perhaps that was just as well. 'Over my dead body,' he'd said, and if she hadn't upset him by her friendship with John Holland perhaps he wouldn't have gone for a walk. He'd be here today.

When Elizabeth answered the door, that rainy day in February, he was standing there. The rain dripped from his nose and ran in rivulets from his thick hair down his forehead , and his brown corduroy jacket was dark and sodden across the shoulders.

She looked at him in astonishment. It was as if he had been conjured up by her thoughts and if she blinked he would disappear and all that she would see would be the empty path and the dripping chestnut beyond.

John rubbed a hand across his face. "Can I come in a moment?"

"Oh, yes. Yes of course. I'm sorry. Do come in." Mentally she shook herself. "Let me take your jacket. You're soaked."

"Thank you. It was fine when I started out. Never know what the weather's goin' to do this time of year."

She took his jacket with trembling hands and he followed her into the kitchen where she draped it over the back of a chair. He watched her as she opened the door of the range and positioned the chair in front of the fire, fussing with the sleeves and straightening the collar.

"You've made the place very cosy," he observed as his eyes swept the room. They took in the dresser with the blue and white willow-patterned plates neatly arranged on the shelves with five matching cups hanging from hooks in front of them, two Windsor chairs with their embroidered cushions set to each side of the hearth, and the oak table, massive and firm, that dominated the room. On it was a tray, set for one.

"I was sorry to hear about your father. He was a nice old boy, even if he did send me packing."

Looking up, Elizabeth saw him give a rueful smile. She found herself tongue-tied now that he was here. All the conversations she had rehearsed in her mind deserted her and she could only say, "Can I get you something to drink? There's some brandy…. That will warm you. My father has some brandy in the parlour. In a decanter. I'll get you a glass." and without waiting for an answer she left the room only to return, a few moments later, with a glass of brandy on a small oval tray. In pouring, she had spilled some and so she took a cloth and wiped the bottom of the glass before she handed it to him.

"My father always said brandy was a good restorative. That's what he took… when he first became ill. With all his medical knowledge he refused to admit that he was ill.

He wouldn't have the new doctor to attend him, even after he took to his bed, and by the time he did it was too late. Doctor Rudd did his best but it was too late…."

John sat, leaning forward, his forearms resting on his knees, both huge hands holding the delicate crystal brandy balloon. His eyes never left her face.

She didn't seem able to stop herself now that she had started but stood, twisting the cloth in her hands, over and over, while she told him how her father had gone out walking and been caught in a storm. His cold had turned to pneumonia and within two weeks, in spite of her careful nursing, he was dead.

And then she told him something that she hadn't told anyone, not even Ruth.

"I feel so guilty. I wasn't even there when he died. All the nights I had stayed up with him, all the time while the fever was with him, I sat beside his bed. And yet when he died, for his final moment, I wasn't there. I had come downstairs to tend the fire. I was so weary that I sat in the chair. I only meant to sit a short while but I must have fallen asleep." she shook her head as if to shake the memory from her.

"What will you do now?"

"Stay here I suppose."

"But how will you get by? It's a long way from the village."

"I know how to look after the house. As

you know, my mother died when I was young. When I was growing up I spent most of my time in our housekeeper's care. She taught me how to cook and clean. My father used to say it was unbecoming for the daughter of a man of his standing, but I think he was glad that I was happy and not a cause for concern. It will all come in useful now. I can manage the horse, too, and anything else I can learn. My father had such plans. He was going to grow vegetables. He even talked about a few chickens and I'd never seen him so excited…."

He nodded towards the fire. "And what about logs? You'll be needing more logs cut soon, I'll warrant. Will you do that too?"

"Well, I thought… I thought that perhaps I could get one of the boys from the village to come…."

It was difficult to hear her words, she had spoken so quietly. She looked vulnerable and so overwhelmed by everything that he rose and, putting the glass on the table, came to stand beside her.

Mutely she stood, under his silent scrutiny, and then he said, "I could cut the logs for you."

Her spirits lifted at the thought of seeing him again and then reality brought her back to earth. She shouldn't encourage him. She wanted to see him again but her father's words echoed through her mind. 'No good will come of it.'

"It's kind of you but I couldn't expect you to come all the way from Chillingford simply to cut my logs."

He was standing so close. She could smell the brandy on his breath, see the hairs on his chest at the open collar of his shirt.

And then he tilted his head to one side and said to her, "I wouldn't have to if you married me!"

# CHAPTER FOUR

In the village, Bella Faddon was banging her mats against the garden wall, and wondering what she could cook for her husband's tea, when her next door neighbour appeared on the other side of the wall.

"Hello, m'dear. Still a-cleaning are you? It takes a while to get into a routine, don't it? I expect you'll get yourself sorted out soon. After all, you haven't been married long, have you?"

"No, Mrs Caldwell," said Bella, thinking that, judging by the state of Mrs Caldwell's curtains and the washing on her line, she had never got into the hang of things herself.

Jesse Caldwell shrugged, adjusting herself so that her great breasts sat comfortably on her folded arms. "Happen we'll have another wedding in the village soon."

Jesse let the statement hang in the air for a

moment. She was an expert at making the most of any snippets of information that came her way.

"Oh? Who's that then, Mrs Caldwell?" Bella had learnt that there would be no stopping Jesse until she had had her say.

"Parson's daughter. She's a-meeting someone on the sly."

"Never! Not Miss Greenway?"

"That's surprised you, ain't it? Surprised me too if I hadn't seed it with me own eyes, 'cos she's no oil painting, is she?"

Bella's interest was now aroused. "And just what was you a-seeing with your own eyes?" she asked.

"Every week, this last month, she's taken herself up to Doc Gilbert's cottage. I didn't think much of it at the time 'cos I knowed her and Miss Gilbert's a bit thick. And what's more natural that she should go a-visiting her friend? 'Specially now she be on her own since the old doc died."

"So why are you a-thinking she's got a young man?"

"I noticed that on the same day, p'raps half an hour or so later, after Parson's daughter has crossed the bridge, someone else goes over the self same bridge and walks in the same direction."

Bella sighed. Why couldn't the old witch come out with it and let her get back to her work? She hadn't made the beds yet or riddled out the grate. "And who was that, Mrs Caldwell?"

"Not anyone from 'ere. Some nice-looking feller. Not the kind you'd think would take a fancy to Miss Greenway. Must be from Chillingford 'cos he gets off the carrier's cart, all spruced up he is, and goes over the bridge too." She gave Bella a meaningful look. "It's easy to put two and two together, ain't it? Too much of a coincidence each week. And what's more, my Alfie's seen 'em."

"What? The two of them?"

"He was up that way last week and he seed 'em come out of the doc's cottage together. Bold as brass, they was, and the doc's daughter a-waving goodbye to the two of 'em from the gate. They walked back to the village together and she said goodbye to 'im at the bridge."

"You wouldn't think Miss Gilbert would have anything to do with summat like that, would you?"

"And I'm surprised at Miss Greenway." Jesse sniffed . "The old parson would 'ave a fit if he knowed she was a-taking up with the likes of 'im. Alf says he's not much more than a common labourer. Well, stands to reason, he's not the kind of person for a parson's daughter, is he?"

"Well, I'd say  good for 'er." said Bella.

"It's about time she learnt there's a bit more to life than playing her  bloody organ!"

It was on the last day of August that Elizabeth and John got married; a beautiful summer's day with the sun shining in a cloudless sky. Cornflowers grew among the hedgerows and everywhere the clean yellow stubble of cleared fields.

John and Florrie took the carrier's cart to Barkwell. They jolted along the turnpike, each lost in thought. John couldn't believe that today he was actually getting married. He had never thought to see the day he'd settle down. And to an educated woman like Elizabeth too. She had insisted on having a chaperone all these months of courting and the parson' daughter, a plain little piece, had obliged.

But tonight, there would just be the two of them and as the cart made its ponderous journey along the quiet lanes, he tortured himself with the anticipation.

Florrie would rather have not come. It had been a shock when he had first come home with the notion that he wanted to marry, but even more of one when she had found out who the lass was. Fancy her brother marrying a doctor's daughter! Ideas above his station, she thought, and did her best to dissuade him. She had argued until she was blue in the face but he hadn't budged. Fair wed to the idea he was and she thought the use of that word was funny 'cos before the day was out he would be wed, wouldn't he?

She hadn't met this Elizabeth Gilbert but from what she'd heard, from John, she was all the saints rolled into one. Well, she'd give credit where it was due; he'd done well for hisself. He'd be set up for life now 'cos by all accounts the cottage belonged to her. No rent to pay and a horse and gig as well. To think that her brother, a Holland, would be going round like that. It'll be sixpence to speak to him in future if she wasn't mistaken.

Pity he wasn't marrying Nan though. Poor Nan had had her cap set at him for as long as she could remember. At one time, she thought John was going to pay Nan particular attention. It would have been nice if her brother had married her best friend, and he could have done a lot worse for hisself 'cos Nan was a fine looking lass, but since he'd met up with this fancy piece there was no talking to him.

Nevertheless, he was her brother and the least she could do was come to his wedding and put on a bit of a show. She had dressed in her good blue and white sprigged print and pinned forget-me-nots on her bonnet. I'll miss him, she thought. It won't be the same on me own. No man to cut the logs or put some silver on the table come Saturday night.

Florrie looked about her. They had arrived

at Barkwell. John jumped from the cart, paid the carrier and helped her down.

Under the great spreading oak tree on the green, some ten yards from the well, was a white painted seat and it was here that the old men sat on summer afternoons.

Tom Potter, squat, flat-footed and toothless, sat sucking on his gums. Beside him, Jack Benson leaned forward, his age-mottled hands resting on an ash cane.

From this vantage point, with their backs to the woodland, they could watch the comings and goings of the village. The seat commanded a view of most of the cottages that lined one side of the green, the general stores, butchers, Miss Bryant's dress shop, the forge on the other side and straight ahead near the bridge was the Scarlet Arms that was set next to the graveyard.

It was said that more people worshipped at the bar in the taproom of the Scarlet Arms than in the little church next door whose spire, covered in ivy, could be seen above the chestnut trees.

Tom and Jack were watching a carriage pulled by a perfectly matched pair of greys. The sun glittered on well-polished harness while the cockaded coachman drove the carriage round the green. In the carriage sat a matronly figure in blue silk holding a white fringed parasol against the sun and next to her sat a small pale-faced man.

"There goes the Marsdens' coach, said Tom. "They do say she'd dropped another. Daughter this time."

"That be three now. I don't know how he do do it. There's not much of him with all his clothes on, let alone…. And she's a big woman ain't she?" Jack screwed up his eyes as he watched the carriage's progress.

"Plump as a partridge, too. How do you think he managed another one, Jack?"

Jack lifted up his cap to scratch his head. "Ah, you've got me there. But 'tis said she's a real dragon, so I do reckon she just tells him and the poor bugger has to do as he be told!" He chortled and replaced his cap.

The carriage disappeared over the bridge and their attention was drawn to the couple strolling past the shops.

"Eh, that be John Holland!"

"He's all done up in his Sunday best. Must be today he be a-marrying Doc Gilbert's lass."

"Who's the woman a-hanging on his arm then?"

"That must be the sister we've heard about."

"Scrawny bit ain't she?"

"Mmm…. Funny sort of do, Miss Gilbert not wanting to come back to the village now her father's gone."

"Quiet out there, ain't it?"

"Must have been convenient for courting' though."

"No one to see what they got up to, was there?"

Parson Greenway emerged from the dimness of the church, blinking his eyes for a moment as if he was stepping into a world he had forgotten existed. He was a large man, middle-aged, with a bald head surrounded by a fringe of grey hair. A mild and agreeable man in the village, slipping sweets into the children's hands, but in the pulpit he was another character.

Sometimes he would speak quietly. Old Mrs Benson, who was a little deaf, would strain to hear his words but there were some, prone to dropping off on occasion, who would be lulled for a while. But not for long would their heads nod, for the next moment he would deliver the word of God with a roar that would startle the congregation and make more than a few sit up a little straighter. With arms outstretched he looked like some great bird of prey who, at any moment, may swoop down and carry them off to the purgatory they must surely deserve.

But today he had a wedding to perform and he would be glad to get it over. He was of the strong opinion that man was divinely appointed his lot in life and he frequently preached of submission to this established order. It didn't do to go against the run of things and he was sure that if James Gilbert was still alive, this wedding would not be taking place.

He looked impatiently across the graveyard towards the lych-gate. Where was that daughter of his?

John and Florrie, with an hour to spare, had decided to take a stroll about the village and had now completed their circuit of the green. Florrie, having turned up her nose at all that could be seen in the little shop windows, sat on a seat near the bridge to wait for Elizabeth. John had been all for going up to the cottage for her, or at least meeting her along the lane, but 'no' she had said, 'I will meet you on the green,' so he stood, without taking his eyes off the bridge, until he saw her.

Elizabeth had dressed herself in a dove-coloured gown with rows of narrow blue ribbon edging its many flounces. On her head she wore a tiny velvet bonnet with wide velvet strings tied in a bow under her chin. Her face was pale but her eyes gleamed with suppressed excitement.

John could only stare at her when she smiled at him. He took into every detail of her lovely face and it was a moment before he came out of his reverie and remembered Florence.

"This is my sister, Florrie."

"I'm so pleased to meet you."

"Charmed, I'm sure."

"We've come on the carrier's cart and she'll have to catch it at four," John continued. "We've got a nice day for it. If it had been last week, when it poured, we would of got soaked." His nervousness made him talkative and he spoke of the journey over to Barkwell and their walk around the village, not noticing that the two women were summing each other up, taking in every detail of the other's appearance and both disliking what they saw.

She doesn't like me, Elizabeth realised. It's fortunate that we won't have to see too much of each other. She's not a bit like John. She reminds me of a sparrow with those beady eyes and sharp nose. I've obviously ruffled her feathers, taking her John away.

And Florrie could see why John was smitten. She had to admit Elizabeth was a good-looking lass. He always has kept his brains in his breeches, she thought. What he wants is someone who can cook and keep house for him, not this doll who looks like she'll spend all her time combing her hair.

The church was chill after the summer warmth outside and Parson Greenway did little to dispel the gloom. "Come on, come on. Let's get on with it. Haven't got all day," he grumbled as, with arms outstretched, he shepherded them into the church and down the aisle.

Ruth Greenway blinked myopic eyes behind her thick-lensed spectacles. She was the only other witness; a short, stubby young woman with a pink and white skin and rather plain features. Her tightly-dressed brown hair drawn back from a broad forehead gave her a severe look. Until she smiled. When she did, it transformed her face and made her look charming. It was a pity that she had so few occasions to do so.

But this was one such occasion. Wasn't it all so wonderfully romantic? Just like the stories she read in the penny novelettes she kept secreted beneath her mattress. She didn't care what her father said. This very morning he had voiced his misgivings but she had stood up to him and defended her friend. She would always be loyal to Elizabeth who, after all, was the only person who had ever claimed her friendship. Her father had been angry and Ruth shuddered to think how much angrier he would be should he discover the part she had played in the romance.

But her father wasn't the only one who had something to say about the match. Since the banns had been called there were those in the village who had smiled and nodded knowingly over their ale in the taproom of the Scarlet Arms. They said that John Holland hadn't wasted time getting his knees under the doctor's table. And women at the well, or waiting to be served in the general stores, put their heads together and clicked their tongues.

"My word, haven't he got a nerve, setting hisself up like that," said Jesse Caldwell.

"Won't allus be sunshine and roses for them two," Nellie Benson predicted, bristling with righteous indignation.

"Stands to reason, you've got to summer and winter a man before you can pretend to know him and that cuts both ways don't it?"

Whatever their opinions, the deed was now done. The ceremony over, John enthusiastically shook the parson's hand, causing him to wince a little, and thanked the blushing Ruth for coming. He and Elizabeth saw Florrie off on the carrier's cart. John promised to call in to see her the following week and they both waved goodbye until the cart disappeared round a bend in the road.

Elizabeth looked about her. "There seems to be a lot of activity in the village today," she observed, trying to keep a straight face.

John, raising his eyebrows, followed her gaze and with a wry twitch of his long mouth said, "Yes, my dear. Perhaps something special is happening today."

He took her hand, pulled it through the crook of his arm and together they walked sedately over the bridge. Turning left, they took the river path and once out of sight of the inquisitive eyes (that they knew had been peering from behind curtains and garden hedges) the surreptitious glances of gossiping women and the open stares of children, he took her hand and they ran, laughing, until they reached the stile.

He leapt over, turned to help her and she stepped down into his arms. Her bonnet hung by its strings down her back and he brushed stray tendrils of hair behind her ear.

He took a long indrawn breath and it seemed as if he had inhaled the very essence of her. The fragrance of her was in his nostrils; he saw her shining eyes, those incredible eyes, as she looked up to him, felt the soft yielding of her body against his and his chest swelled with pride and tenderness, love and wanting and happiness.

And then his hands were in her hair, grabbing fistfuls of it as he pulled her to him. His lips were on hers and all the longing of the past year was in that kiss.

And such was their hunger for each other that the neatly pressed linen she had placed on the bed that morning would have to wait to be crumpled, for he took her there, amid the long grass by the river, while a mallard and its mate swam quietly by.

# CHAPTER FIVE

It didn't take a summer and winter, as Nellie Benson had predicted, for Elizabeth and John to get to know each other and to realise that their differing backgrounds would be the cause of clashes in their marriage.

Elizabeth expected certain standards at the table and towards herself but John was found wanting. He, in turn, thought that Elizabeth shouldn't stand on ceremony so much and should let her hair down.

She had looked forward to keeping house and welcoming John home at the end of the day with a lovingly prepared meal; of evenings at the piano with John and his fiddle. She had spent the months before their wedding in joyful anticipation making the cottage comfortable, embroidering tablecloths and antimacassars for the parlour chairs.

John refused to eat in the parlour. It had been difficult for her to get used to eating there after the spacious dining room of the house in the village but to be expected to eat in the kitchen was even harder. The linen napkins lay ignored and he made fun of the vase of flowers she had placed on the table.

"I can't eat these," he had laughed. "Now if they had been sweet peas...."

And she had laughed with him, but she had been hurt.

Florrie came to tea. John went to fetch her in the gig. It was an uncomfortable afternoon, both women having agreed to the arrangement, at John's suggestion, for his sake.

"I see you're using the vase I gave you," were his sister's first words as she removed her bonnet; the same one she had worn for the wedding.

"Yes. It's very...er...unusual."

The vase stood on the window sill. Privately, Elizabeth thought it was a hideous thing but had kept her opinion to herself when it was obvious that John had been delighted with Florrie's wedding gift. She had filled it with masses of bronze chrysanthemums and was glad that the foliage hid most of the gaudy decoration.

Florrie, with darting eyes, took in the cottage, the garden, Elizabeth's clothes, a whole tea service that matched and the silver teapot too. She was determined not to show her jealousy and sat in sullen silence at the table.

Elizabeth made every effort to be the perfect

hostess. She had baked scones and a sponge cake and there were little ham sandwiches, cheese, thinly sliced bread and the strawberry conserve she had made that summer.

"How do you like living in Chillingford?" she asked.

Florrie extended her little finger and sipped her tea. "It's all right."

"I've always lived in Barkwell but sometimes I like to go to Chillingford for the market."

"Oh," was all that Florrie said.

They had nothing in common and little to say to each other. After a while Elizabeth, too, lapsed into silence. John was left to carry the conversation until the grandfather clock struck five and it was a relief that it was time to take Florrie home.

It was a pity that Elizabeth and Florrie couldn't be friends. Elizabeth found her life lonely, isolated as she was from the village. Her father's friends and acquaintances, upon whom she had previously relied upon for company, were cold towards her since her marriage and the village women were slow to accept her. As the doctor's daughter she had an established standing in Barkwell, but now she was regarded as neither fish nor fowl. She might be wed to John Holland, not much more than a common labourer, but with her fine clothes and different ways she made them feel uncomfortable.

Her only visitor was Ruth. She would trudge up from the village, even in bitterly cold weather, when the wind was fierce and her ears were cold and sore in spite of the woolly scarf tied firmly round her head. She would spend an hour gossiping, often making Elizabeth laugh with her remarkably apt impersonations of some of the village folk.

Elizabeth was grateful for her friend's visits, especially as her romantic visions of cosy evenings with John were dashed when she realised that his idea of a good evening was to spend it down the Scarlet Arms, supping ale and giving them a tune on his fiddle.

He didn't have the same problem making friends. His fiddle was his passport to social acceptance in the Scarlet Arms.

John soon established a particular friendship with Patrick McGiveney, a man noted for his ready wit and roguish smile. Patrick played the penny whistle and it wasn't long before he and John were in great demand. They set feet tapping, most evenings, with their lively music. The village men requested all the old favourites and the women, coming to the back door for a jug of ale, lingered to listen.

They made a strange pair; John, tall, dark and broad shouldered, and little Patrick with his mass of iron-grey hair, a beard that reached halfway to his waist and clear green eyes that almost disappeared beneath shaggy brows when he laughed.

As a young man, Patrick had come over from Ireland seeking work and was taken on when the new wing was built on to Marsden Hall. It was then that he met Mary, a good catholic girl from Chillingford, courted her and when the work was finished, stayed on and married her. Patrick had been trained as a stonemason but he could turn his hand to most things and over the years found that it was just as well because, in such a small rural community, there would not have been enough work to sustain him otherwise.

And just as the passage of time had mellowed the stone of the new wing so that it blended in with its new surroundings, so had Patrick mellowed with age and fitted into the village life. Only his accent was as strong as ever.

His wife, Mary, was short and stout with thin legs. She had rosy cheeks and her once red hair, now flecked with grey, had a tendency to escape the bun at the back of her head. Patrick adored her. They had raised ten children, all of whom had survived, and it was quite a sight to see them all, decked out in their Sunday finery, traipsing over to Chillingford for early Mass. The little ones darted hither and thither, their mother admonishing them to keep clean, the two eldest girls whispering and giggling behind gloved hands, and Patrick and Mary bringing up the rear, his hand at her elbow to help her over the stiles.

Elizabeth asked John if he would accompany her to

church and was dismayed by his reply.

"Hatches, matches and despatches," he said. "That's what you'll get me there for... and then only under sufferance. I don't hold with all that religion. Where was your God when me ma and pa died of the fever, and me brother, Jed, too? He was only fourteen with all his life in front of him and precious little behind. No, I'll leave you to do the praying, but if you ask me, you might as well rely on a rabbit's foot for all the good it'll do. After all is said and done, it's all superstition."

So Elizabeth went to church alone which set the tongues wagging. John walked with her down to the village and waited on the village green, talking to the old men to while away the time or sometimes he would leave her at the bridge and go on to Chillingford to see Florrie.

On those days Elizabeth, returning to the empty cottage, felt the loneliness engulfing her. She would look over the silent fields and wonder how she was going to cope with the life that she had made for herself. All she could see were the years stretching before her and more than once she thought she heard the echo of her father's voice saying, 'He's all wrong for you. You mark my words; no good will come of it.'

Yet she only had to see John's familiar figure striding up the hill for her spirits to lift and she would then rush to the gate to meet him.

And at night, when he took the pins from her hair so that it fell in a golden cascade to her waist, held her in his arms and made love to her, she would know that without doubt she could never want to share her life with any other.

In November John sold the gig. When he came home that day with Jess straining up the hill, pulling the unaccustomed load of a farm cart, they had their first quarrel.

"How could you do such a thing? I can't believe that you would sell my father's gig without consulting me!" Elizabeth exclaimed, banging the kettle down on the hob.

"I had a chance to take over the business from Tom Harris. He's getting on a bit now and he's packing it in. he said if I bought the cart he'd let me have the tools. I got the ladder, three long-handled knives, a spare cradle full of shearing hooks and so on… oh, and all the iron hooks and needles I'll ever need and he gave me all the sways and liggers he had left over. I expected those 'cos he won't have any use for them and it was me who cut them all for him when it was quiet earlier this year."

He paused from shovelling peas into his mouth with his knife and wagging the blade towards her added, "I've arranged with Matt Fuller to have the wheat straw from three acres. If I reap and thresh the grain for him, without pay of course, he'll let me have the straw for the thatching."

"So you've had this all worked out for some time then?"

"Makes sense don't it? I met this man over

Chillingford way and he bought the gig off me. Don't look like that Beth. I could hardly carry the thatch in a gig, could I? I got a good price for it and it's been lying idle anyways…. I needed the money for the cart don't you see?"

"If you had asked me I could have given you the money. You didn't have to go selling the gig behind my back."

"Look, we've had this out before." He finished his meal and pushed the plate away. "I told you when we was wed that I was going to be the wage earner. It's a poor show if I can't support me own wife. What kind of man do you think I am? I'm not living off you and if we don't have all the things you've been used to then I'm sorry, but I've got me pride. What kind of a man do you think I'd be if I was always holding me 'and out?" He was shouting now, his hands fisted, his face red and glaring.

"I'm sorry John." She hated to see him so angry. "But I still don't see why you couldn't have spoken to me first." She turned her back on him not wanting him to see how he had upset her.

"You haven't heard a word I've said, have you? Can't you see that if I'm to be master in me own house I'm going to have to make me own decisions?" His voice softened. "Beth. Beth, try to understand."

He came and stood behind her and put his arms about her waist. "I thought you'd be pleased I'm going up a step." He kissed the back of her neck knowing the exact spot that gave her pleasure.

Elizabeth turned, as he knew she would, and then he was kissing her. She found herself responding. And their first argument, as all the others that followed, was forgotten as he made love to her, skilfully and with a thoroughness that left her breathless.

# CHAPTER SIX

At Christmas Elizabeth gave John her father's gold watch and the news that she was pregnant. The baby was due in July, soon enough for the villagers to start calculating on their fingers but late enough for those who were looking for gossip to be disappointed. John was delighted and Elizabeth considered it to be an answer to her prayers, an antidote for her lonely days.

Ruth called, as often as she could, bringing gifts for the expected child; tiny bootees she had made and one day a beautiful quilt, a patchwork of tiny hexagons of cloth, each embroidered exquisitely with a different flower. Elizabeth realised that it must have taken many hours of painstaking work to complete and was touched by her friend's kindness.

There had developed between them a close friendship, born of loneliness but grown in mutual regard for each other and it was Ruth, not John, who was there with Elizabeth when the child quickened in her womb. Elizabeth was startled by the sudden fluttering movement and they laughed, delightedly, together.

A cold night air swept the valley in place of the dusty heat of day when Sarah Ellen Holland, named after the two grandmothers she would never know, was born. She arrived with clenched fists, a chaos of brown curls and a contented disposition. Elizabeth was enraptured by the tiny bundle that had the same wide mouth as John and her own startling eyes. John was a proud father. He couldn't wait to get down to the Scarlet Arms, next day, to celebrate.

At the Scarlet Arms, windows were thrown open to the summer's twilight and on the soft evening air came the sounds of children playing; little girls chanting *Poor Mary is a-weeping, a-weeping, a-weeping. Poor Mary is a-weeping on a bright summer's day,* and boys yelling at each other as they kicked a tin can.

George, in company with the white-whiskered old men and a few young ones who gathered on the benches that lined the wall of the taproom, pondered as he drew on his pipe. "Well, I don't understand it. I really don't. Flummoxed I am. How can his delphiniums have grown that high? I been a-growing 'em for nigh on forty years and I can't get 'em more'n three feet."

Young Freddie shifted in his seat and winking at his friend said, "Happen his missus empties the chamber pot on 'em, George."

"God a'mighty! You young 'uns come out with summat. Never knowed such a lot in me life. If I'm going to get remarks like that I might as well of stayed at 'ome."

"You'll more than like be glad you didn't," said Walter. He jabbed George with his elbow and nodded in the direction of the doorway. "'cos here's John and he's got his fiddle with him. Happen he'll give us a bit of a tune."

Albert Cooper nodded to John over his foaming ale. "Hello, John. How's the missus? My Jenny tells me you've got yerself a family now." Albert was married to the village midwife.

"She's doing well thanks, Albert." John grinned.

"What did you 'ave? Boy or a girl?" someone asked.

"A girl."

An opportunity for some good natured banter was not going to be passed by and it was Ed Parry, a small wizened old man with watery blue eyes and more hair on his face than on his head, who started it. "Ah... they do say it takes a man to 'ang the fruit on."

Slyly, he winked at John as he wiped the ale from his moustache with the back of his hand.

Patrick McGiveney joined in then. "I'll be thinking, perhaps, you'll be needing a bit more practice, John." He pushed his tankard across the bar for a refill. "Sure and didn't I have to have three daughters before I got it right?"

Wilfred Hoskin's grey eyebrows lifted sardonically as he gave Patrick his ale. "Well, you must be losing your touch then 'cos if I remember rightly the last two were girls again."

At this, they all laughed and Ed Parry had to mop his eyes. Wilfred's wife, drying pots behind the bar, tossed her head and sniffed. My goodness they were a coarse lot!


Within a year a second child was born, this time a boy. John was overjoyed and they named him James Edward. But he was a sickly infant who cried constantly and failed to thrive. Five months after he had struggled into the world he quietly left it in his mother's arms.

Elizabeth was inconsolable. As they lowered the tiny coffin into the ground on a day of high winds and fine driving rain, she heard Parson Greenway intone, "The Lord gave and the Lord hath taken away," and told herself that there would never be another child to love and to lose.

Hugging Sarah closer to her as she leaned for comfort against her grim-faced husband, Elizabeth remembered John's words when he had said, 'Where was your God when my brother died?' And she asked herself, now, the same question. No she would never have another child who could be taken away. She didn't think she could survive the pain another time.

It was the tail end of October and the

shedding trees looked as if they were shaking angry fists of leaves at the darkening sky. Elizabeth was glad the weather was so austere. She didn't think she could have borne it if the sun had shone.

But she was already pregnant and when she came to realise her condition there was not the rejoicing that had accompanied the discovery when Sarah or little James was expected.

She left it as long as possible before she told John and was surprised that he greeted the news with pleasure. He couldn't understand how she felt and she couldn't find the words to explain. All he could think of was the possibility of another son to replace the one that he had lost. He didn't tell her how much a son would mean to him and how much he too had suffered their loss. At the time all he could think of was to be strong for her sake. She hadn't seen the times when he had climbed the downs to be alone and there, with just the silent hills as witness, had given vent to his grief in anguished cries.

It was a girl who arrived in June after another long labour. She was the image of Elizabeth with the same wide-spaced eyes, a wisp of honey-coloured hair and the promise of dimples. They named her Margaret Ann but from the beginning, despite Elizabeth's protests, John called her Polly.

Elizabeth was relieved that her ordeal was over, that the child cried lustily instead of the mewling cries that had accompanied James. John was disappointed that it wasn't a boy but if he showed it she was too weary to notice, and the men down at the Scarlet Arms, mindful of his loss the previous year, made no remarks this time.

Elizabeth was sometimes too protective of her children but she gave thanks that they were well and strong. She wished that she too felt the same but since Polly's birth she was easily tired. When the girls went for their afternoon nap she was glad of the respite from the demands of two young children and took the opportunity to rest herself. But always when John returned home at the end of the day she would be there waiting for him with a welcoming smile and his dinner on the stove.

Ruth was concerned for her. Elizabeth didn't have a strong constitution and three pregnancies in less than three years was taking its toll. She was glad that for more than a year there was no sign of her friend having another. She loved the girls and found it no hardship to take them off Elizabeth's hands for an hour or two. She would take the black, wicker baby carriage, and with Sarah clinging to the handle, push it, creaking and rattling, down the lane.

Elizabeth was grateful and happy to see them together. Ruth had once confided in her that she was unlikely to marry; she had neither the inclination nor, it seemed, the opportunity and her only regret was not having children of her own.

Elizabeth viewed her fourth pregnancy with mixed

feelings. She was constantly tired, frequently sick and dreaded the thought of coping with another child. When this one was born Sarah would be nearly four and Polly still less than two. She hoped that it would be a boy. John adored the girls. He would play with them before bedtime often, much to her consternation, throwing them in the air and catching them until they squealed with delight.

"Careful John," she would cry. "You'll hurt them!"

He always laughed and said, "Not my girls. They're made of sterner stuff." Sarah and Polly would plead for more.

But she knew, even though nothing was said, that he yearned for a son.

The baby was expected in the middle of March and by then Elizabeth felt as if she had always, and would always, be pregnant. She was uncomfortable and found every little task an effort. The days were long, the due date passed and she looked forward to the baby's arrival with a mixture of anticipation, impatience and dread.

On the first of April, when a few violets began to show their faces and shafts of sunshine broke through the clouds, the pains began. All night, unable to lie comfortably, Elizabeth's sleep had been fitful, but she waited until she heard the clock in the parlour strike six before she shook John's shoulder.

"John. John, dear. Wake up."

His voice, still thick with sleep, muttered back. "Mmm…. What is it?"

"You have to go for Jenny. My time has come."

John was awake now. He threw the covers from him, leapt out of bed and hauled his nightshirt over his head. He flung it on the bed and grabbed his trousers from the chair. "Will you be all right while I'm gone? I won't be much above an hour…. What about the girls? How will you manage?"

"Don't worry about me. There's plenty of time and the girls will sleep for another hour. And don't forget to call in at the vicarage. Ruth will have them for the day…. You haven't buttoned your shirt properly." She smiled at him as he stood there, looking lop-sided with his shirttails hanging down.

He laughed at her. "A time like this and you're noticing my buttons!"

She could tell that his laughter was a cover for his anxiety and it felt good to have someone to care for her. All of a sudden she felt the need to reassure him as if he was the one who was giving birth and not her.

"Everything will be fine. I promise you." And then she softly added, "I love you."

At this, John paused in his rushing and sat on the edge of the bed. He took her face in his big hands and with his own very close to hers answered in a low voice, "And I love you too Beth…. My very own Beth."

A contraction gripped her and she gasped

with pain. John was at once stirred into action. At the bedroom door he declared that he would not be long and then his heavy boots clattered down the wooden stairs. The door opened and closed and once more the cottage was quiet save for the ticking of the grandfather clock. Suddenly a blackbird burst into joyful song in the laburnum tree.

She eased herself in the bed. Thank God it would soon be over.


By seven thirty both Ruth and the midwife had arrived and they lost no time in packing John off to work.

"This be women's work m'dear," said Jenny Cooper, tying the strings of her apron round her ample waist. "She'll be all right with me. I been a-seeing the beginnings and ends of everybody for forty years. Lost count of the babes I brought into the world... or the number of bodies I've laid out."

Her remark sent a chill through both Ruth and John even though they knew she was referring to her two separate occupations. Jenny was a kindly soul with a bustling manner and had been with Elizabeth for each of her confinements.

Jenny saw John hesitate in the doorway and flapped her hand at him. "Go on now. Off you go. You'll only be in the road and it will no doubt be all over by the time you get back for your tea."

John needed no more persuading.

But it wasn't all over when he returned that evening. Ruth had taken the children to the vicarage for the day and had come back to cook his dinner. She stood in the kitchen, wearing one of Elizabeth's aprons, stirring a pot on the stove as he came through the door, a look of eager enquiry on his face. Before he could speak, he heard Elizabeth's agonised cries in the bedroom above and turned to climb the stairs.

Ruth stayed him with her words. "John, I think you'd better go for the doctor. It doesn't look good and Jenny would rather he came. We've been waiting for you to come back. I would have gone but the children... I couldn't leave the children, though if you hadn't come when you did I would have dressed them and taken them with me."

Sarah was clinging to her skirt, anxiously sucking her thumb, frightened by the noise she could hear. Polly slept, unconcerned, in a cot by the fire.

When Doctor Rudd arrived he took over with quiet efficiency. He was dedicated to his work and the villagers had, although hesitant at first, come to trust him.

Ruth tried to persuade John to eat. She had cooked a meat pudding with cauliflower and spinach and baked a rhubarb pie. She was not offended, but understood, when he said he had no appetite and left the warmth of the kitchen with all its cooking smells to go into his garden.

He wandered aimlessly down the path trying to quell the fist of fear that grabbed him and churned his belly so that he had to fight the urge to retch. It was the thought of losing his Beth. Dear God. Oh dear God don't let her die! The man who thought he might as well carry a rabbit's foot was praying.

For an hour he stood there in the dark, heedless of the cold. He wanted to put his hands over his ears so that he didn't have to hear her cries but, somehow, to hear her agony increased his own suffering and he felt that in some strange way he shared her pain.

He was standing at the garden gate when the doctor came hurrying down the path carrying his black bag and pulling the collar of his coat about his ears against the chill night air. John couldn't tell by the young man's expression what news he was bringing.

"Well, John. It's all over."

John searched his face for a clue. "Dammit man. Tell me. How is she? My Elizabeth? Is she... is she all right? And the baby; is it well?"

"You have a fine healthy child." The doctor sighed wearily. "But I must tell you, John, that your wife has had a very bad time. The strain has been hard on her heart. So hard that I doubt if she will wholly recover. She'll need plenty of rest." Thrusting his face towards John's he added, "And I feel it would be a dereliction of my duty if I didn't advise you that another child would surely kill her." He clapped John on the back and became brisk. "You can go up to see her soon. Give Mrs Cooper a few moments to tidy them up."

He was through the gate and climbing into his gig when he paused and said, "Oh John... congratulations! It's a boy."

John stood there. It was a full minute before he could assimilate the full import of the doctor's words. When he returned to the kitchen he hovered awkwardly by the fire. He took down his pipe and tobacco from the high mantel and put them back again, his mind in a turmoil of pride, dread and relief.

Ruth fussed round him. "Congratulations, John. You'll be able to see them in a minute." She pulled on her coat and tied a muffler about her ears. "I'll walk down with Jenny when she's ready. I've put the little ones to bed. Polly's dead to the world but perhaps you'll look in on Sarah. All this has no doubt unsettled her. I don't suppose she'll get to sleep for a while. You will do that, won't you John?"

"Yes. Yes I will," he answered absently.

"Perhaps you'll fancy something to eat now. I've left it warming over a pan."

"Thank you, Ruth. Thank you for all you've done. I don't know what we would have done without you."

Ruth flushed with pleasure. "Oh, it was nothing. All I've done is cook a meal and tidy up a bit."

Upstairs, Jenny Cooper carefully laid the baby in Elizabeth's arms and then called down to John. He came bounding up the stairs, two at a time, and burst into the bedroom only to hesitate in the doorway. Jenny gently pushed him into the room and closed the door behind her.

Elizabeth, propped up against clean bed linen and wearing a fresh nightgown, looked pale but had never appeared, to him, more beautiful. She looked up from the bundle that lay in the crook of her arm. Her face, although tired, was radiant, her eyes triumphant.

"Come and see your new son, John."

John sat on the edge of the bed and Elizabeth pulled the shawl from the baby's face. He looked down at the tiny perfect features that were so like his own.

"Oh my dear…my dear," he managed before the tears spilled from his eyes. He was unable to express all that was in his heart.

# CHAPTER SEVEN

It took a long while, as the doctor predicted, for Elizabeth to regain her strength and she knew that she would not fully recover.

Although it was never discussed, they were both aware of how near she had come to dying; that they would not take the chance again, and that was why they no longer made love. It saddened Elizabeth for she felt that something very beautiful had gone from their marriage.

In other ways, though, they had grown closer over the years.. Her values had changed. His ways no longer jarred her sensibilities and she, in turn, had ceased to concern herself with the social graces that had, at one time, seemed so important. What did it matter if they ate in the parlour or the kitchen providing there was good food on the table, or if he changed for dinner as long as he was there?

He evoked in her the same feelings, the same desire, but the fire and passion that had coloured their early days together had given way to a quiet, more enduring love, and although there were nights when, sleepless, she longed for his touch, she was still able to count her blessings. She was getting better, she told herself; John was a good husband who worked hard and cared for them all; she had three beautiful children. She was content.

She wondered how John felt about the situation. He often stayed overnight at his sister's when he had work on the other side of Chillingford and those nights away were becoming more frequent. It occurred to Elizabeth that perhaps he had a woman there. A man like John would find it difficult to suddenly lead a celibate life.

But she asked no questions and got told no lies.

Patrick sent up one of the girls to help out. His eldest two were away in service and Agnes was now waiting for a position. In the meantime she was glad to come and look after the children while Elizabeth gained her strength. Agnes was a pleasant girl, strong, with bouncing red hair, the same twinkling eyes as her father and a scattering of freckles over her nose.

She attended to the children with efficiency and good humour and laughingly remarked to Elizabeth, "Sure, after helping to look after seven brothers and sisters, I'll be thinking that three is child's play."

The children loved her.

When the weather got warmer Elizabeth was able to sit in the garden. It was good to quietly enjoy the still beauty of the flowers. Daisies spangled the lawn and blood-red poppies with a delicate new-born look turned their faces to the sun. A cuckoo called, insects droned, and she was dozing when Mrs Tulley hobbled up the lane.

The side of the old woman's boots had been cut away to accommodate a painful bunion and her hands were gnarled and swollen with arthritis. She had a long face with high cheekbones, a dark skin wrinkled as a walnut from a life spent outdoors, and sparse white hair that she wore high on her head in a tight little bun. Her dress was old, faded and worn, but spotlessly clean and was covered by an equally old and equally spotless apron.

She brought a jar of honey and told Elizabeth, with pride, "Now, this be honey from me own bees, m'dear. Got three hives y'know. Feeds off the heather they does, and you won't find better honey than that for miles around. And I've brought you up one of me herbal remedies. I'm not going to tell you what's in it, m'dear, but you make an infusion with a spoonful of this and, I promise you, you'll be feeling fit as a fiddle in no time. A real pick-me-up that be."

She pressed a brown paper package of herbs into Elizabeth's hand. It smelt strongly of Rue. Elizabeth, mindful of her father's remarks about Mrs Tulley's potions, thanked the old woman and said she would take some later.

Mrs Tulley sat for a while. "Ain't he a beauty!" she exclaimed when she saw the new baby.

"What have you called him?"

"Robert John," Elizabeth told her. "After my husband's father and himself."

Mrs Tulley had brought her grandson with her. Ned's mother had died giving birth to him and it was left to his granny to raise him. He was a sturdy five year old, big for his age, with a mop of unruly fair hair and an engaging smile. A lively child, full of devilment, his granny said, but Elizabeth could tell he was the apple of her eye.

Ned was a year older than Sarah. The two of them ran wild in the garden, climbed the apple tree and chased each other, laughing and shrieking all the while, with Polly trying to keep up with them. He must be lonely, Elizabeth thought, living away from the village with only his granny for company. She resolved to invite him to come again to play with the girls.

It was the beginning of July before Elizabeth felt well enough to cope with a christening for Robert. The day was one full of sunshine with only a few clouds, delicate and feathery, in a clear blue sky. John took her down to the church in the cart. She carried Robert in her arms and the girls squeezed between them on the high plank seat.

It was the first time she had been as far as the village for months and her spirits lifted as she watched the ducks and their young on the river and shared the girls' delight in the outing. It was a 'good to be alive day' and she was so very glad to be alive.

They stopped for Mrs Tulley and Ned. The boy ran down the path to greet them and stood fidgeting in his best clothes. He grew so quickly that the sleeves of his jacket were already too short. He kept trying to pull at the sleeve hems with twisting movements of his hands in an effort to cover his wrists.

Mrs Tulley followed at a slower pace, shutting the front door behind her. When she saw that they had come in the cart she shook her head and lifted her hand to John. "You go on, m'dears. I'll make me way to church meself. It's very kind of you, I'm sure, but I'm too old to be a-climbing in that there old cart. It's not but half a mile. I shall be glad of the fresh air."

"You'll do no such thing, Granny," John told her. "Don't you know I've spent all morning a-cleaning out this 'ere cart in your honour. We're all travelling in style today." And before she could stop him, he picked her up and heaved her into the cart while Ned laughed with glee to see his granny in Mr Holland's arms with all of her petticoats showing.

Patrick and Mary, with Agnes and two of her brothers, attended the ceremony. A neighbour was keeping an eye on the other children but the boys - twins - were a handful that Mary refused to inflict on any of her friends. They behaved themselves well enough when their father was present, having experienced the painful retribution of sharp clouts to the ear that Patrick was inclined to mete out for their transgressions.

Ruth played the harmonium then joined the group for John and Elizabeth had asked her to stand as godmother to Robert. She was Sarah and Polly's godmother too and was proud to have been asked. She felt that she belonged to the children as much as if she were a real aunt, and it occurred to her that she was more of an aunt than their real one. She noticed that John's sister hadn't come today and was secretly pleased. She didn't like Florence, any more than Elizabeth did, although she'd only seen her twice; the first time when John and Elizabeth were married and then at Sarah's christening. John had excused his sister's absence when Polly was christened saying she had a cold and didn't want to pass it on. Ruth wondered what the excuse was this time. In her opinion, Florence was jealous of Elizabeth and John and therefore preferred to stay away.

Parson Greenway looked kindly on the little family. He had, long ago, overcome his misgivings about their marriage and about his daughter's friendship with the Hollands. He thought she spent more time than was necessary trudging out to see Elizabeth when she could be doing more good works in the parish but, to be fair, she didn't neglect her duties and as long as she didn't he was more than content to let things be. He had too many calls on his time; his mind was on higher things.

It was four o'clock by the time they got back to the house. John, with Patrick's assistance, set up a table on the front lawn. They brought the ladder-backed chairs from the kitchen and the Windsor chair for Elizabeth who, at John's insistence, sat there with Robert in her arms while the women bustled between the kitchen and garden.

Mary and Ruth brought baskets of food and Mary, coming from the kitchen with an enormous raised pork pie and a fruit cake, said to Elizabeth, "I'll be thinking we have enough food to feed an army, Elizabeth. Ruth has made one of her sponge cakes. Light as a feather they are and no mistaking. And Mrs Tulley has made sandwiches and brought you a jar of her honey."

"And there's a ham in the larder and I've made blancmange for the children so I think you may be right. Did you find the salad and the dish of strawberries? Oh, there's cream in the larder. It's in a blue and white jug. Perhaps I should come to help you. I feel lazy just sitting here."

"Let ye give over, Elizabeth. It's not often ye'll have so many willing hands to wait on ye so make the most of it."

"Thanks be to God you're getting better," Patrick added. "It's grand you've got the roses in your cheeks back. Like a pale ghost ye were, if ye'll pardon me honesty. Me and Mary were fair disturbed, that we were. But now ye'll be blooming it makes me heart turn over just looking at ye."

Elizabeth liked Patrick. He always paid her extravagant compliments, usually ending them with an enormous wink, as he did now, before returning to the house for one more chair.

Soon the table was laden, Ruth brought out the silver teapot and Mrs Tulley a jug of ale for the men.

Elizabeth was overwhelmed by the kindness of her friends and their concern for her well-being. It was good to have an occasion to celebrate. She wondered what her father would have said if he'd been able to see his quiet retreat now. It rang with the peals of children's laughter, women's chatter and the deeper tones of the men as they discussed Gladstone's proposition to give the vote to country labourers.

Would he have been pleased for her that she had made a life for herself with the man he had called a scoundrel? Would he have admitted that he had been wrong when he had told her that no good would come of a marriage between them? She watched Sarah and Polly playing with Ned and the twins. They were chasing each other round the laburnum and the girls, pigtails flying, were squealing with excitement. How proud she was of her family. For a moment, she was saddened that her father had never known his grandchildren.

Remembering her father, she thought back to the life she had led before she met John. It all seemed so far away now, and with surprise she realised she hadn't touched the piano since before Polly was born. At one time, music had filled her life and she reflected that very little else did then. Now, she had a fine husband, three beautiful children and good friends to enrich her days. She looked about her and smiled.

The sun was low over the chestnut tree in the lane and the river was bathed in the orange glow of dusk by the time the table was cleared and John brought out his fiddle.

"What'll it be?" he asked.

"Give us something we can dance to," said Patrick. "Let us be having a bit of jollification, John."

So John played for them and Patrick took Mary in his arms and they danced up and down the path. Agnes hauled one of the twins to his feet and Sarah and Polly, giggling together, copied their elders. Soon the garden was filled with their whirling and twirling until the music came to an end and Mary collapsed into a chair, laughing and fanning her face with her hand.

John started up again and Patrick turned to Ruth. "I'm thinking we might have a dance, you and me, Ruth."

"Oh no, Patrick. Thank you for asking but I can't dance."

"Sure, if ye can walk, ye can dance! We'll have a go at it."

Ruth could tell that he wasn't going to take no for an answer. Self-consciously she got to her feet and they were off round the lawn. Patrick, who only came up to her shoulder, spun her round and round until the pins from her hair fell loose, her cheeks were flushed and she was laughing.

Elizabeth watched her friend and not for the

first time she thought that it was a pity that Ruth led such a quiet existence. She had so much vitality, so much to give and she deserved so much more than she appeared to get out of life. Elizabeth was glad they had asked her to be godmother to their children. Somehow, it made her seem to belong to them.

Patrick brought Ruth back to her seat next to Elizabeth and, as she sat, gave her a courtly bow accompanied by one of his enormous winks.

Ruth nodded her head and smiled. "Thank you, Patrick. I enjoyed that." She turned to Elizabeth and looked down on the sleeping Robert. "I don't know how that child can sleep through all this noise. It is nice that he is such a contented baby."

"Yes. Nothing seems to disturb him. The girls can be shrieking and making a great din but he'll sleep through it all. I think I'll take him in now. The air's getting cooler and it's really time the girls were in bed."

Protesting, the girls were led away and by the time Elizabeth returned it was dark and everyone was preparing to leave.

"I'll get the cart out, if you wait a minute, and take you back, Mrs Tulley," offered John.

But she wouldn't let him. "No, m'dear. I'm quite capable of stepping down the lane. You've done enough already. I don't think I'm up to being thrown in the back of that there cart, like a sack of taters, three times in one day."

"We'll walk the way back with you, Mrs Tulley," said Patrick, taking her hand and tucking it under his arm.

It was a merry group going home, with lanterns swinging, down the long dark lane. John and Elizabeth watched them go from the gate, John's arm about her shoulders. They watched the small light dwindle and vanish round a bend in the lane.

"It was a good day, wasn't it?" he said.

"Yes, John. It was a very good day." She had never felt so happy.

It was halfway through October; autumn was well advanced and the days were dull and misty. Leaves, driven by the wind, covered the grass and collected round the roots of the lately pruned roses. Flocks of starlings gathered noisily in the huge golden-leafed chestnut tree in the lane and all over the valley smoke from numerous bonfires scented the damp air as allotments and gardens were cleared and tidied before winter.

Elizabeth was in the kitchen cooking and the air was filled with the warm fruity smell of boiling jam. Blackberries and apples had been plentiful this year and she looked forward to adding the jars to an already good supply on the larder shelves.

Robert, six months old, sat on a rag rug, a wooden spoon engrossing him. He kept turning it over in his plump baby hands then beating the air to some internal rhythm and laughing to himself. He was a placid child with huge eyes like brown velvet that were alert to every movement about him.

At the end off the table, Sarah and Polly were painting. Christmas presents, they said. Although Elizabeth knew they would probably lose them or change their minds by the time Christmas arrived, it amused them and she wanted to make soup. She had been grateful for help but now that Agnes had gone away into service it felt good to be pottering about the kitchen again.

She reached for the heavy copper pan that hung from a hook above the range.

John was working in the garden. He enjoyed growing vegetables. There was something satisfying about growing your own. You couldn't get them much fresher, pulled from the garden and straight into the pot. Let Elizabeth grow her lavender and lupins, hollyhocks and roses; he liked to grow things you could eat. The beans had produced well this year but now they were finished and he wanted to get the poles put away.

He had collected a bundle together and was carrying them across the vegetable garden when Sarah came flying down the path calling his name, her breath a ragged ribbon streaming behind her on the chill air.

"What's the hurry, Sarah? Where's the fire?"

"There is no fire." She always took his questions seriously. "Ma said to come and get you.

She said 'Go and get your father quickly,' so that is why I'm running."

"Is she all right? What's the matter."

"I think she is all right but she looks peculiar. She dropped the big pan and —"

The beanpoles clattered to the ground and Sarah was almost knocked over as John rushed to the house. It's her heart, he thought. She's had a heart attack. His mind cried out in fear as he flung the door wide.

Elizabeth was on the floor. She knelt in front of the baby, talking to him.

"Aw, Elizabeth! I thought you was ill. You gave me such a fright sending Sarah for me like that. Dammit, if it's just to tell me he's said his first word it could of waited." He flopped down into a chair, heedless of the mud falling from his boots.

Elizabeth picked up the child and turned to him. He straightened, then came up and out of his chair when he saw her stricken face. Something was very wrong.

"What is it, Beth? What's happened?"

She opened her mouth to speak but, for a moment, no words came. She swallowed and tried again. "It's Robert... I... I think..."

John searched her face anxiously. What was she going to say? It wasn't like Elizabeth to be lost for words.

"John...the girls...."

He understood then that she didn't want to speak in front of the children.

"Sarah, take Polly into the parlour for a while," he said. "Your ma and me, we want to talk."

He dutifully admired their paintings, ushered them from the kitchen, shut the door and waited for Elizabeth to speak. When she did, her voice was little more than a whisper. "John…I think the baby is deaf." Her lips trembled and her eyes were bright with unshed tears.

"What makes you say that?"

"I was going to make some soup so I got the big pan down. I was bringing it to the table when that wretched kitten got under my feet. Why Patrick had to give the girls that kitten is beyond me. It was a nine days wonder and is more trouble than it's worth."

"Never mind about the animal. Just tell me what happened."

"I tripped and dropped the pan."

"Well? Go on."

"The pan made such a clatter on the floor. It made the girls jump and Polly shrieked. But Robert…. It was right behind him and it didn't disturb him. Not at all." Her voice rose in fear. "John, he didn't hear it!"

"You mean…."

Elizabeth could only nod.

They experimented. John banged pot lids together behind Robert. He shouted. He yelled. And as Elizabeth's fears were confirmed, he bellowed his rage and his disappointment that this child, his son, his only son, was unable to hear.

It was only later that he was fully to realise what that would mean.

They took him to see Doctor Rudd whose examination of Robert was as rudimentary as their own; his conclusion the same.

He sent them to see a specialist in Chillingford. Ruth took the girls for the day and John and Elizabeth, with Robert, went over in the cart. It was November, cold and damp and miserable; fitting weather for the way they felt, especially on their return journey.

They had been given no explanations, no reasons, no hope. Robert was completely deaf. He was unlikely ever to learn to speak, communicate, be educated.

During their silent journey home John mulled over the implications. The specialist had only confirmed what they already knew. But they had hoped. Hoped that something could have been done. Now, without that hope, a bitterness crept into his soul. First, James had died, and now Robert, his perfect child, was not perfect. What had he done to deserve this, he asked himself. He didn't ask for much in life. Damn well didn't get it either.

He knew he should be saying something to Elizabeth. He ought to be giving her some words of comfort but what could he say? He knew his pain was hers too but he couldn't trust himself to speak; couldn't hide his disappointment.

Elizabeth hugged the child to her, pulled the

shawl closer about his face as they rattled down the rutted lane. She could only guess what John was thinking. She glanced sideways at him. His face had that set look that she had only seen once before. That was when their other baby had been buried.

At least this one is alive. Thank God for that. He may not be perfect but he was alive. And if bitterness was born in John that day, then in her was born a fierce determination that Robert would lead as normal a life as possible. He would be loved as much, if not more, than any child. Didn't he have that right? Life was going to be hard for him but she would dedicate her life to his well-being.

# CHAPTER EIGHT

Chillingford could be divided into two separate parts. Upper Chillingford was not much bigger than Barkwell and was the original village made up of a scattering of cottages, a church dating back to the Normans, a blacksmith, an inn called The Black Swan and a few shops. Then the factories sprang up on either side of the river; the candle factory where Florrie worked, the rope works, a tannery, a brewery, and a sawmill that supplied two large furniture workshops. Such a mixture of odours filled the air, of wax and leather, sawdust and ale.

Soon dwellings, mean ugly little back-to-back houses, grew up like fungus about the factories to house the workers. Lower Chillingford, as it was called, became bigger so that a newcomer could be forgiven for thinking that Lower Chillingford was the original town and Upper Chillingford a limb that sprawled up the hillside reaching out to a patchwork of farmed fields and woodland.

The nearest school to Barkwell was in Upper Chillingford and that meant a four mile walk for

Sarah and Polly and two miles for the village children.

When the Education Act had been passed by Gladstone's Liberal government in 1870, there were a lot of folk who didn't hold with schooling. 'Brains ain't no good for a working boy,' they said and 'what does a young lass want to do with larnin'? She don't need all that for keeping house and bringing babes into the world.'

How much the two pence a week charge per child influenced their thinking was a matter of conjecture, but now it was 1880, for four years the National School had been compulsory and free, and a lot of mothers were glad to get their children off their hands. Not only that, if the children didn't go for their 'edication' the Attendance Officer would come knocking on the door expecting to know why.

There was talk in Barkwell that they would one day have their own school built on the edge of the green; a plan that met with approval from the parents but not so the children.

For them, the walk in the early morning and mid-afternoon was the best part of going to school. Freed from parental restrictions it was a time to explore the hedgerows, chase one another over stiles and generally run wild. It was a time for catapults and climbing trees, for bird nesting and scrambling down the bank to pick watercress and forget-me-nots, and in winter they would slide on icy puddles and throw snowballs at each other.

Once, they found a newly shot pheasant in a

cluster of brambles at the foot of a poplar tree and another time they discovered a hedgehog with her five blind babies, little bundles of soft white prickles.

It was in the afternoons on the way home that, at the right time of year, they would hunt for blackberries, stuffing them into their mouths like starving sparrows. This delightful occupation was reserved for the afternoons because Miss Trotter - or Trotsky as the children called her behind her back - was a stickler for neatness and cleanliness and they dare not arrive with hands and faces stained with the sticky purple juice.

Ned Tulley went with them. Sarah and Polly had to pass Granny Tulley's cottage on their way down to the village. Each day they waited for Ned, swinging on the garden gate until he came running down the path, shrugging on his jacket and sometimes with the last of his breakfast still in his hand.

Together they walked down to the village and once over the bridge were joined by other children spilling from their homes in varying degrees of eagerness. They followed the river path and more boys and girls swelled their ranks until reaching Upper Chillingford they had become a band of some twenty children.

The schoolhouse was a large one-roomed wooden building with plank steps to a door that was crowned with a big shining bell. every morning, Miss Trotter stood on the top step, ringing the bell in her usual vigorous manner. Sometimes the children were still some way off and, hearing the bell, they would have to take to their heels in order to arrive, breathless, but just in time to follow the Chillingford children into the school.

Miss Trotter lived in a tiny two-roomed cottage next to the school. She was not always liked but well respected. 'Never let bad behaviour spread' had been the parting advice of her mentor before she took up the post. It was advice she had not forgotten and it was implemented with the aid of a long ash cane that hung on a hook by the blackboard.

The classroom was well lit with several windows. On their wide ledges were stacked slates and bead frames and on some, in springtime, things grew in jars; beans and seeds and frogs' spawn that turned into wriggling tadpoles.

The only heating was a monstrous black pot-bellied stove surrounded by a square fireguard. It stood on one side of the room with its chimney angled to go through an opening in the wall high up by the ceiling. It had a voracious appetite and devoured, at an alarming rate, the logs that the school keeper kept stacked outside.

Miss Trotter thought Ned a helpful boy, always offering to bring in more wood, until she realised that it was his way of getting out of the lessons he hated. He didn't seem so helpful when she suggested he replenish the fuel during the morning or midday break.

Sarah liked going to school and came home full of the things she had learnt that day. "Did you know, Pa, that there are people in the world who live in tents and ride camels and are called nomads?" Or "Ma, Miss Trotter says that it is necessary to have one collar and two socks. That means that the word necessary is spelt with one C and two S. Isn't that clever?"

She was quieter than Polly. Where Sarah walked, Polly ran. If something made Sarah smile it would make Polly laugh, and if a grazed knee made Sarah cry it was nothing compared with Polly's wailing after a fall.

Polly liked the reading and painting lessons and very little else. She couldn't understand how Sarah could be so interested in everything and was, herself, quickly bored. She would rather play with her dolls or join in the singing games on the grass outside the school.

Elizabeth was grateful that she had Robert at home with her although when she remembered why he would never attend school she felt guilty. But it was good to have at least one of her children there. She missed Sarah and Polly's chatter and Robert missed their presence too.

Polly didn't take much interest in Robert. He had ousted her from the position of youngest child and she thought he got too much attention just because he was deaf. Although her pa never seemed to take much interest in Robert, her ma made a fuss of him and Sarah spent most of her free time in his company.

All one summer Sarah took him down to the bottom of the garden and sitting beneath the apple tree taught him a rudimentary form of communication. Patiently she flapped her hands together and pointed to a bird flying high in the sky. Robert laughed and copied her. Soon he learnt that crossed thumbs wagging together was a butterfly and two index fingers pointing upwards on either side of her head represented the cat. Polly thought it was fun at first, a bit like playing charades, but she soon lost interest and went back to her games. By the end of that summer Robert was contributing signs of his own; the river, a fish, he was hungry or thirsty.

John took little interest in Robert. Just seeing the boy made him angry. No matter how much he tried he couldn't accept the situation. His anger was directed at himself for this inability, rather than at the child, and because it made him feel a lesser person he preferred to keep out of his way. Because Robert and Sarah were inseparable his seeming indifference included her too and it was Polly who had his attention.

Elizabeth tried to talk to him about his attitude, which she regarded as favouritism, but any discussion developed into an argument. What Sarah and Robert lacked in paternal interest was compensated by her doting concern and as the years passed the Holland family were thus divided.

From signs Sarah progressed towards words

and painstakingly taught Robert to say 'Ma' by holding his fingers over her lips while she formed the word and then over his own while his features contorted in his effort to imitate.

Elizabeth cried when she heard him address her for the first time. She had argued with John, years ago, when she had wanted the children to call them Mama and Papa. John had disagreed and been adamant. He didn't want to be addressed in such a namby-pamby way. Ma and Pa it would be. It had been good enough for him and would be good enough for his children.

Now, to be called Ma was the sweetest sound in all the world. She stroked Robert's hair and held him to her while the tears spilled from her eyes and her heart swelled with pride. Such tenderness she felt for this child in his silent world.

Sarah was not so successful with the other names; Pa sounded like 'Baa', Sarah became 'Say-a', Polly was 'Boll-ee' and Ruth, 'Rue'. Every word was accompanied by those contortions of feature that Polly said made him look quite mad, a remark that Sarah ignored and earned Polly a tongue-lashing from her mother that reduced her to tears.

Apart from adding a 'Dan-oo'  for thank you, it seemed that Robert had defined his world, a world of family and the wildlife of the countryside about him, and he made no further attempt to speak.

He was a gentle child, handsome like his father with wild black hair and a wide smile. Quiet and thoughtful, he was inclined to sit gazing in space, thinking his own thoughts and dreaming his own dreams. He had an innocent rather than a vacant expression. Sometimes he would burst into loud inarticulate cries that were taken for laughter. He was given to wild gestures and grimaces that caused the village folk to be wary of him. They said he was a bit soft in the upper storey but his strangeness came from his affliction not his mind.

He loved all the wild creatures and his bedroom, a tiny narrow space partitioned off from the girls' bedroom, usually housed a bird or some other small creature that was injured or motherless.

Elizabeth was convinced that had things been different he may have become a doctor as her father had been, but humans held no interest for Robert; it was to the animals that he was drawn. In some way he was able to identify himself with the dumb creatures and they, in turn, sensed that they would come to no harm in his gentle hands. So it was they, his mother and Sarah that comprised his world.

Robert was accustomed to walk to the village each schoolday afternoon to wait for the girls by the bridge.

"Why does he have to come down to meet us?" Polly asked one day. "The children call him names and say he's daft. They've called him the April Fool ever since Sarah told them his birthday was the first of April. Jimmy Caldwell says he ought to be put away. He says it's not right that he should be out loose." She cried into her mother's skirts.

"You are the one who is daft for listening to them," declared Sarah. "It's only because they're ignorant and don't know any better. Robert is more intelligent than they are even if he can't speak properly. *They'd* have a job to speak if they were deaf!" She was furious; furious at the children, at Polly who should know better, and furious at the fates that had made her brother different.

Elizabeth could only make soothing noises as she stroked Polly's hair. Sarah had said all there was to say and she could add nothing more. How had she managed to raise two sisters who were so different? And from where did Sarah get her wisdom? She had more sense than a lot of folk twice her age.

It was a warm spring afternoon, the first warm day that year, and the band of children coming home from school had taken off their coats. They slung them over their arms so that some trailed along the ground.

As they came near the bridge they saw Robert waiting for his sisters. Robert saw the girls and, waving his hand, came running to meet them.

"Here comes the April Fool," cried Jimmy Caldwell.

"Yeah! Been to any good shoots lately?" asked another boy and the children laughed.

The last time there had been a shoot, organised from the Hall, Robert had caused a great disturbance when he had realised that the men with the guns were going to shoot birds. He became agitated, yelling in his incoherent way and flapping his arms in such a manner that Sarah had to pull him away and take him home. But it was not before his reputation as someone 'not all there' was reinforced.

Suddenly Jimmy shouted, "Let's get the April Fool!" He was a big boy, a bully, and most of the children followed his lead.

It was doubtful if Jimmy would have picked on Robert had Ned been there. It was well known that Ned Tulley and his granny were in thick with the Holland family and Jimmy knew from past experience that Ned wouldn't stand by where they were concerned. But Ned was at home with a cold and Jimmy knew that nobody else would challenge him. He faced Robert, his fleshy lips a cruel smile, and pushed Robert in the shoulder with the flat of his hand.

Robert was puzzled. He tipped his head on one side and frowned. Jimmy hoped that he would run away. It would be fun to lead the children in a chase. But Robert stood his ground. Jimmy pushed him again. Robert lifted his arms more for protection than in an aggressive way.

"Ah, so you want to fight, do you, Dummy?" sneered Jimmy and landed a blow to Robert's stomach.

Robert's eyes widened in surprise. When he didn't hit back Jimmy lunged at him and together they fell to the ground. The next moment Jimmy was astride Robert in the dust.

Sarah, her eyes blazing, tried to pull Jimmy off. She tugged at his shirt and yelled. Robert tried to cover his face with his arms. Meanwhile Polly jumped up and down shrieking for help. The children surrounded the two boys, shouting with excitement, punching the air as they shouted their encouragement.

Suddenly they were pushed aside. Their cries subsided when they saw that it was the parson.

"Boys! Boys! Boys! What do you think you are doing?" he cried. He hauled Jimmy to his feet and shook him.

"He started it," Jimmy accused, scowling.

"Jimmy Caldwell! May God forgive you for your wickedness. And please do not compound it by lying. You should be ashamed of yourself. I've watched from the bridge and witnessed the whole sorry episode. There's no doubt in my mind that it was you who picked on this poor boy." He shook his head sadly. "This kind of behaviour will not do. It simply will not do."

Most of the children had scuttled away at the sight of the parson but those that remained were subjected to a sermon on the sins of fighting and telling lies. It was a full five minutes before they were allowed to leave.

Robert was obviously bewildered by what had happened. Parson Greenway fished in the pocket of his black frock coat and pressed a sweet into Robert's hand. He patted the boy on the shoulder and, without a glance at Sarah or Polly, set off across the green, shaking his head and muttering to himself as he went.

Sarah watched him go and the thought came to her that it would take more than a peppermint to make things all right.

# CHAPTER NINE

The church of St Thomas was small with roughcast walls and a stone-flagged floor. It had a cold, damp earthy odour that seemed more pronounced after the fresh morning air outside.

Lord and Lady Marsden and their family had pews on either side of the chancel with their backs to the wall. Between them stood two long benches for the schoolchildren. Below the steps, down into the nave, Ruth played the harmonium. She had played for every service – apart from two consecutive Sundays when she had had a fever – ever since she was sixteen. Over the years her body had thickened and now it was impossible to see the stool on which she sat. Her plumpness and full skirts completely enveloped it. Sarah smiled, imaging that in fact there was no stool and Aunt Ruth was merely squatting there.

Parson Greenway read the lesson. His deep, rich voice relished every word. "Then he will answer them, *Truly I say unto you, as you did it not to one of the least of these, you did it not to me.*"

Sarah watched Polly plaiting the ribbons of her hymnal. Polly was always bored with the Sunday service except when they were singing the hymns. She had a good voice and sometimes Sarah thought Polly quite deliberately spun out the Amen at the end so that her voice could be heard a full second after the rest of the congregation had stopped.

Robert liked to come to church. It was funny that, because he couldn't follow anything. What drew his attention were the stained glass windows. Dutifully, he stood and sat, taking his cue from Sarah, but all the while his eyes were fixed in fascination on the windows that shone jewel-like on either side of the altar. The one that he seemed to like the most was of St. Francis of Assisi who stood in a brown robe with his hand uplifted. On his finger rested a dove and another flew about his head in a forever blue sky. At his feet, on an emerald grass, lay a lamb. It was beautiful in its simplicity.

Today, the Marsden family were all here. The poor old lord seemed, to Sarah, to be getting smaller. He must be very old, she thought. His face was all wrinkles and folds of flesh as if his skin was too big for his body; as if he was shrivelling up inside. He sat, leaning forward slightly, resting both hands on his silver-topped cane, his eyes drooping and his mouth ajar as if he was about to drop off to sleep.

Lady Marsden sat beside him. She was very

much younger than her husband. She sat erect, back so straight you'd swear she had a board tied to it. She had an air about her as if she owned the church and all the people in it. To some extent she did for there were not many families that didn't have at least one, if not more, members working up at the Hall.

Mr and Mrs Benson's eldest son worked in the stables. Mrs Cooper's daughter was a kitchen maid and Mr and Mrs Potter had two sons working in the grounds and were hoping they could put in a good word for their sister, Rose, now she had reached her twelfth year. Sarah had heard Mr Bishop say that if it weren't for the Hall his butchers shop wouldn't do enough business to keep the wolf from the door.

So perhaps she did have a right to look as if she owned the place. She couldn't own the church though. Oh no, it was God's church. Parson Greenway looked after it, with the help of the women of the village who polished the pews and arranged the flowers at Easter and Harvest Festival, and Mr Stockton who stoked the stove and dug the graves, but it was God's church.

The young Marsdens didn't have to sit with the village children. They sat next to their mother; Samuel, the eldest, square and solid with a set expression of concentration but a faraway look in his eyes; Joseph, leaning towards his sister, whispering in her ear, and Margaret, like a little dark-haired doll in her blue coat and matching bonnet, laughing behind her dainty white-gloved hand. Polly would take an hour cataloguing every detail of her outfit when they got home and Sarah would be expected to discuss everything from the trimming on the collar to how the bonnet was tied just so.

But it wasn't Margaret's outfit that claimed Sarah's attention. It was Joseph. Sarah couldn't help taking sly glances at him. Ever since Christmas, when he had come home from that big school, she had been aware of him. He must be the most beautiful young man in the whole of England, she thought. He had dark, restless eyes and a way of looking about the church just like his mother. Once, he had looked straight at her and caught her staring at him. She was embarrassed and had to look down at her hymnal. She felt foolish and excited at the same time. Such a mixture of feelings she had these days.

Wouldn't it be wonderful if she could be beautiful and capture his attention like the heroine in the book she was reading. She wished she looked more like Polly who had a pink and white prettiness and big blue eyes. Polly would look like their mother when she was older. She had the same fine hair and candid way of looking at people. Sarah had heard her father say that Polly would break some man's heart one day but she had never heard him say that kind of thing about her. She wished she wasn't so tall and her feet were smaller, her mouth not so wide. And her hair? Well, that seemed to have a mind of its own. Yes, Polly was just like Ma, Robert had inherited Pa's good looks, but she didn't seem to take after one or the other.

Robert nudged Sarah in the ribs with his elbow and she looked, automatically, to his hands. He was signing to her but the first thing that crossed her mind was that he had outgrown his jacket. Granny Tulley would say that his hands looked as if they had had an argument with his sleeves. She smiled at the thought.

Robert nudged her again so she paid attention to his signing. His thumbs were crossed as he waggled them. She followed the direction of his gaze across the church.

There, hovering over Mrs Fuller's flowered bonnet, was a butterfly. It must have come in through the open door. It wasn't a beautiful thing, just an ordinary cabbage white, but the sight of it in church was diverting. Gleefully, they watched it move on to investigate the shining bald head of one of the congregation and then held their breath while they wondered if it would settle.

Sarah felt Polly grip her knee. What could she want? Reluctantly Sarah dragged her eyes from the butterfly and, glancing sideways at Polly, was surprised to see that her sister's face was a bright red and she was squirming uncomfortably in her seat. What had upset her now?

Curiously, Sarah looked about her and gradually became aware of the surreptitious glances cast their way. She saw Ma self-consciously fiddling with a tendril of hair at the nape of her neck and, next to her, Miss Bryant peering over her spectacles with a sympathetic smile.

It was some seconds before she made the connection between the parson's words and the congregation's interest.

"It is abundantly clear that the Lord was telling us to respect our fellow men," he was saying. "We are all God's children...."

Jimmy Caldwell sat staring at his knees, his head pulled down into his shoulders.

"The richest and the poorest, the greatest man in all the land and the most insignificant...."

Now Sarah realised he was referring to Robert and felt the heat rising to her face.

"...and care for the afflicted." Yes, he was talking about Robert. That was why Ma looked uncomfortable. And Polly too. It seemed that everybody knew that the parson was talking about Robert. Everybody, except the Marsdens, who all wore the glazed expressions of those whose thoughts were elsewhere.

"So when you come across a man or child who suffers a sickness, some deformity, or is lacking in senses of the mind or physically...."

Robert, oblivious to the attention, watched the butterfly as it flew high up in the church.

"...and say to yourself; there but for the grace of God, go I."

A smile settled on the parson's face. Satisfied with a sermon well served, he paused before saying, "Let us pray."

Dutifully the congregation waited until the Marsden family had left their pew before following them up the aisle into the sunshine. While Elizabeth was exchanging pleasantries with Miss Bryant, Ruth steered the children to the side of the path, away from the congregation; those hurrying to get home, their duty fulfilled for another week, and those who lingered to socialise with friends.

"I have a gift for Robert," she said. "Nothing big or special mind, but I happened to come across it and thought it might interest him." She ruffled his hair and he looked up at her. Having gained his attention, she reached into her bag and drew out a small book. It was bound in blue leather and showed signs of wear. The girls were curious.

"Robert can't read, Aunt Ruth," said Polly, put out that Robert should have something and not her.

"I know that, Polly, but I thought that he would enjoy the pictures. It's a book of birds. There are some fine illustrations and I feel sure he will recognise quite a few."

She held it out to Robert, nodding her head to indicate that he should take it. She could hardly wait to see his reaction when he discovered the contents. Coming across the book in a musty second-hand bookshop in Chillingford, she had known at once that it was just the thing for Robert. Her intention had been to keep it for a birthday present but when her father had returned from his home visits, two days earlier, full of anger over Robert's ill-treatment, she had decided to give it to him now.

Such love she felt for this child; she couldn't love him more if he were her own. She often wondered if it was born of compassion for his affliction or the look of wide-eyed innocence that made the breath catch in her throat so that she wanted to hug him close.

Robert opened the book. His eyes rounded and his lips parted in wonder at the contents. He turned page after page and each had an illustration of a bird; a blackbird, a chaffinch, crow, eagle, jay, kingfisher, magpie, swallow, swift, wren and so on. It was a beautiful book and he was so engrossed in it that when Ruth touched him on the shoulder to say goodbye he misunderstood and, reluctantly, closed the book and held it out to her.

"No. No, Robert, it's for you." She pushed the book towards him and then laughed with pleasure at the astonished delight that lit his face.

Sarah thanked Ruth on Robert's behalf. "I expect he will be out all the time bird watching now," she said.

"Dan-oo," said Robert as he opened the book again; the book that was to become his constant companion.

# CHAPTER TEN

The years flew by and, in turn, Sarah and Polly left school. Elizabeth rejoiced that there was no need to make immediate decisions for their future. John, always busy with the thatching and other odd jobs that came his way, was frequently away from home, staying overnight in Chillingford. A lot of his work seemed to take him in that direction.

She was glad to have the girls at home for company and they were a great help to her. Her health was delicate and she tired easily. Sarah and Polly took over a lot of the chores and Robert made his contribution, fetching and carrying and drawing water from the well.

That summer of 1888 was hot and dry. There had not been rain for the whole of July and August. The earth cried out for water. Now that the harvest had been safely brought home everyone prayed for rain.

At the beginning of September the storm

clouds gathered, the air was heavy and oppressive. At last the rains fell; great sheets of rain, driven by a south-west wind, that washed the dust from the leaves of trees and hedgerows and made the countryside green again.

Sarah, returning from the village with a basket of groceries, had just crossed the bridge when she heard her name called.

"Sarah! Sarah, wait."

She turned, saw Ned Tulley lumbering towards her, and put the heavy basket on the ground while she waited for him to catch up.

"Can I carry your basket for a while?" he asked. "I'm going up to the 'all for Mr Bishop so I can carry it as far as the turn-off." His big open face smiled down at her. She thought he must be all of six feet now and wondered if, at sixteen, he had stopped growing.

"That's kind of you, Ned." She waited while he tucked the paper parcel he was carrying under one arm and lifted her basket as if it had been empty.

He set off, his long legs taking great strides. She quickened her pace to keep up with him but even so, for the next few minutes, he had to toss his words back over his shoulder.

"I reckon Mr Bishop's getting past it. He's allus forgettin' things. I've already been up to the 'all this morning. The cook, Mrs Tatlow, she allus checks the order. Likes to make sure it's all of the best quality, she says. Only the best'll do for up there. Well, you should of seen her carry on when she found he hadn't put her mutton in. Allus has mutton on a Monday. You should of heard her. You'd think it was my fault. I told her I didn't make up the order, I only delivered it. Now, I've got to go up there a second time.

Sarah could tell that he didn't really mind. He liked to be outdoors.

"How's your granny?" she asked. "I haven't seen her for a while"

"Oh… 'bout the same. Still moaning that her feet 'urt. Never knowed a time when they didn't. spends a lot of time with her bees, just a-sitting there with the 'ive. Takes her knittin' with her and talks to 'em. Daft, I calls it." He paused and then, trying to make it sound like a casual enquiry, asked, "How's Polly?"

Sarah suppressed a smile. So that's why he had been so eager to catch up with her. It had been obvious for some time that Ned was smitten by Polly. Sarah thought back to the good-natured teasing Polly had been subjected to as a result.

"You'd be all right, Poll," their pa had said. "Just down the road with Ned and his granny. Plenty of honey and near enough to come home for your tea." How he had laughed his big belly laugh!

Polly drew in her breath and shook her head at her father. "Oh, Pa!" she exclaimed with exaggerated patience.

"You could do worse for yerself, Poll. Working at the butcher's like he does. Well, you'd

118

never go short of a bit of meat, would you? And any left over you could send up to us." He looked across the table and winked at Ma, who was smiling back at him.

"Huh! I wouldn't marry Ned Tulley if he was the last man on earth. Have you seen his ears? He's got lugs on him like jug handles!"

Sarah glanced sideways up at Ned. Polly's right, she thought. He has got big ears. Funny, but she'd never noticed them before. Everything about him was big; big hands, big feet and a big smile. He was nice though. She'd never known him to be nasty to anyone. And she thought it a pity that Polly would never be interested in him. Polly had big ideas.

"She's very well, Ned. She's helping Ma at home today."

Ned stood there, awkwardly shifting his weight from one foot to the other, his face red with embarrassment. Sarah encouraged him with a smile.

"Will you... will you tell her I was asking after her?"

"Yes. Yes, I will. And you must give my regards to your granny…. Thank you." She indicated, with a nod of her head, the basket that he still held and seemed to have forgotten.

He looked down as if surprised to find it in his hand, passed it to her and the next moment went striding up the hill towards the Hall with the parcel of meat swinging by his side.

She waved goodbye to him and climbed

down the bank so that she could take the river path. She much preferred to be down by the river.

The day before had been one of constant fine rain that had continued through the night so that water still dripped from the eves that morning. It had left the air smelling fresh and clean. It's a 'good to be alive day' as her ma would say, she thought, and was glad that she had been asked to go down to the village. She had left her mother bending over the wash tub, her sleeves rolled up and a sacking apron covering her skirts. Polly had been feeding the sopping sheets into the wooden rollers of the mangle while Robert turned the iron wheel.

Sarah reached the stile and stopped to rest the basket. As she looked to the hills she felt a restlessness. She had felt like this for weeks. It was as if she was waiting for something, but for what she wasn't sure. There's a whole world beyond the downs, she thought, that she'd never seen. Sometimes it seemed as if she never would. Part of her wanted to go somewhere, anywhere, travel and explore new sights, new sounds, new smells, new experiences. But the other part of her wanted to stay safe at home. She wanted change. She wanted everything to stay the same.

Although Polly was younger she already knew what she wanted. She wanted to go and work in Miss Bryant's dress shop. She wanted to be fashionable and learn everything she needed to know about making gowns and then go up to London to open her own dress shop. Somewhere

where all the aristocracy and famous people would come to be dressed by Miss Polly Holland. And one day, the brother, or son, or nephew of one of her customers would walk into the shop and fall in love with her. They would marry and she would be kept in a life of luxury. That was Polly's dream. Sarah had heard variations of this dream countless times. Often, as they lay in the big double bed, Polly would go into minute detail of the gowns she would wear and the fine house she would have. That a degree of skill with a sewing needle was required – a skill that Polly didn't possess – was a mere detail that Polly chose to ignore.

Polly never asked Sarah what her dreams were and Sarah thought that was just as well. She would not own to a dream that lay much closer to home. A dream that included Joseph Marsden. The difference between Polly and Sarah was that Sarah had a streak of realism. She recognised the fact that her dreams were simply that; silly, girlish dreams.

She sighed and gazed out over the tranquil river. A flash of brilliant colour caught her eye as a kingfisher dived from an overhanging tree. It swooped down towards the water before flying off with a small shimmering fish in its beak, water spray catching the sunlight.

Sarah picked up her basket. The sight of the bird had lifted her spirits. She hummed to herself as she resumed her journey, watching the river all the while in the hope that she would catch another glimpse of the bird.

She didn't, at first, see Robert racing towards her but while he was still some way off she heard his cries and looking up saw him running down the hill. He was flailing his arms in the air. She wondered what had caused his wild excitement but, before he was near enough for her to see his contorted features, she realised that something was wrong. She hurried to meet him.

He reached her and grabbed her arm. Urgently he tugged her towards home, crying over and over, "Ma... Ma... Ma!" as the tears coursed down his cheeks.

Sarah dropped her load. It took all of her strength to halt his frantic progress. Once she had, she shook him by the shoulders in an effort to still him for a moment and get his attention.

"Robert. Robert!" she cried, stabbing her fingers in his chest and then pointing in the direction of the village. If Ma was ill she would need the doctor. "Go for Doctor Rudd." She signed with her fingers and pushed him on his way. She said to herself, "Dear God, I hope he understands," and forgetting the groceries, gathered up her skirts to run up the hill.

She threw open the front door calling for Polly as she ran from room to room. Through the kitchen to the scullery, still steaming and smelling of soap, back through the empty kitchen to the parlour. About to climb the stairs, she heard Polly's distraught cries coming from the back garden and hurried outside.

Halfway down the garden, where the last of the garden peas clung to their twiggy supports, she saw Polly kneeling by their ma. She lay on her back, across the path, beside the upturned wicker basket that spilled its wet linen contents on the ground.

Polly was shaking her, sobbing and screaming to Sarah, "Sarah, come and help me. She just fell. I can't get her to move. Sarah, quick! She's not moving. Dear God, what shall we do?"

Sarah hauled Polly to her feet. "Polly, go and see if Doctor Rudd is coming. I sent Robert for Doctor Rudd."

She knew that there was little hope of the doctor getting to them within the hour but Polly was hysterical and would be better out of the way.

With Polly gone, Sarah turned her attention to her ma. But even as she knelt, and before she took her cold white hand, she knew that her ma was dead.

# CHAPTER ELEVEN

ELIZABETH HOLLAND 1851–1888. The stone was new, clean, freshly carved and stood out from the older headstones that had darkened and grown moss with age. Patrick had made it for his friend, intending it as a gift but John had taken umbrage at the thought.

"Do you think I don't have the means to pay for my own wife's headstone?" he had asked, drawing himself up to his full height and putting the diminutive Irishman to disadvantage.

So Patrick reluctantly accepted a payment, did as good a job as he knew how, and the stone had been placed in position that morning. Now, with the afternoon sun still warm in a clear blue sky, Elizabeth's children stood beside her grave.

Sarah stared at the words, BELOVED WIFE AND MOTHER, and felt an awful emptiness. She had never thought she could feel so empty. Perhaps if she could cry she would be able to get rid of this ache that was like a stone in her throat. It threatened to choke her and had prevented her from eating much for days. Maybe it was as well that she couldn't give way to tears because she didn't want to start Robert off . He had howled like a wounded animal for days and she couldn't bear to see him like that again.

Doctor Rudd had said that Ma had always had a bad heart and that was why she had collapsed in the garden and died. And that was a funny thing to say because she had often heard Pa say 'Beth, you've a good heart,' and some of the villagers, who had come to the funeral last week, had said the same. 'She was a good hearted woman,' they had said. Yet she had died of a bad heart. She had just crumpled up and died. Dead like some of the baby birds Robert found and tried to care for. They died because they didn't have a mother to look after them. Perhaps it would be a good thing if we died too, she thought. She wouldn't mind dying right this moment if she could be in heaven with her ma. Parson Greenway had said it was a beautiful place, but she'd seen her ma lowered into the ground in a wooden coffin and the damp earth shovelled on top of her. Where then was heaven? So many things she didn't understand, and her pa going around not speaking.

Sarah's eyebrows drew together and she scowled at the thought of him. She wondered where he was. He had gone off early this morning, after his breakfast, wearing his Sunday suit, which was unusual because Saturday was his day for working in the garden and he only wore his suit on a Sunday when he went over to see Aunt Florrie. He had gone out the kitchen door without a word. With not so much as a goodbye, he had set out towards Barkwell and she had assumed she would see him here. He knew Mr McGiveney was going to put Ma's stone in place today.

The church clock chimed the hour. The bell rang out four times and she realised that they should soon be making  their way home. Pa would be wanting his tea when he gets back, she thought, and nudged Robert who stood pressing his head against her shoulder, his hand tightly holding hers.

He was staring down at his boots and she smiled sadly as she remembered how he had polished them this morning. And this afternoon he had combed his hair with a damp comb in an attempt to control the dark, wiry curls. You'd think Ma could see him, the way he'd spruced himself up to visit her grave.

She nudged him again and he came out of his own private reverie and looked up at her with eyes huge and velvety, sad as a fallow deer's. She indicated, with a nod of her head, the floral mixture in his hand; a cluster of hawthorn berries, some brightly coloured Virginia creeper leaves, a tansy-head and a few dandelions too.

"Fancy him picking dandelions." Polly sniffed, dabbing at her nose with a cambric handkerchief. "We've got all those flowers in the garden. He could have had those but he goes and picks that lot! I told him he'd wet the bed if he picked dandelions but of course he didn't understand."

"He always bought Ma wild flowers so why should he change now? Come on, we'd better be getting back."

They placed their offerings on the grave. Polly had picked all the best blooms from the garden and Sarah wondered what Pa would say when he realised that all the bronze chrysanthemums had gone. They dwarfed Robert's delicate bunch with the dandelion heads already wilting.

The last rays of sunshine lingered over the church roof as they left the graveyard. They went past Grandpa Gilbert's grave, the grandpa they had never known, and the tiny grave of James Holland, the brother they had hardly known, and past the grave of Jimmy Caldwell's father who had died last year. He had died after the drayman's horse had bolted. It was whispered in the village that it was Jimmy Caldwell, himself, who had kicked the tin can that had startled the horse, but no witness had come forward. Mr Caldwell had been knocked down and his head crushed when a full barrel of Ridley's best ale had fallen off the cart. Didn't stand a chance, they said. Young Freddie Cheeseman made the remark that he had always thought the drink would get him in the end. It wasn't a thing to joke about because poor Mrs Caldwell was now struggling to make ends meet with seven children to raise and only Jimmy's wage from odd jobs he picked up and some help from the parish.

Through the lych-gate and down the lane, past the Scarlet Arms and over the bridge, the sad little group silently trooped. They turned into the lane and saw Joseph Marsden and his sister, Margaret, as they came galloping down the hill, racing each other. They were well matched, both in their abilities and their horses, and came, at the same time, to a halt at the fence that separated Marsden land from the lane.

Margaret was laughing, her head thrown back, her eyes shining. "I won! I won!" she cried.

Joseph was laughing too when he said, "No you didn't you little minx. You cheated."

Polly's eyes lit up as she took in every detail of Margaret's tight-fitting blue habit with its long flowing skirt and the saucy little bowler hat balanced on her bright curls.

But Sarah's thoughts were very different. She was bitter that there was laughter when her ma was dead. She felt as if the whole world should be grieving for her, that the sun shouldn't be shining, that the birds shouldn't sing. How can everything be the same when it will never, could never, be the same again?

Even the sight of Joseph Marsden could give her no pleasure today. Angrily she pulled on Polly's arm. "Come on, Polly, we've got to get the tea," she snapped.

And when Polly still lingered, Sarah strode

out with Robert close behind.

John had been sitting on a rocky outcrop, high up on the downs, for the last hour but now, with the sun gone down, he was, reluctantly, making his way home.

Well, he'd done it. The deed was done. He didn't have much choice, did he? he asked himself. It wasn't an easy decision to make and it wasn't going to be easy breaking the news either. They'd be wondering where he had been, dressed in his best suit on a Saturday. Well, they'd know soon enough.

But they'd never know the reason. Not the real reason. Nobody would know that. Because even in those hours before the dawn, when it was hardest for truth to hide behind self-delusion, he found it hard to admit to himself that the feelings he had for Polly were not right for a man to have about his own daughter, his own flesh and blood.

She was growing to be the image of her ma; exactly the same way of holding her head on one side when she smiled, and the direct way of looking that had attracted him to Beth. For months now her presence had disturbed him and it was getting worse. So what he had done today was for her own sake… and his own.

When he came into the kitchen it was getting dark. It was the time before the lamps were lit when the fire cast dancing shadows on the walls. His dinner had been put to keep warm over a saucepan of water on the stove but he had little appetite for food tonight. Sarah sat by the window trying to read a book in the fading light and Robert was stacking some logs by the fire. The cat rubbed herself against John's legs and meowed as he took off his jacket.

Sarah looked up from her book. "We wondered where you'd got to, Pa. We've had our teas. Yours is keeping warm. Shall I bring it to the table?"

"In a minute. I'll go and change first." His voice sounded surly although he hadn't meant it to.

Polly passed him on the stairs and came into the kitchen. "He's back then," she said. "'Did he say where he'd been?"

"No, but wherever he went, it didn't bring him much joy. He hardly said a word. But then he hasn't had a kind word to say these past ten days. I know he's taken it hard but so have we. It's as if he's closed in on himself and shut us outside."

"Well, he hasn't had a kind word to say to me in months. It's not just since Ma died. He's changed somehow and — " She broke off as she heard he pa's footsteps on the stairs.

Robert had gone to bed and the lamps had been lit before John spoke. He had hardly touched his food and soon pushed his plate from him and took down his pipe and tobacco tin from the mantelpiece. He took time filling his pipe. First, he cut a plug of tobacco into pieces with his pocket knife, rubbed it into flakes between his hands, filled his pipe, pressing it down carefully with his forefinger and then lit it from the fire with the aid of a taper .

Sarah wrinkled her nose as the puffs of pungent smoke wafted across the room. She's just like her ma, John thought. Beth had hated the smell too. He knew what his daughter was thinking and felt ashamed. She was thinking that had her ma been alive he would not be smoking in the house.

"I 'spect you're wondering where I've been today," he began. He didn't want to look at them; didn't want to see their expectant faces, so he stared into the fire as if it would give him the courage to go on. He would have given a year of his life, more, to have everything go on as before. Why did Beth have to die? Why did he feel as he did? He had been asking himself these questions for days now and he knew that even if Beth had not died, something would still have to be done. At least he didn't have to answer to Beth now. For how could he have told his wife that he had to send Polly away because he didn't trust himself with her?

"I've been up at the Hall," he said.

Sarah was drying the plates. She stopped and waited for him to continue. By the tone in his voice he had something important to say and was having difficulty in the telling.

Polly sat in the chair opposite him. She leaned forward. "What did you go up there for, Pa? We thought you'd gone over to Chillingford, to see Aunt Florrie, only you usually go on a Sunday don't you? We wondered where you were when we didn't see you in the village. We went to see Ma's stone. Mr McGiveney set it up this morning and it looks—"

"I went to see Mrs Tatlow," he said, interrupting Polly's chatter. "She's the cook up at the Hall. Knew your ma when she was young. She's had a word with the housekeeper, put a good word in like, and you're to start up there on Wednesday, Polly. They need another housemaid as the old one has had to leave, sudden like. She's given me a list of what you need to take with you. The uniform's provided and you're to get twelve pounds a year. Lucky to get the position 'cos they usually takes them younger than you, but as I said, there's a vacancy to be filled and Mrs Tatlow's put a good word in." He fished in his pocket and brought out a folded sheet of paper that he placed on the table.

Polly's jaw dropped. It took a few moments for her to grasp what he was saying and the look on her face was as if he had physically dealt her a blow for such was the pain it showed.

"You can't mean what you're saying. I don't believe that you would do that. Why Pa? Do you hate me so much you would send me away?" Her voice was low, incredulous.

"It's about time you earned a living. You've had it easy too long. It's a good position and a good wage."

"But why not Sarah? Why me?"

"Because Sarah's needed here to look after me and Robert."

"Well I'm not going." Her voice began to rise. "And you can't make me. If Ma were alive she wouldn't let you send me away. I hate you! I'll... I'll never speak to you again if you make me go."

She was shouting now and Sarah, who had stood by in stunned silence, came to her side. Polly had risen from her seat, shaking with anger. Sarah put a hand on her shoulder.

"Yes, why Pa?" she asked. "Can't you give us a better reason? I know how to market, Ma taught me well, and I'm sure we could manage. It can't be the money.... We can manage, can't we, without this? It's only fair that Polly be given an explanation."

"I don't need to give you reasons, girl. I'm your father. If I say she's going, then she will. I'll not have either of you questioning me. It's all settled and she's going on Wednesday."

John went to the door and took down his working jacket that was hanging there. He had to leave. He couldn't give them a reason and he couldn't look at Polly; couldn't bear to see the stricken look in her face. It was a face filled with pain and hatred.

"Mrs Tatlow said you're to be there Wednesday morning at eight and not to be late," he said, busying himself with his jacket. "That's the time they have their breakfast. And she tells you to ask at the gatehouse and they'll point out the footpath that takes you round to the side of the house. It brings you out by the stables and anyone there will tell you which is the kitchen door. She says on no account are you to go up by the carriage drive else there'll be hell to pay."

And with that, he left them.

# CHAPTER TWELVE

It rained during the night but when Polly awoke a watery sun was doing its best to pierce the thick valley mist.

Polly opened her eyes and remembered. I have to go today. And again she felt the resentment that it should be her and not Sarah who was being sent away. Why did Pa hate her so much? He hadn't always been like this. Ever since she could remember, it had been she who had been favoured, she whom he petted the most. Ma used to say that she could twist him round her little finger. It had been true. She only had to look at him with her head on one side, eyes wide and a coaxing smile and he would laugh and say 'Oh, go on then,' whether it was a ha'penny for a paper of sweets or an extra ten minutes before bed.

But for the past six months he'd changed. He didn't smile at her any more or stroke her hair and once, when she had tried to sit on his knee, he'd pushed her away from him and left the room. Well, if that was the way he was going to be then she could be the same. She would go up to the Hall today and she wouldn't come back, not even for holidays. See if she cared! But she would miss Sarah and Robert. Oh yes, she would miss them.

She looked about the room. Since a partition had been put up to make a separate room for Robert it had been very cramped. A blue curtain hung on a short pole across the corner of the room to the left of the window and, in the triangular space behind, were their clothes hanging from two hooks on the wall.

The curtain matched the ones at the tiny casement window. When she had been little, she had climbed out into the laburnum tree and sat among its yellow tassels, watching Robert play with the cat on the grass below. He hadn't known she was there and she had felt like God watching over the world until Pa had seen her and threatened to tan her backside if she didn't get down that minute. She hadn't known who Ma had been the most angry with; her for climbing into the tree or Pa for using such words, but she remembered that she had been sent to bed without her tea.

All her life, she had slept in this big old bed with the mattress that dipped down in the middle and the springs that creaked if you bounced about. Ma had made the quilt, piecing it together in the evenings when her work was done, and on summer afternoons sitting in the shade of the apple tree. Aunt Ruth had given her quite a few of the scraps, bits left over from her sewing. She recognised the lavender print from a dress that had suited Aunt

Ruth so well and the plain blue that didn't suit her at all. Ma had cut up an old petticoat for the red bits and Pa had laughed and said she'd feel the draught so that her girls would be cosy on a cold winter's night.

It seemed so long ago that she'd heard Pa laugh his big, deep down laugh. At one time, they would sit round the kitchen table listening to him telling tales that made her shriek with laughter. She always hoped that Ma wouldn't hear the clock strike eight and pack them off to bed. There were tales about when he and his brother, the one who had died young, had gone scrumping apples and been caught with their mouths and pockets bulging. The farmer had boxed their ears and they daren't tell their pa or he would have boxed them again.

And he'd tell them about the time when his ma was chased down the lane by a pig and their own ma would smile her gentle smile. And then she would suddenly remember the time and they'd be sent up to bed to lie under the quilt that had robbed Ma of her petticoat.

She and Sarah would listen for the latch to click and hear Pa whistling as he went down the hill, knowing that he was going down, with his fiddle under his arm, to see his friends at the Scarlet Arms and Ma would sit by the fire with her sewing until he returned. It had always been good to snuggle down. She had felt safe, secure. Now, with Ma gone, Pa had changed and she was off to the Hall. Nothing would be the same again. There was nothing she could be sure of, could depend on, and she was frightened.

Polly fought back the tears and turned her head to see Sarah still peacefully sleeping beside her, one arm above her head resting on the pillow, her hair a tumble of dark curls. For some moments, Polly watched her and would have liked to curl up close and stay in bed, but instead, she gently pulled back the covers and, wrapping a shawl about her shoulders against the chill morning air, crept down the stairs and unlatched the front door.

Standing barefoot in the grass, she bent and ran her hands over the damp blades then washed her face with the dew. I won't be able to do this again. Oh, dear God, find some reason for me not to go today... or ever.

Sarah found her there, gazing over the downs, frail and childlike, hugging her shawl. The hem of her nightgown was wet and clinging to her ankles. Her feet were blue with cold.

"Come on, Poll, you'll catch your death." She touched her arm. "Come and have some breakfast. We'll have to make an early start."

They set out, the three of them, in gloomy silence, Robert carrying the basket that they had carefully packed the night before; six pairs of drawers and her second best frock along with her hairbrush and ribbons and, on top, she had placed her copy of *Gulliver's Travels* wondering if she would have the time to read.

The stile was wet and slippery as they clambered over, Robert going first with the basket and the girls following. Wrapped in their own thoughts, as they approached the Tulley's cottage, they didn't see the tweak of the curtain but soon saw Ned's granny as she hobbled to the gate.

"Off to the 'all are you today, dearie? Mind you be a good gal now and does just as you be told. You'll be back for your 'olidays before you knows where you are."

"Yes, Mrs Tulley." It was a wan smile but it was all Polly could manage.

The old woman thrust a package into Polly's hands, her narrow lips working in and out as she sucked on her teeth.

"Thank you, Mrs Tulley," said Sarah. She took Polly by the arm and propelled her down the lane, at the same time waving to the bent figure who stood leaning on the gate watching them go.

"I don't know how she's found out but if we'd stopped she'd have been on for hours about her young days in service. Ma always said she could talk the hind leg off a donkey. But it was kind of her, Polly. It was kind of her to give you something. What is it?"

Polly looked without interest at the package. She opened it and started to smile, then to laugh, a brittle laugh, and handed it to Sarah. Soon Sarah was laughing too for there in the crumpled paper were two thick slices of wheaten loaf and, peaking out between them, a pink, greasy rasher of bacon.

"That'll keep your strength up, Poll." Sarah handed back the gift and they leaned against each other, their heads touching and their shoulders shaking with their mirth. Robert watched them with a puzzled expression, but he hoisted the basket up higher under his arm and smiled when Polly held out the package and indicated that he should take it.

"Food will never go begging as long as we have Robert," Sarah said as they watched him devour Granny's sandwich.

But their laughter didn't last and by the time they reached the old ivy-clad walls that bounded the estate, they were once again subdued. The trio followed the high walls until they reached the entrance. Over the gate was a wrought iron arch with a lamp hanging from its highest point, and set into the wall on the right was a bell. They could see the lodge keeper's house through the gate and a wide gravel drive that, in the distance, disappeared behind a group of elms.

"I can't see anyone about." Sarah peered at the little house. "You'll have to ring the bell."

They stood silently for a moment, each reluctant to say goodbye. Robert examined an acorn he had found.

"It won't be long before you are visiting and I'll look forward to hearing all about it," Sarah encouraged. "I don't think we've forgotten anything but if you find we have then you can perhaps send a message down with Ned when he calls…." Her voice trailed away. They had said all there was to say the night before.

"I'll never forgive him you know. Not ever." Polly needed her anger at this moment of parting otherwise she knew she would cry. She reached out and rang the bell with an angry jabbing movement and then picked up the basket that Robert had set down on the ground.

"You can go now. I'll be all right. I'll find my way." Polly turned her back on them but Sarah and Robert remained until a stooped man in a green baize apron came and opened the gate.

"Bye Poll…." Sarah raised her hand to wave but Polly left them without a backward glance.

The lodge keeper was an elderly man with a craggy bad-tempered face. He indicated, with a wave of his hand, the footpath that would take Polly to the back of the house. She crossed the drive and found a sodden path behind rhododendrons that had leaves still dripping with last night's rain.

Standing there, for a moment, she felt abandoned and sorry for herself. She would have given a lot to turn round and run back home, back to all that was familiar. If that sour man was anything to go by she didn't think she was going to be very happy here.

Some raindrops trickled down her neck. She hunched her shoulders and hoisted her basket a little higher. Well, Margaret Ann Holland, it's no good dilly dallying, she told herself. You'll be in trouble for being late before you start.

She hurried along the path and turning a

bend was startled to suddenly find herself at the entrance to a courtyard of cobbled stones. To the right was a row of eight stables, their upper doors latched open, and three horses were greeting the morning, ears pricked forward at her approach. In the centre of the courtyard, a tall beanpole of a youth groomed a sleek chestnut mare. He paused to stare, open-mouthed, as Polly headed towards him with a look of fierce determination on her young face.

"Good morning. Excuse me, but would you be kind enough to show me the kitchen door?"

He swallowed and his Adam's apple bounced up and down on his scrawny neck. He had never seen such a lovely child, for child she certainly was with her long fair plaits and wide blue eyes. If this was the new maid they were expecting, they were in for a surprise in there. And she'd be in for a surprise too for she sounded more like a lady than a maid. Poor little mite. He wondered how long she would last.

"It's that one over there." He pointed to a heavy oak door opposite the stables.

As she turned, it opened and a girl in a dark maroon alpaca dress appeared. She wore a white cap that was trying, unsuccessfully, to contain a shock of red curls, a large apron that enveloped her ample frame and hid most of her skirt, and had her sleeves rolled up to her elbows.

"You coming to breakfast, Ted?" she called to the boy, and as she caught sight of Polly. "You the new maid we're expecting? Better come in then." And without waiting for an answer, bundled Polly through the door.

The kitchen was huge. Polly had never seen such a kitchen, not even at the parsonage which was the largest house in the village.

She wasn't to take in the details until much later because, in the centre of the room, was a massive oak table and around it sat a dozen or more people. And a dozen or more pairs of eyes, openly inquisitive, watched her as she made her way, clutching her basket before her, towards the table. She stopped in front of an enormous woman who sat at its head attacking a whole ham with a carving knife.

"Excuse me, ma'am. I'm Polly Holland and I'm... I'm the new maid." Her timid voice was hesitant, hardly above a whisper.

"Oh you are, are you?" As she nodded her head, her many chins rearranged themselves and settled. "Well, I'm Mrs Tatlow and I'm the cook here. And that's what you'll call me. Cook or Mrs Tatlow. You can save your ma'ams for those that warrant them. Although I must say," she added, looking round at the servants assembled there and fastening her eye on Ted, who was attempting to gain his seat inconspicuously, "a bit more respect from someone, who I'll not mention, wouldn't go amiss."

She smiled kindly at Polly. "Sit yerself down over there, next to Agnes, and have a bite with us, then Fanny can take you up to yer room. You'll be sharing with her. After that you're to report to the housekeeper. She's expectin' you at nine. She'll tell you yer duties."

Polly drew out a chair and sat down. She looked about her at the faces that scrutinised her. These were the people that she was going to have to work with, eat with, and live with for the foreseeable future, and she wondered how they were going to get along.

# CHAPTER THIRTEEN

November brought cold raw days and frequent fog. Sarah, hanging some sheets on the washing line in the back garden, had little hope of getting them dry. She pushed the clothes prop up against the line with hands bright red from the icy water. She daren't have a proper hot wash more than once a week or Pa would start asking questions. You could always tell a washday by the steamy windows and smell of Sunlight soap and she didn't want to have to explain to him that Robert had started to wet the bed. She didn't think  he would be sympathetic, so wrapped was he in his own thoughts these days; unapproachable and bad-tempered.

Sarah's footsteps crunched on the frosty leaves as she hurried up the garden path, anxious to reach the warmth of the kitchen and get on with her chores. She washed the breakfast dishes and returned them to their place in the dresser, scrubbed the table and swept the floor, all the while reflecting on how life had changed so drastically in one day; the day that Ma had died.

Making her bed, shaking out the top sheet, she watched it billow above the bed and settle softly. She bent and tucked it in under the heavy feather mattress, and as she plumped up the pillows, she thought of the years when she had yearned for a bed to herself. One that she could stretch out in and nobody to share it with. Nobody to take all the covers on a cold winter's night; nobody to disturb her with their tossing and turning; alone to think private thoughts instead of listening to Polly's inconsequential chatter. Well, she had got her wish, hadn't she? But now she wished she could put the clock back and have Polly here again.

She had not seen Polly since she had gone to work up at the Hall and she missed her. The cottage was so quiet these days, what with Pa off to work at first light and Robert rushing through his chores and disappearing for hours. All she could hear, at the moment, was the clock ticking and, somewhere in the distance, the barking of a dog. Well, you'd better get used to it, she chided herself, because this will be the pattern of things and it's no good moaning about it.

She made her pa's bed and dusted the brass rails. As she shook the duster out of the window, she noticed the gathering storm clouds and wondered how she was going to get Robert's sheets dry. It was then she remembered that Ma kept some spare sheets in the tin trunk under the bed.

She dropped to her knees and pulled out the heavy trunk that had always housed Ma's possessions. As a child, Sarah had enjoyed tracing, with her finger, the flowers and birds that were painted on the lid and sides. Now, as then, she ran her hand over the pink and white roses, followed the lines of the intertwined leaves, touched the delicate outstretched wing of a bluebird. It was a reverent movement. This was Ma's trunk and, inside, all the possessions she had cherished.

Sarah hesitated a moment. Ma had always kept the contents away from her children and she wondered what Pa would say if he found out that she had been rummaging down it. She would just take the sheets. Only until the ones she had washed today could be dried, she told herself. It was more important that Pa didn't find out about Robert's problem.

She opened the lid and smelled the lavender. Its delicate perfume permeated all Ma's things. For as long as she could remember Sarah had associated lavender with her ma. It grew down each side of the garden path, right from the gate to the front door, and in summer their skirts brushing the flowers as they passed would release its fragrance into the balmy air. Her ma filled sachets with the dried flowers and kept them tucked between her linens.

Topmost in the trunk lay an embroidered tablecloth. Sarah remembered Ma working on it, skilfully stitching all the yellow daisy petals and green leaves. And she remembered special occasions when the cloth had been brought out. Times when family and friends had gathered round the table and there had been scarcely enough room for them all in the tiny parlour. Whose birthday had it been, Polly's or hers, when Ned had dropped beetroot on the cloth and Granny Tulley had cuffed his ear? Ma had been gracious and smoothed things over, sprinkled salt on the cloth and said it didn't matter, but it had taken several washes to remove the stain and you could still see a trace of it if you knew where to look.

Sarah lay the cloth on the floor beside her, added an apron and two tray cloths, then lifted out a small box. She knew what was inside. Forgetting, for a moment, her search for the sheets, she removed the lid and her eyes softened as she looked upon Ma's cameo brooch. The images came tumbling one after another into her mind: Ma, in her best blue dress, pinning the brooch between the two points of the lace collar. She had worn it on Sundays and any special time and Sarah could picture Ma's happy face at Christmas sitting beside the fire, smiling as she watched them all opening their presents. And her ma, coming up to kiss them goodnight, the cameo glistening in the candlelight. Another of her; sunlight shining on her face, beautiful and dignified, sitting on the plank seat of the old cart as they made their way to church. Such an overwhelming sadness, she felt, and yet she remained dry-eyed.

It had been two months now and still she

kept her grief locked inside her, even in the sleepless nights when Polly had at last fallen asleep, tears still wet on her cheeks, she had stared wide-eyed into the darkness, unable to cry.

She sighed and, thrusting the cameo and her memories from her, soon found the sheets. She would have quickly replaced the tablecloth and the other linen had her attention not been drawn to a small leather bag at the bottom of the trunk. She had never seen it before.

Curiously, she lifted it out. But the drawstring had not been tied adequately to secure the bulging pouch and before she could save it the contents had spilled into her lap.

Sovereigns! Golden sovereigns! More than she had ever imagined she would see in her life. For some moments she sat motionless, staring at the coins in astonishment, eyes round with wonder and her mouth agape.

There must be a hundred sovereigns here, she thought, feeling the weight of them as they lay in her skirt. She returned them to the bag, mechanically counting them. All the while, questions pulled at her mind. Where have they come from?…forty-five, forty-six…Who do they belong to?… sixty-two, sixty-three… Why are they here?… eighty-four, eighty-five….They most certainly can't belong to us or Pa wouldn't still be working so hard. And where would he get such a large amount? She had finished counting. There were one hundred and twenty sovereigns.

Sarah was still staring at the bag when she heard the footsteps on the path, the front door opening.

"Hallo. Is anybody there?" Polly's familiar voice called up the stairs.

Sarah quickly buried the bag beneath the linen and scrambled to her feet. "I'm up here, Polly."

"Shall I come up?"

"No. No, I'll be right down." Sarah tossed the sheets onto Robert's bed from the open doorway and hurried downstairs.

Polly stood in the kitchen with a red knitted muffler about her ears, rubbing her hands together. "It's freezing out today." She turned, was puzzled by Sarah's distracted expression. "Are you all right, Sarah? You look queer. Are you ill?"

Sarah forced a smile. At any other time she would have been delighted to see her sister. "No I'm fine. You startled me, that's all. Why didn't you send word with Ned that you were coming?"

"I haven't had a chance to see him. I'm always somewhere else when Ned delivers." She didn't say that she always made sure she was somewhere else when Ned came up to the Hall. His moonstruck countenance irked her and she was embarrassed by the way his gaze never left her face. He fastened on to a smile like a puppy on a table scrap. Agnes, the red-haired maid, had noticed and sniggered, whispering behind her hand to the other servants and Polly had been furious.

"I'll put the kettle on. Take off your coat and get yourself warm." Sarah noticed Polly's pale face, the shadows beneath her eyes, and thought how tired she looked.

"Oh Polly, I have missed you. What's it like up there? I want to hear all about it."

As Sarah collected the tea things together, Polly looked about her. "I hadn't realised how small this place is," she said.

Sarah looked up with a rueful smile. "It doesn't seem small when I am on my knees scrubbing the floor."

"Don't talk to me about scrubbing floors. It seems as if I spend my life on my knees. If I'm not scrubbing or polishing I'm brushing the stairs. You could sit this house in the kitchen up there and still have room to spare."

"Do you have to scrub the kitchen floor?"

"Of course not. That's scullery maids work. I'm a housemaid."

"What's the house like?" Sarah asked eagerly. "Is it as grand as they say?"

"I haven't actually seen the house. Not where the family live. My work's confined to the servants' quarters, the back stairs, the housekeeper's rooms...oh, and the butler's too. Miss Passmore - that's the housekeeper - she's horrible. Looks down her nose at you and sniffs a great deal. Well, she says it will be a long time before I'll be allowed above stairs, but if I worked hard and kept a civil tongue in my head, I would get there one day.

You'd have thought she was offering the moon the way she said it."

Sarah handed her the tea and for a moment Polly looked down at the steaming cup, and when she raised her eyes the deep resentment she harboured was plain to see.

"I still can't forgive Pa," she said. "I don't understand why he has changed towards me. I thought he loved me. He was always such a loving father but something has caused this... this hostility he has towards me. Perhaps, if I could understand, I could come to terms with the way things have turned out. I could try to forget and find some peace. But I can't just forget... or forgive. When I left home, it was as if a part of me died. I never thought I could feel this empty and yet so... so full of anger at the same time."

Sarah listened to Polly's pain but felt helpless to ease it.

"I try to make the best of things, Sarah, and some of the servants are nice. Mrs Tatlow likes to appear fierce but she's soft inside and Fanny... I like Fanny. I share a room with her and one night she told me about her life. She's had a hard life and she's such a little thing. She came from the workhouse and you wouldn't believe what it was like there." She sipped her tea and edged closer to the fire. "But it's freezing there. I've never felt so cold. You'd think that with all their money they could keep the place warm. Agnes - she's the second housemaid - says that it's always like that.

They put on a show when guests are staying though. Last week, some distant cousin and his wife stayed for three days and you should have seen all the coal that was lugged about; all the hot water they sent for. And when they'd gone, the cinders had to be sieved and the clinker saved for another fire."

"Do you have to do that? What are your duties?" Sarah wanted to draw Polly away from thoughts of their pa.

Polly told her of the long hours. How she and Fanny crawled out of bed before dawn, dressing hurriedly before they could lose the bed-warmth from their bodies and then scurrying down the back stairs to go about their tasks. She spoke of the long hours black-leading grates and whitening hearths with a scouring stone; of the fire irons that had to be polished and how her hands had cracked from the hard yellow soap with which the floors were scrubbed; of falling asleep as her head touched the pillow only, too soon, to have Fanny shake her awake the next morning.

Sarah didn't tell her about the wet beds or the money she had seen in the tin trunk. These things she kept to herself. In fact, they were pushed to the back of her mind as she listened, and was surprised when Polly exclaimed at the time.

"Did the clock strike four? I'd better be going. I have to be back by five."

# CHAPTER FOURTEEN

It was perhaps fifteen minutes after Polly had left and Sarah had washed the cups that she thought of Robert. She hadn't seen him all day and that was unusual. He had done his chores in the morning and gone off to the woods, and now his evening chores needed to be done. Water had to be drawn and the logs brought in.

She sighed and it was with some irritation that she laced up her boots and wrapped a shawl round her shoulders. As if I didn't have enough to think about, she thought. I shall have to go and look for him while there's still light.

First, she climbed to the spinney at the back of the house. The trees, bare of their summer greenery, stood tall against a leaden sky, angular and unwelcoming. But without the leaves it was easy to see that Robert wasn't there so she retraced her steps and made her way down to the river. The watery sun was low as she followed the path upstream, hugging her shawl to her against the cold.

Ahead, hawthorns grew down to meet pale reeds that rose from the water's edge. Here, the path petered out to wet mud and she had to clamber up the bank to the lane. She stood here, for a moment, looking about her in the fading light. Clicking her tongue against the roof of her mouth, she spoke to herself. Robert. Robert, where are you? What a nuisance you are. It's a good job Pa's not coming home tonight because I wouldn't have his dinner ready. And she thought, as she had done on similar occasions, how frustrating it was not to be able to call out to Robert. Perhaps he has gone up to see the animals at the farm. Mrs Fuller sometimes let him feed the chickens and he liked to help Walter with the big shiny-backed cart horses.

Dodging the puddles in the lane and the wet slippery leaves, Sarah hurried towards the farm. She wished that she had worn her coat as she eyed the gathering storm clouds and the wind began to rise. She almost ran over the wooden bridge that spanned the dark swirling water with its cargo of bouncing twigs and leaves and was glad to see the farm before her. The lights from the low stone farmhouse were welcoming.

Her annoyance at Robert's absence was turning to anxiety. What if he wasn't here? Where else could she look?

Lantern light spilled from the cowshed onto the flagstones of the yard and she could hear old Snowy gently chiding the cows. "Come on now, Pansy, let's be having yer. We've not got all night.

That's the way, Daisy. Good girl. Good girl."

She picked her way across the yard and called from the open door. "Have you seen Robert lately? Has he been here?"

Old Snowy shook his head as he blew his nose loudly into a red handkerchief. "He be 'ere a while ago but I ain't seen him this last 'our. Happen he's up at the 'ouse. Go'n ask the missus. She'll be the one to ask."

Mrs Fuller, herself, opened the door to Sarah's knock. She stood with her face flushed from baking and her eyes crinkled at the corners when she smiled at her visitor.

"Why it's Sarah. What be you a-doing out this awful weather? I reckon we're in for some rain. The cat's been licking her tail all day and that be a sure sign that rains a-coming. Come in. come in, m'dear."

She ushered Sarah into the kitchen. It was warm and full of the smells of cooking; of apples and cinnamon and pork roasting in the big black stove. The firelight shone on the polished brass fender. It was a big room with a low-beamed ceiling and a grey flag-stoned floor brightened by a rag rug in front of the hearth. In the centre of the room stood a massive oak table with trestles on either side. Sage and thyme and rosemary hung from hooks in a beam and a picture of the queen, stout and cross-looking in her blue garter ribbon, and another of roses and one of cows, decorated the walls. Everything was neat and clean, cosy and comfortable, and it was a relief for a moment to come in from the cold.

"Mrs Fuller, have you seen Robert?" she asked anxiously. "I've searched for him everywhere, in the spinney and down by the river. I can't find him anywhere."

"Lordy, dear, why he's been and gone this hour or more. He's allus up here with the animals but he didn't stay above an half hour today. He's not been looking hisself lately. Proper down in the dumps, but I s'pose that's to be 'spected, what with your dear mother passing an' all. I wonder where he's gone though."

The kettle sang on the hob and Mrs Fuller picked up a big brown earthenware teapot. "Sit yerself down a second and have a cup. Get yerself warm. Dan'll be in any moment and he might know where the boy is."

"I don't think I should wait, thank you all the same. I'm anxious to find him and get home."

"Two minutes won't make no difference and it stands to reason if Dan knows where he is it would save you time in the long run."

Sarah had to agree. "Yes, perhaps you're right if you're sure he won't be long."

"He'll be here any moment. He's just seeing to the pigs." She pushed back the grey hairs that strayed from the bun at the nape of her neck. "And anyway," she laughed, "he can smell the teapot a mile away. Now if you'll excuse me, I won't sit down with you. I want to get this little lot away."

Sarah liked Mrs Fuller. She thought of all the years this fat little woman had presided over the massive tea urn when all the cottagers assembled for their annual Harvest Home supper, always laughing, always talking, and how she was known in the village for her kindness to her workers, everyone getting a joint of beef at Christmas and never forgotten when sickness came.

She sipped at the scalding liquid, grateful for the warmth, as Mrs Fuller bustled about the kitchen. She took a red and white checked cloth, lifted the roasting dish out of the oven and basted the sizzling meat with the juices from the pan. She returned it to the oven and cleared the table of the remnants of her baking. Wooden barrels of flour and sugar were restored to their shelves and butter and eggs to the pantry.

Sarah watched her and remembered, too, that years ago Mrs Fuller had walked with a limp. The children of the village had followed her round the green, stiff-legged and laughing. But Dan had fashioned boots for her, the right one built up to compensate for her shorter leg. Dan was kind, like his ma.

The door opened and it was as if her thoughts had conjured him up. She watched Dan wiping his feet on the mat, telling his ma how hungry he was and she laughing and saying she had a horse in the oven and would that do? They exchanged an affectionate glance and Sarah thought what a happy household this must be. Mrs Fuller obviously doted on her son and he was a fine young man.

Tall and fresh-faced, he had grown broad shouldered and strong from following the plough and lifting bales of hay. He had sat next to her in school one year and what she remembered most of that time was his kindness.

Dan's hazel eyes lit up when he saw Sarah. He strode over to where she sat by the fire.

"Hello, Sarah. What are you doing here? It's a nasty night to be out, isn't it?"

"Oh, Dan, have you seen Robert?" She rose from her seat. "Your ma thought you might know where he is."

"He was here earlier. Helped me to rub down old Nellie, he did. But I've not seen him for some time."

Mrs Fuller asked, "Do you know where he was going after?"

Dan raised his eyebrows at his ma. It was with a wry smile, but in a kindly way, that he answered her. "Well, he couldn't exactly tell me, could he?"

Mrs Fuller looked embarrassed. "Aw, I'm sorry Sarah. I didn't think. I meant no offence."

"And no offence is taken, Mrs Fuller. Thank you for the tea. I'd better get along. Robert's without his coat and I'm worried for his safety."

"And so are you without a coat. Just you wait a moment." Mrs Fuller rummaged in a cupboard and brought out a thick grey coat. "Here.

159

Take this. It's seen better days but it'll keep the wet off."

"I'll go with you," Dan offered. "It's dark now and you'll be needing a lamp."

Without waiting for an answer, he took his big black coat out of the same cupboard and picked up the lamp.

The wind had reached the force of a heavy gale as they set off together and with it singing in their ears they had to shout to make themselves heard. Dan asked her where she had looked and when she told him he said, "Shall we make our way down towards the village on this side of the river? If you didn't light your lamps before you came out, and he's returned home, then we should see a light shining and can double back."

"Yes, yes we'll do that," she cried. The wind whipped her hair across her face, into her eyes and she struggled to tuck it under her shawl that now covered her head.

Suddenly, the storm broke. The icy rain fell in torrents and within minutes they were soaked. Bent against the wind, that hurled the rain into their faces and made it difficult to see, they slipped and struggled to remain upright on the muddy paths.

The river, to their left, rushed bubbling by with a noisy rumbling sound. Weeds were lashed from side to side in the fast-flowing current; the water brown with swirling mud. The chestnut trees, devoid of their huge golden leaves, provided no shelter. By the time they reached the spot from where they could see the cottage, they were staggered by the fury of the storm.

Sarah's spirits sank. No lights could be seen from any of the windows.

Dan took hold of her hand and helped her over the slimy stile. "Look! there's the village," he shouted. "We're nearly there. Happen someone can tell us where he is. Mayhap he's just sheltering from the storm."

Sarah was grateful for his encouraging words and for the hand that held her own. She looked up at him, saw his light brown hair now dark and glistening, the rivulets of water that ran down his face and dripped off his chin, and thought how kind he was. How many people would come out with me on a night like this? And she knew that she would never forget his kindness.

At the outskirts of the village, Dan spoke again. "He may be at the smithy. If he's not there, I'll ask at the inn if anyone has seen him. Let's cut through the churchyard. It'll save a few minutes."

They paused at the lych-gate. Sarah said, "Perhaps we should call at the parsonage. Aunt Ruth, Miss Greenway, may have him. If he was there, when the storm broke, I'm sure she wouldn't have let him leave." But even as she said it, she knew that Robert should have been home long before then and she was afraid.

Not even the looming headstones or the creaking elms or the pile of fresh earth over a newly-dug grave could increase her dread. Nor the dark shape next to her ma's gleaming new headstone.

"Wait! Wait, Dan, wait!" She pulled her hand from his and ran over the slippery turf towards the grave. "Oh, Robert, Robert, my dear, my dear!" she cried as she pulled him to her and rocked him in her arms.

Robert cried out in his misery. His keening seemed to rise above the wind and the driving rain. It was a cry of such loneliness and despair.

Dan bent and took the boy from her. "Come on," he gently said. "Let's take him home."


Dan lay on his back staring into the darkness. He couldn't remember the exact moment that he realised he was in love with Sarah Holland. Happen it was from the time when he had sat next to her in class. She was two years younger than him but he remembered how bright she had been. Or had it been from the time she had started to bring her brother up to the farm to see the animals and he had noticed how she was growing? He didn't know.

Since he had left school the farm had taken up most of his time. He didn't want his ma getting a new farm manager when Grimshaw retired. He wanted to run it himself and it took time to learn all he needed to know. And so he hadn't seen much of the Holland girls.

A lot of folk said that her sister, Polly, was the prettier of the two girls and it was true that she was pretty in a doll-like way. But compared with Sarah she was a colourless creature and he detected a peevishness in her nature that showed in her eyes and about her mouth.

But Sarah... Sarah, with her wild good looks and startling blue eyes; it was \Sarah he couldn't get out of his mind.

His ma had started hinting that it was about time, at seventeen, that he got out more. 'Can't understand why you don't start enjoying yerself,' she said. 'God alone knows and He won't tell us. Surely there's somebody you'd like to be stepping out with.'

Yes, there was, he thought. He'd like to be stepping out with Sarah Holland and he couldn't understand why he hadn't made any moves in that direction. Why couldn't he just come out with it? Come out with what? I'm in love with you, Sarah Holland. No, he couldn't say that. That would never do.

It would be different if it was Jane or Betsy. Jane was housemaid for his ma and Betsy worked in the dairy. Only the other day, Betsy had waylaid him as he was bringing the empty churns into the dairy. She was always throwing herself at him with her inviting smiles and the way she thrust her large breasts out when he had to pass her in the narrow passage between the milking sheds and the dairy.

It was tempting to have his fun with her; she was asking for it and he was a man now after all and with a man's needs. No, Betsy may laugh, mocking him for his blushes and later he would usually see her and Jane giggling in a corner, but he would rather go without if he couldn't have Sarah.

Well, why didn't he go and see Sarah, ask her if she'd like to keep company with him? She could only say no and then at least he would know where he stood. He had nearly spoken to her at this year's Harvest Home. He had asked he to dance. Round and round they had spun and whirled about the yard with the young folk and all the cottagers singing;

> *You should see me dance the polka,*
> *You should see me cover the ground.*
> *You should see my coat tails flying*
> *As I dance my way around.*

When the music stopped, she had looked up at him, laughing, and it was all he could do not to take her in his arms and hug her to him. The memory of it and the fresh apple smell of her hair had stayed with him. He should have asked her then but Ned Tulley had come over and asked her to dance, whisking her away so that he had missed the chance.

He had still been full of good intentions but put it off, always making excuses to himself, and then Mrs Holland had died and he knew he would have to bide his time.

Tonight was the first time he had seen her since the funeral and he had had the chance. There, under the lych-gate, when she had looked up at him with those beautiful, frightened eyes, he had wanted to say something but she was so concerned for her brother that he'd kept a still tongue. So why hadn't he asked her when they had got back to the cottage? It didn't seem like the right time then either. Always a reason not to… or were they excuses?

Dan groaned as he rolled over onto his stomach. Burying his head in the feather pillow, he tried to push the image of her from his mind.

# CHAPTER FIFTEEN

All night, Sarah's mind had been filled with the happenings of the day; thoughts of Polly and Robert and Pa.

She tried to examine her feelings for her pa. Suddenly he had become a stranger. Why was there this animosity towards Polly? She had wondered about that since Polly had gone up to the Hall. What had brought about such a change when she had always been his favourite? And where did all that money come from? All those sovereigns in the tin trunk. She could not believe that they had not been honestly come by but, for the first time, she questioned the periods he spent away from home.

Night passed, morning came and her head throbbed when she rose at seven. She was concerned about Robert. When she and Dan had brought him home he was soaked to the skin and shivering. But strangely enough he wasn't affected by his drenching and, confined indoors by the adverse weather, had tried to help her about the

166

house. It was his way of saying sorry for the trouble he had caused, she supposed, and was glad of the help for, as the day wore on, her headache persisted and she felt both physically and mentally battered.

The next two days were a struggle for Sarah. She managed to keep going but the prickle in her throat developed into a soreness that made swallowing difficult. Her head continued to throb, her eyes smarted and she alternated between shivering and feeling hot.

On the third day, she had to admit that she couldn't go on much longer. She would have to go to bed. She made a big pot of stew with some scrag-end, and carrots and onions from the garden. That will feed Robert and Pa for a couple of days, she thought. I'll just take a walk up to the farm. I'll take Mrs Fuller's coat back. The air might do me good if I wrap up.

She could have sent Robert, she knew, but she felt the need to see Mrs Fuller's kindly face. Perhaps she could suggest a remedy for the sore throat. The horehound and honey  she was taking soothed for a while but had done nothing to improve. Yes, she'd just go up to the farm and come straight home and go to bed.

Robert went with her. The air was crisp and frosty as they walked up the lane but her skin felt hot and dry. Robert stopped to watch a moorhen skate over the now tranquil water. She left him to catch up with her. It was an effort to put one foot in front of the other and the sooner she got there, and back to her bed, the better. She had left a brick to bake in the oven and would wrap it in a piece of flannel when she got home and take it to bed to sweat the cold out of her.

Jane opened the door and ushered her into the parlour. The housemaid had a stolid little face and wore her dark hair parted in the middle with smooth plaits wound round her head.

"I'll tell the missus you be 'ere. She's out the back with the chickens." She left the room only to stick her head round the door and add, "Oh… and please to take a seat," before disappearing once more.

Sarah sank into a rocking chair by the fire, the coat folded over her knees. Gently, she rocked herself and looked about her. Gleaming wooden floorboards covered in the centre by a carpet; pink roses on a grey-green background. Gate-legged tables and a horsehair sofa. Every surface crammed with ornaments; photographs, rows of pewter, figurines and tall vases, and on a tripod table, a huge aspidistra in a big china plant pot. There were three diamond-paned windows with window seats, all in a row, and through the nearest she could see into the courtyard. She could see the granary with its outside staircase and the stable with the stamping cart horses. Robert was there, watching them.

It was a big room and only a small fire, so why did she feel so terribly hot? She really didn't need this scarf around her neck. She got up and moved away from the hearth. She blinked her eyes.

The room was spinning. Fire coursed through her veins, a pulse beat in her head, an unremitting throb. She must go outside. She must get some air.

Sarah felt herself being lifted up, her sodden nightclothes pulled over her head. Cool water on her skin, refreshing cool water and new fresh-smelling linen.

Her ma was caring for her. "Ma..." she murmured.

Muffled voices. They seemed to come from a long way away. Her eyelids flickered open and through the blur of dazzling light and moving shadows she was able to make out the figure bending over her. It wasn't her ma. Ma was dead. She wondered who was looking after her but the effort to concentrate her mind was too much.

She slept again and when she woke fingers of sunshine felt their way through the casement window and she could hear a blackbird joyfully greet the morning. Looking about her, she realised that she was not in her own bed. This room was bigger. Knotted, darkened beams ribbed the sloping whitewashed ceiling and brightly coloured rugs covered the wooden floor. Apart from the bed, a washstand, a dressing table and a wicker armchair with a patchwork cushion were the only furnishings. Yet in spite of its sparseness it managed to convey an air of cheerfulness with rose patterned curtains and embroidered samplers on the wall.

Her attention was drawn to a painting that

hung to the right of the window. It was a picture of the crucifixion of Jesus. Written above the cross were the words 'This I have done for thee' and below was the question, 'What hast thou done for me?' The inscription made her feel uneasy. It bothered her but she couldn't say why. She didn't want to see the agony the painter had portrayed; didn't want to see the pierced and bleeding body. She turned her head away.

She slept again. When next she opened her eyes, she could hear the sound of voices, the clopping of hooves, the jingle of harness.

"Take them up to the top field, Walter. I'll follow up there a bit later and we'll have a look at that fence while we're about it."

Sarah recognised Dan's voice and she knew then that she was at the farm. Now she remembered bringing the coat back, how warm the parlour had seemed, how hot she had felt. And with the remembering came an anxiousness. She must get back home. Pa would wonder where she was. He would want his dinner. And then she couldn't remember if he was coming home tonight or not but she did remember the sheets. She'd left the sheets on the line. She had to get them in. and what about Robert?

She pushed back the bedding and attempted to stand, only to fall back on the bed, surprised at how weak and groggy she felt. Her head spun and she closed her eyes.

Mrs Fuller found her there, half out of the

bed. She gently lifted Sarah's legs so that she lay straight and was covering her with the quilt when Sarah opened her eyes.

"Mrs Fuller? How long? How long have I been here?" Her mouth was dry, her voice no more than a rasping whisper, each word a painful croak.

Mrs Fuller smiled. "Nigh on a fortnight. Well, 'twill be tomorrow. How are you feeling, m'dear? It's good to see you a bit better. Fair worried, we were, I don't mind telling you. Found you, all of a heap, on the parlour floor."

Sarah was astonished. "A fortnight! It's not possible. I have to get back." She made to rise. "I have to see to —"

"Now don't go a-frettin' yerself." Mrs Fuller stayed her with a gentle hand. "Everything is taken care of. Your pa is staying with his sister over at Chillingford. He came to see you, asked if there was anything he could do, was concerned about you, I don't mind telling. He was a-wanting to take you back home but you wasn't fit to be moved. I told 'im you was best left where you was and that me and Jane and Betsy could do all that needs doing. He be a-coming over tomorrow, so you can see 'im then."

"And Robert? How's Robert? Is he over at Aunt Florrie's too?"

"No, m'dear, he's right here. Has been since you took sick. Sat with you for hours, he has. Right worried he's been, I can tell you. He'll be glad to know you're better. He's with Walter, up at the top

171

field, just now. Likes being with the animals, don't he? Got a way with 'em too. He'll be down for a bite to eat come midday so I'll send 'im up to you then."

Sarah watched her fuss about the room, folding a towel, adjusting an ornament of a shepherdess a fraction so that it stood exactly in the centre of a crocheted mat.

"Mrs Fuller... about Robert..." Sarah was diffident about broaching the subject. "Robert has a problem... at night.... He has been—"

"Don't you fret yerself, m'dear. I know full well what you're on about and it's all sorted out. He had that... that problem for the first few nights but he's been right as ninepence since. Happen the excitement of spending so much time with the animals has taken his mind off things.

'It's a hard time for boys when they reach eleven or so. They're old enough to go out to work, like to think of their selves as grown-up young men, but they're still little boys inside. Must have been hard on the lad when your ma died. You can't talk to 'im and he can't say how he feels, can he? He do love them animals, though, don't he?" She wiped the marble top of the washstand and then turned, and with her arms folded under her ample breasts, approached the bed. "Now, do you think you could fancy a bite to eat, m'dear?"

Sarah looked up into Mrs Fuller's friendly face. "Oh, Mrs Fuller ... Mrs Fuller..." She started to cry. Her face crumpled and now the tears came. It

172

was the last thing she wanted to do; cry in front of this kind woman. But it was her very kindness that prompted the tears. So long, it seemed, had she wanted to cry but couldn't and now it was difficult to control her weeping. She felt weak and foolish. Her ma had always said that tears were for shedding in private and she would possibly have composed herself had it not been for Mrs Fuller's next words.

Seeing Sarah's distress, she sat on the edge of the bed and took her in her arms. "There, m'dear, you have a good cry. You'll feel a lot better after, I dare say. It's all been a lot to cope with, hasn't it? What with your ma going and Robert disappearing and young Polly off into service. And now this illness on top of everything. It's a lot for a young lass to have on her plate. Yes, you have a good cry."

Sarah's head rested on Maisie Fuller's breast.. Her plumpness was comforting. Maisie had a smell about her that was both clean and earthy. It was the smell of soap and fresh air and newly baked bread, not at all like her ma who had always smelt of lavender, or the cologne Pa had bought her one Christmas.

She cried for a long time; great heaving, racking sobs that shook her narrow shoulders, purged her of all the hurt and anger and pain of her ma's death and left, in its wake, a terrible sadness.

And when her tears were spent, Mrs Fuller took a handkerchief from the capacious pocket in her apron and handed it to her. "There, m'dear, you blow yer nose. I'll go and fetch some water and you can freshen yerself up a bit. Rinse yer face and you'll be as right as rain again in no time."

"I'm sorry Mrs Fuller. I shouldn't have behaved like that. You've been so kind—"

"Now don't you go a-worrying yerself. 'Tis but nature to want to cry at a time like this and 'twould do more harm than good not to."

It was another week before Sarah went home. During that time Mrs Fuller fussed and fed her and brought her warm frothy milk to drink straight from the cow. It was nice to have such attention but as soon as she felt well enough she wanted to be home.

Dan brought the dogcart round to the farmhouse door and Sarah, wrapped in blankets against the cold, said goodbye to Mrs Fuller.

"Don't thank me, thank God I'm able," Mrs Fuller told her. "Now, you think nothing of it. Get yerself home and keep warm. 'Twon't do to go a-catching cold again. Here, I've put a few things together for you. I made one of them cakes that you liked – I put in a good sprinkling of raisins – and some new-laid eggs, the brown speckly ones. I allus think they're the best. A pound of fresh butter, there is, and a milk pudding, so mind you don't go a-tipping it up." She wedged the basket in the cart, next to Sarah's feet, as Sarah thanked her again.

With a twitch of the reins Dan had the long-tailed pony clattering out of the yard. Sarah looked back to wave at Mrs Fuller, standing at the open door. The woman, who had shown her such

174

overwhelming kindness, waved back.

They had crossed the wooden bridge before Dan spoke. "You mustn't mind Ma fussing the way she do. I think she gets lonely, stuck out here without another woman to talk to. I think she's enjoyed mothering you..." Suddenly he looked confused.

It occurred to Sarah that perhaps he thought it was a tactless remark bearing in mind her ma had just died. "I think I've enjoyed being mothered... and I don't think Robert has stopped eating the entire time." She laughed and then became serious. "We will never forget your kindness, both yours and your mother's."

The sun cast shadows across the lane from the high trees and the wide bars of light and dark gave it a striped look. Dan stopped the cart under a chestnut tree and turned to face her, his broad shoulders sloping as he leaned his elbow on one knee. She thought he was about to say something but he hesitated, gnawing on his lip, and looked about him as if he searched for the words he needed.

He looked down at his hands and fidgeted with the reins he held. "Sarah, I was thinking,' he said at last, 'well, I was wondering...." He took a deep breath and the words came tumbling out in a rush. "...if you've a mind to keep company with me."

There was nothing that Sarah would have liked more and she thought his grin was going to stretch from ear to ear when she answered.

"Yes, Dan," she said. "Yes, I would like that very much."

# CHAPTER SIXTEEN

Down in the village, on the far side of the green where the brambles and long grass grew, Betsy pushed Jimmy's hand from her and buttoned her bodice.

"Leave off now, Jimmy Caldwell," she laughed, "I got to get back for the milking."

She straightened her skirts. "Aw, look at that! Grass stains on me petticoat. What ever's Jane goin' to say when I put it in the wash on Monday?"

Jimmy grinned as he stood and buckled his belt. "Happen she'll have to get used to seeing them soon," he said.

Betsy's eyes narrowed as she looked up at him standing between her and the May sunshine. "What you getting at?"

"I was talking to old Snowy in the Arms last week and he said they could do with another 'and up at Fuller's. I'm going up there first thing the morrow. If I get taken on, we'd have more chance to get them grass stains on yer petticoat." He laughed suggestively.

"Well, there you're in for a disappointment 'cos he's just taken on the 'olland boy. He won't be a-needing anyone else now."

The smile left Jimmy's face. "That bloody loony!" he ground out. "What good's he goin' to be?"

"He's not so daft as you think… nor ain't his sister neither. Ever since she took sick last winter she's been coming up to the farm nearly every week. Real thick with 'em, she is, drinking tea and gossiping with the missus. I reckon she's got her eye on the farm and she's set her cap at Dan…and 'im, poor devil, can't see what she's about. She's too clever by half and he's running after her, making sheep's eyes and grinning all over his face."

Jimmy wasn't listening to her. His thoughts were of the job he had missed and the nagging his ma would give him if he didn't find work soon. That bloody loony! He had never liked him. He hadn't forgotten the lathering his pa had given him, all those years ago, after he'd laid into the boy. He had only done it for a laugh but nobody had seen it that way. They all said it was a disgrace, especially after old Greenway's sermon. His ma had said she couldn't hold her head up in the village for a long time after. They'd soon forgotten, but he couldn't forget the feel of his pa's belt and the way the other boys had turned against him.

"And there she was last week looking as if butter wouldn't melt in her mouth. And another thing —"

"Aw, stop yer blethering, Betsy. I'm off home."

Betsy watched him stride off without her. With his head down and his hands thrust deep into his pockets, he crossed the green without a backward glance.

Robert had grown both in stature and confidence since he had gone to work at Fuller's farm. "And lucky he was to get taken on, considering," John said.

At first, Dan arranged to have him clearing ditches with the other men, but they teased him in their rough way and, because he couldn't understand their laughter, he became frustrated. Provoked enough, he threw sticks or whatever was at hand. Once, he threw Walter's dinner frail. A rosy apple rolled into the mud and bread and cheese fell from its wrapping.

Walter was much upset and complained to Dan. "If you ask me, he's a bit soft in the upper storey. He shouldn't be a-working with us men if he can't behave hisself."

"Well, you must have done something to start him off, Walter. He's a good worker till you lot start on him."

"We were only having a bit of fun like. That's no cause to be sending me dinner a-flying."

So Dan put him to work at the house. Robert was strong and lifted bales of hay without effort, carried the milk churns to and from the dairy, chopped wood and fetched and carried for Mrs Fuller. He liked, most of all, to feed the livestock and was happy to muck out sties, stables and hen houses. Anything as long as he could be near the animals.

Mrs Fuller would often beckon him from the kitchen window as he crossed the yard. He would walk over, then, and stand waiting with a grin on his face, for he knew there would be something good for him to eat; some apple pie or a Banbury cake that, when eaten, flaked and crumbled down the front of his shirt. She once gave him a wedge of cherry pie, warm from the oven, the pastry encrusted with sugar. When he bit into it, the juice oozed out and dribbled down his chin, and he had flung back his head and laughed.

When Robert had worked his first week at the farm, Dan placed three half-crowns into his outstretched palm. "There you are, Robert. There's seven shillings and sixpence. You've earned that this week." Dan smiled as he spoke. He knew Robert couldn't hear what he was saying but somehow it didn't seem to matter. 'Just keep talking to him,' his ma had said, all those years ago when he had first asked her about Robert. 'He don't understand but he seems to like it.' And she had been right, Dan thought. It must be lonely to be deaf and most people thinking you were daft.

His face contorting, Robert framed his words. "Dan-oo." He swelled with pride as he looked at the three coins in his hand and Dan smiled at his pleasure.

Each week, on his day off, Sarah and Robert walked to the village. She would leave him while she made her purchases at the butchers or called into Miss Prior's for thread or a paper of pins. Sometimes she visited the parsonage to borrow a book from the parson's vast library.

Wherever she left Robert, she would always be sure of finding him in the same place, and that was outside Emily and Harold Water's store. In winter, he would be bent with his nose, red from the cold, pressed against the window pane. In summer he stood on the green opposite, his head tilted back against the sun.

The general store had something that greatly interested Robert. It was a magpie in a wicker cage. In winter the cage was in the window, balanced on a flour barrel next to the copper pans and the tea service with the pink roses painted on the cups. On warm summer days it was hung on a hook to the left of the red shop door.

Robert had been waiting for Sarah when he had first noticed the cage. She was inside buying sugar for her preserves. He looked up and caught sight of the cage swaying gently under the eaves. He paused to stare at the bird who sat quite motionless on the single perch, its long black tail feathers jutting through the bars. Robert walked across the street, his eyes never leaving the little cage, oblivious to Ed Parry passing by with his wheelbarrow loaded with manure. "Why can't you keep out of the road?" Ed yelled.

Close to the cage, Robert brought his face up to the bars and made little murmuring noises deep in his throat. At first, the bird remained quite still, his eyes dull and lifeless and then it turned its head, cocking it to one side, and looked straight back at Robert.

Robert had tears in his eyes.

It was a year since Robert had started work; a May day, bright and sunny, and he and Sarah were going to the village. Since first light Robert had been going about his chores with a lightness in his step and, at the same time, an urgency to get finished.

Sarah watched him as he brought water from the well. He's happy, she thought. For the first time he feels really useful. Not just doing work about the house but having a job and earning money. It didn't seem a year since that first night when he had dropped his wages on the table, just as his pa did on a Saturday night.

Every Saturday Pa would put his half sovereign down, as he had when Ma was alive, and just as Ma had, she would give him a shilling for his pocket. She didn't know what he did with it. She knew that he got paid in ale for playing his fiddle at the Scarlet Arms, so he didn't take it for ale money. And why did he need pocket money when he had all that in the tin trunk? She could never ask him. She

182

wasn't supposed to know it was there. She wondered, too, what Robert was going to do with the pocket money he had accumulated.

Now, he was tapping her on the shoulder, her double-lidded basket in his hand. He nodded and smiled at her.

"All right, all right, all right. I'm just coming," she laughed, untying the strings of her apron. "I don't know what you're in such a hurry for today, but I must confess it will be good to be out in the fresh air."

They walked along the path by the river and as the mist began to rise over the water, the smell of may and cow parsley flowers hung on the air. On the other side of the river were mustard fields, great stripes of yellow rising to meet the hills.

Sarah paused to breathe the fresh morning air. She, too, was happy, contented was the word. Ever since Dan and she had been friends, things had been different. She no longer felt so alone, with all the years stretching before her. Years of nothing but keeping house for Pa and Robert. She enjoyed her visits to the farm and the times when Dan could get away to walk the downs with her.

Polly seemed to have settled down too, she thought. What was it that Dan's ma had said only last week? 'There's one above who knows what's best for us though we may not see it ourselves at the time.' Yes, that's what she said and she was right. There's a lot of good sense that Mrs Fuller comes out with. She hurried to keep up with Robert's purposeful strides.

They reached the village and Sarah left Robert outside the butcher's and went inside. She wanted to buy some beef bits to make a meat pudding and she had gathered some raspberry leaves for Mrs Bishop. Mrs Bishop's youngest daughter was expecting her third and an infusion of raspberry leaves was supposed to be just the thing needed to ease the pains. Mrs Bishop said she swore by it but Sarah would prefer not to think about such things.

As soon as Sarah left him, Robert made his way over to the general stores. He stood aside to let Rosie Potter out the door and then entered Mr Water's store.

It was dim inside after the sunshine. He sidled up the narrow passage left between the sacks of flour and sugar on one side and the potatoes and cabbages on the other. The general store had always fascinated Robert. He seemed to like the mixture of smells. He stood and sniffed the air. Over there, were the spices and the cask of vinegar, the smell of cheese and pickles and polish, and in the far corner, where the garden tools were stacked, was the rich odour of paraffin.

And there was so much to see; gleaming copper pans you could see your face in, and ropes of onions hanging from the ceiling, fly papers and candles and boot laces, all higgledy piggledy on the shelves. It was a matter of wonder that all this could be fitted into such a small shop and how Mr and Mrs Waters could fit themselves behind the wide counter at the back.

Emily and Harold were perfectly matched like a pair of pepper pots. They were both very short and very round and had a way of ducking their heads forward and saying 'And what can I get you?' to whoever entered the store. Harold covered his baldness with a long length of hair that he combed from the parting across the crown. Over the years, as the baldness increased, the parting got lower and the length of this hair got longer. He lived in fear of going out in the wind without a hat for the slightest breeze would lift the hair, sending it skywards like the sail of a ship.

Today, Harold stood at the top of a stepladder stacking some rolling pins next to some cheese graters on the highest shelf, and Emily, an enormous white apron covering her faded brown dress, stood behind the counter weighing tea into cones of blue paper.

"I hope he don't go a-knocking nothing over, Harold," she said, anxiously watching Robert as he came towards the counter. "And what can I get you?" She ducked her head towards him then seeing Harold smile, added, "I know he can't hear me but I've got to say something, haven't I?"

Robert beckoned her to follow him and picked his way back to the door. He stopped and looked over his shoulder to see if she understood. Emily eased herself carefully from behind the counter and, pausing only to straighten a package on a shelf, followed him outside.

Robert pointed up at the black and white magpie in its wicker cage. It was the third one that had been here since Robert first saw them. The first had been sold to Doctor Rudd for his niece's birthday and the second to a sailor passing through on his way to Chillingford.

"You want to buy that m'dear? It's two shillings you know." She held up two fingers, patting the air in front of Robert's face. "Two shillings," she repeated, smiling and nodding.

Robert drew a red handkerchief from his pocket. He carefully unfolded it, extracted two shillings and handed them to Emily.

"Dan-oo," he said, taking down the cage from its hook on the wall. Gazing intently at the magpie, and murmuring to it, he carried the cage onto the village green.

George Potter sat under the oak tree with Albert Cooper. He nudged his friend and the two men watched Robert's progress. Jesse Caldwell, carrying water from the well, put down her pail and shielded her eyes from the sun, the better to see, and Sarah came out of the butcher's in time to see Robert set the cage down on the grass and open the door.

He took hold of the fluttering bird with both hands and held it lightly to his chest. Suddenly, in one quick movement, Robert lifted his arms, opened his hands and the bird, dark against the blue of the sky, flew away.

Robert burst into loud inarticulate cries.

186

They were cries of laughter and perfect joy.

Over the next few months Robert marched six times into Emily and Harold's store. Six times he bought a magpie in a wicker cage and six times he went onto the green and released a bird.

The cages were not wasted. He lined them up on a shelf in the shed and soon they were filled with the injured birds he found and nursed back to health; a blackbird with a broken leg, sparrows, swifts and swallows, house martins and starlings and a little wren. All found temporary homes in Robert's cages until they were well enough to fly away.

Down in the village Rosie Potter was showing Nell Benson the contents of the parcel that had been delivered that morning. The room was bright with the reds and blues and lilac and cream stripes. Skirts, dresses and blouses were draped over a chair and the kitchen table.

"Just look at this one! Tilley says in her letter that big sleeves are all the go now. I've never seen so much material in a pair of sleeves. Reckon I could make a dress for both the little'uns out of these." She held the maroon velvet against her chest and stroked the fabric.

"I wouldn't say it'll be practical," Nell sniffed, "but she be a good girl to send it. All the way from Lunnon too."

"She's been in her place for two years now

and she never forgets us back home. Last year, when she had her holidays, she brought us no end of stuff. They've got pots of money, the lady she works for, and she's allus a-throwing things out."

Rosie carefully folded the dress and was about to examine a green serge skirt when there was a tapping on the open door. The two women looked round to see Jesse Caldwell standing there, flushed and breathless from rushing, her eyes alight with laughter.

"Can I come in, Rosie? I've got a bit of a tell. You'll die a-laughing when I tell you, you will."

"Come in then and sit yerself down." Rosie lifted the clothes to clear a space for her neighbour and Jesse, easing her bulk into the chair, mopped her eyes with a grubby handkerchief.

"Oh, I haven't heard the like for a long time. You should of bin there."

"Well go on then," urged Nell, leaning forward. "Don't keep us in suspense."

"All right. Let me catch me breath…. I've bin over to the stores. Went there for some split peas and who should come in but that Sarah Holland. You know her brother's bin buying all them birds and letting them loose on the green – he's a bit soft in the upper storey, if you ask me – well, Harold said to her 'I was thinking' as if it had just occurred to him, sly old bugger 'cos he must of bin thinking about it. He was after making hisself a profit. 'I was thinking' he says, 'that it might help your brother if I took back the cages.' Offered her sixpence each for 'em, he did, and then he said, 'that way his little 'obby of settin' birds free wouldn't be so expensive.' All nice and innocent like, he be, as if he be doing 'em a favour."

"And what did she say?" asked Rosie.

"You'll never believe it. 'Oh no, Mr Waters,' she says in that tip-tongued way of hers." Jesse wagged her head from side to side as she mimicked Sarah's voice. "Robert needs the cages." Now she was laughing. She mopped her eyes once again. Rosie and Nell looked baffled.

"Was that it? What's so funny?"

"What is the boy a-wanting with the cages?"

It took Jesse effort to control her laughter. "That's what Harold asked her. And do you know what she said?"

"No. Go on."

"She said, 'Why, Mr Waters,' and you should have seen his face. 'Why, Mr Waters,' she says, 'to keep birds in, of course!'"

# CHAPTER SEVENTEEN

Sarah was excited. It was her seventeenth birthday and a picnic was arranged. Dan had promised to get away from the farm for a couple of hours and let Robert have some time off too. 'Good job it's July and not the beginning of August,' he had said. 'We won't have a moment to spare when we're getting in the harvest.' So he was coming at two and Polly had managed to get the time off by changing her afternoon.

They were packing the baskets with sandwiches and the lemonade, that Sarah had made, when Polly fished in her pocket and said, "Look what I've got." There, on her outstretched hand, was a shilling.

"Where did you get that?" Sarah asked. It was obvious by Polly's grin that it was a special coin.

"From the master. He gave it to me."

"The master? You mean Lord Marsden gave it to you?"

"No, it was Joseph Marsden." She grinned

again. "He said it was for a pretty face. I went up with his water the other morning and he gave it to me…. Perhaps he'd been lucky with the cards. Everyone knows that he gambles and there was a whole pile of money on the table." She returned the shilling to her pocket. "Good job it wasn't Fanny who went up there. She would have to pay him the shilling to look at her!" She laughed again and Sarah gave her a shove.

"You are unkind, Polly," she said, but she was laughing too.

"I didn't mean it. She's nice, is Fanny, and I feel sorry for her because she's got nobody…. But she is plain."

Sarah had to agree with her. Fanny had come with Polly one afternoon when their time off had coincided. She was a mousy little thing with a too-big nose and a squint in one eye. She had spent the afternoon trying to hide her sore hands in the folds of her unbecoming skirt. What a terrible existence, Sarah had thought, spending all her days up to her elbows in hot water, scouring pots and pans. What kind of a future could she look forward to? She was intelligent, all right, but not very good at making friends so it was nice that she got on well with Polly.

She was glad that Polly seemed happier now. She must be doing her work well or they wouldn't have advanced her. It was a step up in the right direction, she thought, and remembered that when Polly had been made second housemaid, she had come home and spent the whole afternoon telling her about the house and its furnishings; the heavy velvet curtains and vast expanses of polished wood floors broken by islands of thick carpets. Little parlour chairs with round backs and tables with fringed cloths, stuffed birds and waxed fruit under domed glass cases.

Yes, she was glad Polly appeared happier and more settled but she felt uneasy about the shilling. It didn't seem right to be given a shilling just because you had a pretty face.

Sarah took a tablecloth from the middle drawer of the dresser. As she used it to cover the basket of food, she tried to stifle her misgivings. Nothing was going to spoil this day. She had been anxious all week that today would be fine and she wasn't disappointed. Bright sunshine flooded the kitchen from the open window where the hollyhocks, white, yellow and rose, nodded in the gentle breeze.

"When is Dan coming, Sarah?" Polly asked, preening herself in front of the mirror. She fiddled with her hair and set her straw hat square on the top of her head. "I have to be back at five."

"I hope I haven't kept you waiting," said an earnest voice from the open door.

Sarah and Polly turned to see Dan self-consciously holding a basket and looking tanned from his days in the fields.

"Oh hello, Dan. Have you brought some more food? Sarah's packed enough to feed us for a week."

"Just a few things Ma has sent along for you," he said, holding out the basket.

Polly peered closely at Dan. With an innocent smile but eyes that teased, she said, "Tell me, Dan. Have you had your hair cut or have you had your ears lowered?"

Dan rubbed his hand over his newly-shorn hair and his face reddened.

"Polly, don't be so rude! You look very nice Dan." She took the basket from him, wondering if he would ever get over his shyness. After all, they'd been keeping company together for over a year now and in all that time he had only got as far as holding her hand when they walked the downs. But it was an easy friendship and she felt comfortable with him.

"Polly, be a dear and go and fetch Robert. He's still out in the shed with that stoat he found. It's a wonder he doesn't take his bed out there.... Now, where shall we go?"

They went down to the river. Dan's basket produced a plum cake, strawberries and a jug of fresh cream that his ma had sent with her best wishes.

Dan and Robert helped to lay the cloth on some flat ground while Polly blew dandelion clocks, chanting 'he loves me, he loves me not,' as the seed heads floated through the air. Hearing her, Sarah wondered whom Polly had in mind and hoped that it wasn't Joseph Marsden.

"I don't think I could eat another crumb," laughed Sarah, an hour later, as she cut another slice of plum cake for Dan.

Polly flapped her hand at two flies that were trying to settle on the remains of the pie. "I can't imagine Robert ever saying that, if he could," she said, nodding towards Robert who was attacking his third scone.

"He's a growing lad," laughed Dan. "Ma says he's a bottomless pit. She's always offering him her baking and he never refuses."

"I should hope that he'll soon stop growing. He'll end up all of six feet," observed Sarah. Robert looked up at that moment. He saw her watching him and smiled; a big wide smile showing strong white teeth.

"I'm certain sure I've had enough though," said Dan, patting his stomach. "That was a real feast. Any more and I'll burst my buttons." He lifted his glass of lemonade and saluted Sarah with it. "Happy birthday, Sarah," he said, and his eyes were full of loving tenderness.

"Yes, happy birthday, Sarah," added Polly. She raised her glass and nudged Robert who looked up and raised his too.

"Say-a," he said, and laughed.

This is the best birthday I've had for a long time, Sarah thought. She gazed affectionately at her companions and wished the day would never end.

After they had packed the baskets, Robert signed to Polly. She turned to Sarah saying, "Robert wants to show me a nest. A moorhen's I think. Up near the bridge. I suppose I'd better go." She rolled her eyes and with mock gravity added, "Are you sure you haven't put him up to this so that you two can be alone?"

"No, we haven't!" Sarah laughed. It was a day of laughter. "Go on then...and don't forget the time."

Dan and Sarah watched them scramble down the bank and follow the path upstream. Sarah took off her hat and lay on her back, watching the small puffs of white clouds that scattered the sky. The sun was hot, insects droned and the heady fragrance of meadowsweet filled the air. She closed her eyes and listened to the river's ceaseless babble and whispering to itself. She couldn't remember when she had felt so happy.

Dan watched her. The dark strands of her hair gleamed in the sunshine and he ached to take it in his hands and feel the silky thickness of it between his fingers. He wanted to lift it to him and bury his nose in its depths, to inhale the delicious fragrance of her. So what was stopping him?

He thrust his hands into his pockets and now, concentrating his gaze on the distant horizon, thought of all the months when they had been together; how often he had wanted to gather her to him, tell her how much he loved her. But he couldn't bring himself to take that one step. He cursed himself for his bashfulness. Give her the present, you fool, while you have the chance. Now, while Polly and Robert are out of the way. What are you waiting for?

"Sarah?"

She opened her eyes to see Dan sitting beside her with a small box in his hand.

"Happy birthday, Sarah," he said, holding out the present.

She sat up and took it from him. When she opened it her eyes shone with pleasure. "Oh, Dan… this is beautiful." It was a gold pin, fashioned in a circle, with five tiny seed pearls.

"Do you like it? Here, let me." He took the pin from her and fastened it between the two points of the lace collar of her cream blouse.

"Of course I like it. How could I do otherwise? It's the most beautiful gift I have ever had."

"And you are the most beautiful person I have ever known," he answered before his courage failed him.

She smiled up at him. He looked down on her sunlit face and was awed by the strength of his feelings.

"Sarah… sweet Sarah," he murmured, taking her face in his big hard hands.

They lay back among the oxeye daisies and the grasses that were tall against the sky. He buried his face in her hair, that untameable hair that smelt so good. He kissed her eyes, her cheeks and the soft lobes of her ears. When he kissed her parted lips, they too were soft and responded with a passion that met his own.

As quickly as the kiss began, it finished. He sprang from her. In a rush he was on his feet, his back to her. She could sense his embarrassment. He shouldn't feel embarrassed just because he had kissed her. It had felt so wonderful.

On a laugh, she too rose and, picking up her skirts, ran down the slope to the river, her hair and skirts billowing out behind her.

He realised then that the laugh was not one of derision but that of pure happiness. Letting out the breath that he felt he had been holding forever, he too ran, catching up with her before she reached the water's edge.

"Come on. Let's skim stones!" she cried, every feature on her face reflecting her joy.

The moment had passed. But they both knew that things would never be the same again.

# CHAPTER EIGHTEEN

All too soon the summer gave way to autumn bringing cold raw days and frequent fogs. The trees, all over the valley, were tinted with copper, rust and saffron hues. There were hazelnuts, chestnuts and blackberries to pick in the shortening days and then, suddenly, it was winter and the week before Christmas.

Snow had fallen. Like a silent thief it had come in the night and stolen the outlines of trees and shrubs. It had changed the valley into a picturesque scene with new dimensions, changed proportions and emphasized shapes.

The chestnut mare picked her way down the lane. Joseph Marsden sat on her back, too deep in thought to be aware of his surroundings. His dark eyes glowered as he remembered the argument he had had with his brother the night before.

And to think that when their father died – and that couldn't be long now for his lungs were giving out and he had declined rapidly in the last few months – Samuel would inherit the lot. All the property and land would be his brother's and he would then be dependent on Samuel's generosity, not only for the roof over his head but for the clothes on his back and even the food in his belly.

Well, damn Samuel! If he could only persuade his mother to part with some cash. Just enough so that he could play the tables and win himself the stake to get in on a big game. Then he could win some big money. Then Samuel could go to hell.

If only he hadn't been so stupid, wasting so much money on that silly actress in London. Ah, but he had had his fun with her – such fun, such lips, such thighs – and would be still if his money hadn't run out. His money had run out and so had her interest.

Money. Confound it! It all came back to money. The old girl might come across. She might rule her household, her husband and family with a sharp tongue and an unyielding parsimony but she had always been indulgent as far as he was concerned. He would have to see what he could wheedle out of her when he returned.

The thought of going back did not warm him. He had had enough of its atmosphere of austerity and unsmiling faces. Only in the west wing, where Samuel lived with Dorothy and their two children, was there any gaiety. But there was no welcome for him there. Not after last night.

He had tried to explain to Samuel that he had meant no harm. It was only a bit of fun, a joke, perhaps the result of too much brandy, but Samuel had been white with rage, had yelled at him to keep away from his wife. Samuel had thrown him into the hall and slammed the door.

Life was so unjust. If only he had the money he would get away from them all. Take some rooms in town or, maybe, a trip to Europe. Money! There it was again. How was he going to get round his mother?

Joseph ducked his head under a low leafless branch, mindless of the snow he dislodged that fell on his shoulders and the horse's rump.

Lady Marsden had one weakness and he thought of that now. Chocolates! I'll get her some of those new-fangled confections that she loves. A whole box of them. Some for Dorothy too and perhaps it wouldn't hurt to get some cigars for Samuel as a peace offering. Something for Margaret too.

His face softened and he smiled as he thought of his younger sister with her elfin face and lively disposition. Of all the family, she was the only one for whom he had any real regard. How could he not care for her when she so obviously adored him?

Yes, that's what he would do. He would go down and buy presents. He'd tell them to send the bill and he'd pay for them with next month's allowance or perhaps sooner with a bit of luck.

He turned his horse about, sat straighter in the saddle and urged the mare towards the village.

At three o'clock the sky was white with the promise of more snow. As it was Robert's half day off, Sarah suggested they go down to the village. Muffled against the cold they splashed through the powdery snow, laughing, with their breath all white and steamy on the chill air.

At the smithy, a shaggy fetlocked carthorse was being shod. It stood, docile and unmoving. The light gleamed on the bulk of its body as the smith leaned against it and lifted one massive foot. Robert couldn't take his eyes off the horse. He patted its neck and was nuzzled in return. Sarah liked to hear the sizzling of the horseshoes as they were dipped in water. She stood there for some time watching the sparks from the fire, feeling the warmth from it on her face and inhaling the acrid smoke before she remembered her errands and signed to Robert that she would come back for him.

She wanted to buy some tobacco to give to Pa on Christmas morning. She smiled to herself when she thought of the gifts she had accumulated. Mrs Fuller would be pleased with the fancy soap she had bought last week. It was hidden away under the bed along with the blue muffler she had knitted for Robert and the brown one for Dan. She had embroidered a handkerchief for Polly and made a needle case for Aunt Ruth. Now, as well as the tobacco, she was going to buy a pink sugar mouse to go with Polly's handkerchief.

The snow in the village had been reduced to a dirty wet slush. Sarah lifted her skirts and kept her eyes on the ground where she walked. She nearly bumped into Mrs McGiveney as she passed the butchers.

"It's a good job you've come out today, Sarah," she said, adjusting her parcels and ignoring her youngest tugging at her sleeve. "I'll be thinking that if it freezes tonight the bairns will be out tomorrow making slides and we'll all be breaking our necks on them to be sure."

Sarah, laughingly, agreed. They exchanged a few more words then wishing Mrs McGivney a merry Christmas, she made her way to Ramsey's shop.

It's good to get out of the house for a while, she thought. Just to see another face and pass the time of day. It was at moments like this that she was aware of her isolated existence outside the village. But things were so much better now that she had Dan and she could always wander over to the farm to see his ma. She saw Aunt Ruth now and then too. Not so often as she used to for Aunt Ruth found the distance was too much for her these days. But Sarah would see her on Sundays and sometimes visited the parsonage.

Mrs Ramsey had already lit her lamps. Sarah paused to look in the window at the Christmas display. Sprigs of holly with bright blood-red berries framed the window and on the shelf inside, jostling one another for attention, were whips and tops and bright-coloured marbles, a blue ball, a monkey on a stick, dolls with porcelain heads and humbler rag dolls, barley sugar twists and pink and white peppermint sticks, shag tobacco, snuff and briar pipes.

A bell jingled on a length of string when she opened the door and stepped down into the shop. She was surprised to see a gentleman in front of the counter. His back was towards her but she could tell he was a gentleman by his fine worsted coat and the sleek beaver top hat that rested on the counter. When she saw his profile she realised with a start that it was Joseph Marsden.

It was warm, after the cold outside, so she loosened her scarf from her head. Her nose tingled from the warmth and she could smell the sugary aroma of the caramels that Mrs Ramsey made in the kitchen out the back.

Sarah stayed just inside the door pretending to examine a wooden train while she curiously studied him. She hadn't seen him for a long time. She had heard from Polly that he spent a lot of time in London and was surprised how he had changed. he was very tall. As tall as her pa or Dan, with broad shoulders and thick dark hair that curled over his immaculate white collar.

Joseph moved with an arrogant ease, picking up a rag doll, turning it over, only to discard it as soon as his eye fell on a doll with an exquisite face and a blue velvet coat and bonnet. He added it to the pile he had collected on the counter; a set of toy soldiers in a crimson box, two bright multi-coloured balls, two boxes of chocolates – one larger than the other but both tied with yellow ribbon – and another box, this time of cigars.

"Do you have any sugar mice?" he asked.

"Yes, sir. They've just come in today," Mrs Ramsey simpered, her homely face pink with pleasure. She reached for a box from the shelf behind her.

"I'll take a dozen. No, better make that two. My sister is inordinately fond of them. I can't think why. Too sweet for my liking."

Sarah listened in astonishment. She couldn't imagine anyone buying so many all at one time. Mrs Ramsey asked if he required anything more.

"No, that is quite enough. Have them wrapped and sent up to the Hall. Good day to you."

He picked up his hat and, turning to leave, noticed Sarah for the first time. His silent scrutiny was disconcerting but she stood there, returning his gaze, and saw the speculation in his eyes. He had a hard sensual mouth and she wasn't sure she liked the way he looked at her. At one time she had dreamt that he would notice her. But not now.

He smiled. "Ma'am," he said, inclining his head. And then he was gone, the bell jingling on its string again.

"Well, that's a turn up for the books, ain't it? Never knowed him to come in here before. 'Spect he be a-doing most of his shopping up in

Lunnon." Mrs Ramsey shook her head, marvelling at such a customer. "Joseph Marsden, no less…. They say he be the black sheep of the family though. Allus a-drinking and a-gambling and heaven only knows what else. Not like his brother. Now Samuel Marsden, he be a different kettle of fish, more settled like, not that he shouldn't be with a wife and two children and standing to inherit the lot one day. They say Lord Marsden can't last much longer. His lungs have gone, y'know. Just like my George, God rest his soul. Once his lungs went he didn't last many months…. Now what can I get you, m'dear?"

"I did have it in mind to buy a sugar mouse, for Polly, but perhaps they've all gone."

"Sorry m'dear." Mrs Ramsey smiled ruefully, although Sarah could tell she was pleased. "I felt sure two dozen would see me over the season. Never dreamed they'd all go at once."

"Mmm… I'll take some humbugs then. And an ounce of Nigger Head tobacco please."

No, she didn't like his manner. The way he had looked at her made her feel uncomfortable.

It was already dusk when Sarah went to meet Robert. The horse had left the smithy and so had he. He had wandered over to the bridge and stood thumping his arms across his chest as he watched the moorhens paddling upstream. He stamped his feet to keep warm as he waited for Sarah and didn't see Joseph approaching.

Joseph could have taken his horse around the boy but instead he called "Get out of my way," and when there was no response, yelled, "I said get out of my way!"

Robert happened to turn round, perhaps instinctively sensing someone there, and for a moment he stared, frowning uncertainly, at Joseph.

Joseph was incensed. "You insolent pup! You deserve a good thrashing." He rode at Robert with upraised whip and brought it down on Robert's shoulder. About to do it again, he heard a voice screaming at him.

"He's deaf. Deaf! Do you hear? He can't hear you. You have no right to do that!"

Joseph wheeled his horse about and Robert ran off over the bridge.

For a stunned moment Joseph looked down into the face of the girl he had seen in the shop. She stood before him, quivering in indignation, her astonishing eyes ablaze with anger. And for the second time he was enthralled by the sight of her. Everything from the muffler tied over her ears to her heavy laced boots told him that she was a village girl, but she had fine features. Her mass of hair framed a face with high cheekbones.

Her wide mouth revealed white even teeth when she almost hissed at him. "My brother was not in your way. You could have ridden round him. There was no need…. He didn't know…."

He watched her look about her, apparently lost for words, and following her gaze he saw the boy raise his fist in an unmistakable gesture of defiance before disappearing down the lane.

"And who might you be?" he asked.

Sarah drew herself up and with a sharp lifting of her chin said in a small dignified voice, "I am Sarah Holland, granddaughter of James Gilbert. He was the doctor here... before Doctor Rudd came."

With an effort Joseph suppressed a smile. "Well, Sarah Holland, I shall not forget you."

And he left her standing there, with the snow settling in her hair.

"I think you're jealous." Polly looked amused.

"Of course I'm not jealous. Why ever should I be?"

"Because you've always had a fancy for him. You never said anything but it was obvious to anyone with half an eye, that you were smitten."

"I'm just telling you for your own sake. That Joseph Marsden is not the wonderful person you would have him be. I've just told you what happened to Robert yesterday."

"Well, he wasn't to know that Robert was deaf, was he?"

"And you think that gives him the right to take a crop against him? You've taken leave of your senses." Sarah angrily poked the fire and when she had finished, added, "At one time you wouldn't have taken this attitude. He's turned your head, that's for sure."

Polly had just told Sarah about another shilling. She hadn't told her that Joseph had extracted a kiss from her in return and was glad that she hadn't. Sarah wasn't much fun to be with today in spite of Christmas being only a few days off.

Polly had told her about the frenzied activity, in preparation for Christmas visitors, up at the Hall. She had described all the food that was ready; the plum puddings, the sirloins of beef for roasting as well as a goose, the hams, tongues and pies and piles of almond tarts. Cakes made with walnuts and others of coconut or chocolate. Blancmanges, jellies, and the trifle that Fanny had dropped on the pantry floor.

She had repeated the rude rhyme that the stable lads had made up about the housekeeper and commented that with a name like Passmore it was to be expected. But Sarah hadn't laughed. She didn't seem to be listening half the time.

So be it, Polly thought. I may have to work Christmas Day but we're all going to have a high old time after. It will be a sight jollier that it is here. She was glad when it was time to go.

For the first time, Sarah too was glad when Polly had left. Since her encounter with Joseph Marsden she had been preoccupied with a tangle of thoughts. Although she had grown out of romantic notions about Joseph some time ago, she still chided herself for having entertained such thoughts. He wasn't at all the kind of person her infatuated mind had conjured up. How could she have been such a fool?

And what had possessed her to say what she

had when he had asked her her name? After all, Grandpa Gilbert had died before Ma and Pa were married. She hadn't even known him and Joseph Marsden wouldn't have known him either. Perhaps it was because of the way he'd looked at her, as if she was a common village girl, and she wanted him to know that she wasn't. Did that make her a snob? Why did she care what he thought of her? Anyone who could raise a whip to another person, regardless of the  reason, and especially for no reason, was contemptible and didn't deserve anyone's admiration.

Sarah didn't notice that Polly had left a little earlier than was usual, for added to the jumble in her mind were disturbing thoughts of her sister. She had changed. At one time Polly wouldn't have understood, let alone laughed, at rhymes like the one she had repeated today.

And what about the shilling? It wouldn't be long before that man would want something in return. She had tried to warn Polly but Sarah knew, even as she was speaking, that Polly wouldn't take heed. 'I think you're jealous,' she had said. At one time Sarah might have been, but not any more. And she felt the humiliation of knowing that her infatuation had been so transparent.

But, overriding all these thoughts, was a fear for Polly. "Oh, Polly," she said to herself as she washed the teacups. "Please, please be careful."

# CHAPTER NINETEEN

It was a Friday in the middle of April and the garden was alive with the gaudy reds and yellows of tulips and primroses. Sarah felt her spirits lift at the first glimpse of the sun for five days. She hummed to herself as she did the cleaning and was shaking a mat out of the bedroom window when she was surprised to see Polly trudge up the hill with her basket on her hip. A blustery wind flattened her skirts about her legs and would have been away with her straw hat had she not been clutching it with her free hand. There was something in her manner that made Sarah pause before she called a greeting. Something's up, she thought. It's not like Polly to be dragging her feet like that.

By the time she had rushed down the stairs and flung open the front door, Polly was coming up the path and Sarah could see that she had been crying. Her eyes were red-rimmed and puffy and her cheeks were blotched with tears.

"Polly! Polly, what is it? Come in, come in. Don't just stand there. Get yourself into the kitchen.... Here, let me take that." Sarah took the basket from her.

Polly, without bothering to take off her hat and coat, sank into a chair by the fire and stared into the flames. Sarah watched her for a moment from the open doorway and thought she had never seen her sister look so forlorn. Beaten was the word. As if all the stuffing had been knocked out of her. It's taken something to do that. And her coming with her basket too. A feeling of dread came upon her as she put the basket down.

Addressing Polly's back, she asked, "What's the long face for?" and when Polly didn't answer she persisted. "What's happened? Are you ill?"

Polly dragged her eyes from the fire and slowly turned her head. For a second, there was a trace of the familiar spirit, a touch of bravado as, with a lift of her chin and an almost defiant tone, she answered Sarah. "I've been dismissed," she said, and once again stared into the fire.

Although half expected, it took some moments for Sarah to digest this information. At a loss for words, she busied herself by taking the ironing blanket from a cupboard and laying it on the table. She took one of the two flat irons that had been heating on the range, expertly spat on the base to test its readiness and on hearing a hiss, began to iron one of Robert's red flannel shirts. She pressed both the sleeves before she spoke.

211

"I thought you were getting on so well there. You've had a step up this year and you said, yourself, that the housekeeper was pleased with you…. Oh, Polly! You haven't taken anything you shouldn't, have you?"

"Of course not! How can you ask such a thing?"

"Well, I'm at a loss. What have you done to bring this on?"

Polly didn't answer her at first. What she did was raise herself from her seat, take off her heavy brown coat and turn to face Sarah. She smoothed the folds of her skirt over the mound that was her belly and her eyes implored Sarah not to berate her. She had had enough of that for one day and had no doubt that when her pa came home there would be more to follow.

"Oh no, Polly. Oh no, not that!" Sarah stood shaking her head, her mouth agape and the iron raised in mid-air.

She watched Polly's face crumple and the tears stream from her eyes, hastily put the iron down and took Polly in her arms. And there Sarah held her until she had cried out her wretchedness and her shoulders had ceased to heave.

Only then did she put Polly from her saying, "Sit yourself down and I'll make some tea."

She took the big black kettle from the range and went out to the scullery where she filled it with water that Robert had drawn that morning. All the while her mind was trying to take in the dreadful news. How could she? How could Polly have been so stupid? Pa will kill him. It didn't bear thinking about. At least, she remembered, he would be over at Chillingford tonight. He'd told her this morning not to put up any dinner for him. That gives us a breather but she'll have to face the music sooner or later. Oh, dear God, where will it all end?

When she returned to the kitchen she saw that Polly had resumed her seat and her still contemplation of the fire. Without a word, Sarah put the kettle on the hob and took two cups and saucers from the dresser. She was stretching up to lift the tea caddy from the high mantel when Polly first spoke.

Without taking her eyes from the fire she asked, "What am I going to do?"

Sarah only just managed to refrain from saying that she should have thought about that before. She bit the tart response that sprang to her lips and Polly asked again.

"What is to become of me? I never thought it would end like this. He said he loved me." She whimpered. "I should have known better. That kind of person would never stand by a person like me…. Gave me five guineas, he did, and told me not to let on it was him." She shook her head as if she still couldn't believe it. "Five guineas!"

Sarah swallowed before she asked the question, and she knew as she was asking what the answer would be. "Who gave you five guineas?"

"The father."

"I know that. But who? Who is it?"

And Polly told her in a hollow voice. "Joseph. It's Joseph Marsden."

Sarah lay in the big bed with Polly once more beside her. Just like old times, she thought, but not the same. Nothing would be the same again. Not after Polly had brought this shame on them. Not after she had done what she had.

Although she couldn't bring herself to ask, she wanted to know what it had been like. What did it feel like? What was it like to allow a man to do those things to you; the things they had read about in the books that had belonged to Grandpa Gilbert. The ones they had found in a box in the stable. She and Polly had found them, one rainy day when they had been playing out there, and had smuggled one up to their room.

It had been in this bed that she and Polly had pored over the text and marvelled at the illustrations. It hadn't actually spelled it out, what happened, but they put two and two together. Polly had made a face and groaned, "Ugh! How awful! It strikes me as being very unhygienic." Polly had giggled and then laughed until her sides ached. Sarah had blushed and turned the page.

But now she wanted to know what it was like and the thought gave her a strange sensation. What was it like to be touched by Joseph Marsden, to feel his kisses and to be touched by him? If only it hadn't been him, it wouldn't have been so bad.

She found it hard to admit to herself that, in spite of everything, she would have liked, just once, to have felt his lips on hers, known what it was like to be held in his arms. But never, never in a million years would she have allowed him to do what he had done to Polly. Never!

"Sarah? Are you awake?"

"Well, if I wasn't, I am now. What do you want?"

"I was wondering…. Do you think—"

"Do I think what?"

Polly was silent for a long time and Sarah turned on her back and stared up at the ceiling. It was a clear night. Moonlight, threading its way through the trees, came in the casement window and lit the foot of the bed. As her eyes grew accustomed to the gloom she could make out the oak beams and counted them as she waited for Polly to continue. There were seven. A barn owl screeched.

"Do you think Granny Tulley will give me something?"

"What do you want? Another bacon sandwich?" she asked with some asperity. She simply couldn't hide the impatience in her voice. She knew exactly what Polly meant but some perversity in her made her want to hear Polly say it.

"You know full well what I mean. Why are you being so nasty? I just thought… I just thought that perhaps she might know of some remedy, some herb, that would make things right again… I have heard that pennyroyal or bay tree berries may do it,

215

but I don't know how much."

It was the smallness of Polly's voice that prompted Sarah to soften her own. "Oh, Polly, that's not the answer. You could even make things worse."

"Nothing could be worse."

"Anyway, if Granny Tulley had the answer to what ails you, then surely she would have been able to solve her daughter's problem." They had gleaned knowledge of the Tulley family history from snippets of overheard conversation.

"Instead of which, Ned was born and her daughter died," Polly said and then on a whisper, "I could die too, couldn't I?"

"Stop talking nonsense. We've got enough things to worry about without that. The first hurdle is breaking the news to Pa. Heaven only knows how he'll take it but, as sure as eggs are eggs, he's not going to be pleased."

"Will you tell him for me, Sarah?"

"What good will that do? You'd only be putting off the moment. You'll have to face him sooner or later."

"But he might take it more kindly coming from you. You know that the very sight of me seems to offend him…. Perhaps I'd better go before he gets home. I don't think I can face him."

"And where do you think you'll go? Be sensible. You've no place to go and can hardly wander the countryside at this time of year. Especially in your condition."

"No. No, you're right. But you will be the one to tell him, won't you?"

John was sitting in his shirtsleeves at the kitchen table, the remains of his dinner on the plate before him. He had enjoyed his meal and seemed, to Sarah, to be in a better mood than of late. She wished, in a way, that he wasn't because it made it harder to tell him. She didn't know if Robert's absence was for the best or not. He was up at the farm; had been all hours of the day and night recently for it was lambing time. Oh, why had she promised Polly she would do her dirty work for her?

She steeled herself and told him. He listened to her, sitting still and rigid with shock until a look of slow horror crept into his face; a face so blanched of all colour that his eyes appeared to darken and grow larger as she watched him. She thought that, for a moment, he had stopped breathing and she, too, held her breath as she waited for his fury to erupt. When he did speak, his voice was low and far more menacing than if he had yelled. It filled her with a dreadful fear.

"Where is she?"

"Upstairs."

"Go and get her."

Sarah left the kitchen, shutting the door behind her. She paused at the foot of the stairs, her hand on the banister rail, took a deep breath and let it out on a sigh. Dear God, where will it all end, she asked herself, not for the first time since Polly had

217

come home. Things were strained between them before, but this would surely be the finish. Well, they'd best get it over because it wouldn't improve with the keeping.

And as Sarah climbed the stairs she heard the crash of his dinner plate as it was swept to the floor.

John still sat where Sarah had left him. His head was bowed and his hands balled into fists where they rested on the table. Polly stood in the open doorway speechless with apprehension. Only a whitening of her lips and a faint twitching of her nostrils betrayed her fear.

Sarah wasn't quite sure what she should do. Should she make herself scarce, out in the scullery, or stand by Polly, give her moral support? Undecided, she stooped to collect the pieces of broken china. She picked up the mutton bones and threw them on the fire, all the while watching her pa with a nervous sideways glance.

John looked up, folded his arms and leaned back in his chair. Silently he regarded Polly. Then his lips twisted bitterly and his head jerked towards her.

"So, she's come skulking home with her belly full. The whore…" and the word seemed to fill the room, "the whore has come crawling home! What have you got to say for yourself, now that you have had your fun?"

Polly gnawed on her lower lip. Now she

looked poised for flight. "I'm sorry, Pa. I didn't want… I didn't think this would happen—"

"Well, what did you think would happen?" he roared, his rage terrible to see." That's not a fairy wand he's got between his legs! Or do you think you get a bun in the oven by sitting on the privy seat?"

Sarah hurried into the scullery with the plate pieces and dropped them into a bucket by the mangle. God in Heaven! She didn't believe he could be so coarse. Her hand came up to her mouth as she heard him ranting.

"You're a shameless good-for-nothing. a…a disgrace to this family. I should throw you out on the streets; that's about where you belong. I've a good mind to give you a good thrashing. Should have given you one years ago."

Sarah returned to the kitchen just as he sprang to his feet. In the lamplight his shadow loomed, dark and monstrous, on the wall behind him. The chair toppled with a clatter to the stone floor. He kicked it aside. He was spitting the words out in his rage and in three strides was across the kitchen.

Yanking Polly into the room, he banged the door shut with a kick from his heavy boots and, before Sarah could take in what was happening, had loosened the belt from his waist. Polly cowered in his grip. She screamed in terror. His arm went back and the buckle end of the thick leather belt came down on her back.

Sarah leapt at him, clutched at his sleeve and tried to pull him away. "For pity's sake," she cried, "leave her be. What good will it do? The damage is already done!"

John flung Sarah from him. She crashed into the heavy table. His arm came up and he struck Polly another blow, this time clipping the side of her face as she twisted to avoid the belt. Her frantic screams filled the air.

His face, now, was suffused with anger and the spittle ran down his chin as his words to Sarah were flung over his shoulder. "Get out, girl. Get away from here or it'll be your turn next."

He made to hit Polly again but stopped with his arm upraised and, afterwards, Sarah was to marvel that her words had got through to him when she said, "I'm glad Ma is not alive to see this day."

And in the moment's silence that followed, when he dropped his arm and Polly slumped to the floor, she added, "For had she been, this would have surely finished her!"

Since early morning John had tramped the downs with shoulders hunched, buffeted by a wind that lifted his hair and smarted his eyes. Now, the wind had dropped and he sat on a rocky outcrop, high above the valley. But his eyes drew no pleasure from the sight of the fields of young green wheat swept by cloud shadows, or the river threading like a ribbon through the village spread out below.

He had sat on this rock on previous

occasions, when he had been troubled, and drawn solace from the timelessness of everything. The hills that scalloped the sky had been there all through the ages, long before he was born, and would remain long after he had gone. And he thought that, in comparison, his life and all the lives of all the people below, were like grains of wheat scattered over the earth, growing and flourishing or struggling to survive, depending on what the fates decreed. And in a century from now, would it matter? Who would remember anyway?

But today his thoughts didn't lead in that direction. Ever since last night he had been wrestling with the savage thoughts that battled his mind. He had been churning with passions that seemed in part shame, in part an impotent fury, and in part a panic that he was losing control.

He looked down on his hard-skinned hands that hung loose between his drawn-up knees and was filled with shame that they had been lifted in such anger to one of his own. Why couldn't he have just given her the rough side of his tongue? What had possessed him?

All night long he had tossed in his bed, reliving those moments of madness until he'd heard Sarah's voice as she hurled those words across the room. 'I'm glad our ma's not alive to see this day'. Somehow, that had got through to him and he had been dragged back to his senses.

'I'm glad our ma's not here to see this day,' she'd said and for that few seconds, it was as if he was looking down a tunnel. He could see nothing but Polly's face. It had changed and had become Beth's and the eyes that stared back at him were wide and terrified and filled with hate. And then it was Polly's face that, once again, he looked upon. Polly, with a vivid red welt that crossed her cheek, narrowly missed her left eye and disappeared into her hair.

What had he done to her? Polly. Dear, sweet Polly who had once loved him and sought him out. Polly, whom he had carried shoulder high, whose laughter had filled the house and filled his heart with love. Polly who had grown to fill his mind with more than love. He had been consumed by a wanting that he had never imagined, a wanting that tortured him every moment she was near and so he had sent her away to be safe, and for a while, without her, he had known a degree of peace.

He'd been such a fool! It was more than flesh and blood could bear. To think he'd sent her up there to be safe, only for her to fall into the clutches of someone else.

And it came to him with a force that hit him like a blow, that he was jealous. That someone else, that no-good pup, Joseph Marsden, who was known to the village for his philandering, had taken what he had denied himself. He was full of disgust and self-loathing. With a cry that was half a sob, half a groan, he buried his head in his hands.

What kind of a man was he to have such thoughts, he asked himself. Was he no better than the one who had taken Polly down? If it had been anybody else, would he have felt any different? If it had been a lad from the village, one of his own kind, he could at least have knocked the living daylights out of him and then arranged a quick wedding. She would have been married and that would have been the end of it.

But what was he left with? He could hardly go marching up to the Hall and knock on the door. 'Good morning, your Ladyship. Your son has put my daughter in the family way and I want to know what he proposes to do about it.' He'd soon be sent packing with a flea in his ear.

Blast them to hell! There was one rule for the rich and one for the poor, wasn't there? 'Twas always the same with the gentry. They'd got the land and they'd got the money. They thought they could just take what they wanted and couldn't give a damn for the consequences. What did that young devil care about what happened to the innocent girls he ruined? And he could say girls for it was a pound to a penny that his Polly was not the first and would not be the last. Not by a long chalk.

John sat there gnawing at these thoughts and after a while he took the pipe from his jacket pocket and dug into another for his baccy pouch. But he fastened on something else and when he withdrew his hand he saw that he had taken out his rabbit's foot.

It lay in his open palm. It had grown dingy with years and a strand of tobacco had caught in its once white fur. How old must it be now? He must have carried it around for a good twenty years. Remembered old cock-eyed Tom, with a nose like a blackberry, who had given it to him. Poacher, he was, and had given it to him and said, 'You be all right if you have a rabbit's foot. Nothing'll go wrong if you allus be sure to carry it'.

Fat lot of good it had done him. He'd lost Beth, his son was as near as dammit a deaf mute with half the village calling him a loony, and now his daughter had blotted her copy book. If that was what you called luck he could do without it.

And so thinking, he hurled it through the air and watched it as it fell in a clump of heather some twenty feet below. A couple of partridge rose up from where it landed and flew, low, across the land. And it was as if all that he had ever believed in and all his hopes had flown with them.

His life had never seemed so bleak, so desolate.

# CHAPTER TWENTY

For two days John came and went without a word. Grim-faced and with scarcely a nod by way of acknowledgement to Sarah and completely ignoring Polly, he had eaten his meal and, after splashing his face with water from the tin bowl in the scullery, disappeared.

Long after the fire had been damped down for the night, the lamps extinguished and the girls had retired to bed, they heard him thumping up the stairs, the mumbled oaths as he bumped into furniture, the creak of the springs as he tumbled into bed.

But on Tuesday, after he had eaten, he moved to the chair by the fire. For a long time he sat, motionless, resting his chin in one hand, his eyes narrowed and lips pursed, as he gazed fixedly at the rag rug at his feet; so long that Sarah and Polly had cleared the table, washed and dried the dishes, and were returning the plates to the shelves and the cups to their hooks in the dresser when he moved for the first time.

He strode across to the door and took his cap and jacket from the hook. Shrugging on his jacket, he recrossed to the fireplace, took down his pipe and tobacco and shoved them in his pocket. He left them then, without a word.

Polly peered through the window and, in the gathering dusk, watched him striding purposefully down the lane.

"I suppose he's off to the Scarlet Arms again, to drink himself silly, while I have to wait for him to make his decision. How much longer is he going to take? I've a good mind to leave now and not give him the satisfaction of throwing me out."

Sarah, lighting the lamp, sighed wearily. She lowered the globe over the flame and the room was filled with soft yellow light and dark shadows. "Don't let's go through all that again. We've been through it, over it and under it and I don't know any more than you do what he has in mind…. And he's not going to throw you out. All he said was to stay out of sight, to keep inside, until he decides what is to be done."

"Didn't he say that he has a good mind to put me out on the streets? Said that's where I belong. Why did he say that then?"

"That was in the heat of the moment. He didn't mean it. I'm sure he didn't."

"Something's got to happen. I can't go on like this. When he's here, you could cut the atmosphere with a knife. He looks through me as though I don't exist. What is there to decide? Either I can stay or I can't." She paced the kitchen floor, all the while plucking at the bodice of her dress.

Sarah, taking up some darning, sat at the table for the light and said, "Polly, for heaven's sake, sit down. We'll have a rut in the floor like a farmer's cart track. Do have patience, dear. He'll let you know in his own good time. Meanwhile, you must rest yourself. Think of the baby. Why don't you start some knitting?"

"Knitting! Rest myself! I can hardly believe my ears. I am beside myself with worry. I have to run to the privy to be sick every morning. I've been beaten, and probably scarred for life, and you suggest I sit and knit!"

"What do you want me to say?" Sarah was trying to be patient. The image of her pa's stricken face and Polly, collapsed on the floor with the livid mark spreading like a stain across her cheek, would remain with her for a long time to come. "The sickness will pass and your face is already improving. Give it time and I am sure there will be nothing to show."

"Just listen to you. Give it time and I'm sure there will be nothing to show," she mimicked. "Give it time and there'll be plenty to show! Why must you always sound so smug? Don't you ever do anything wrong?"

"The only thing I've done wrong is try to help you," Sarah replied with some asperity. "And

227

there's no need for you to look so indignant for you know what I say is true."

Robert came in, carrying the cold from outside and the smell of newly-sawn wood shavings on his clothes. He had been out in the shed building yet another hutch that would, no doubt, soon shelter a squirrel, hedgehog, mole, or some such injured creature that he would find and bring home to nurse back to health.

Having taken off his boots in the scullery, he padded in his stockinged feet to the fire where he sat, smiled at Sarah and Polly in turn, took out his bird book, and was soon absorbed in the illustrations.

Sarah finished the sock she had started and took up another. Leaning towards the light, she threaded her needle with the dark grey wool. She looked across the table to where Robert sat. He's lucky, she thought, as she watched him absently stroking his cheek with the bird's feather that he used as a bookmark. Everything washes over him. He doesn't have to put up with all this. But she was immediately ashamed of herself. Poor Robert... poor Polly.... Poor Pa, with the shame of it all.

She, too, wondered what he had in mind. There were few alternatives that she could see. No relatives to take Polly in; not unless you counted Aunt Florrie. No, she dismissed the idea. He wouldn't send her there. Not to Aunt Florrie. She would never be willing to put up with Polly. Not in her condition. Especially not in her condition.

And then a thought came to her that made her stop what she was doing. It was the first time, since Polly had come home, that she had stopped to ask herself how all this would affect her. If Polly left home, there would be no hope of her ever having a life of her own. She'd be stuck here, looking after Pa and Robert, cleaning and cooking and darning socks, till she became a dried-up old maid with nothing to look forward to and nothing to look back on. Nothing to break the tedium of life but the changing of the seasons. Never having known a man or a family of her own.

And if Polly stayed? What would happen when the baby was born? Would Polly remain to keep house for them and leave her free to make a life of her own? What life did she want? But she knew, as she asked herself, for Dan's image had come to her mind.

Dan, with his laughing eyes and homely ways. She would be comfortable with Dan. She would live on the farm and be Sarah Fuller, farmer's wife. It was a hard life but Dan's ma was a good soul. She'd enjoy her gentle humour and quiet wisdom. They would cure hams in winter, make preserves during the summer months, and bake bread. Yes, it would be a good life; Dan to come home to her at the end of the day and for her, too, there would be children. Dan had never said anything but she knew that one day he would propose. But now she didn't know how she would be able to answer because it could all go by the board if Pa had a mind to send Polly away. In spite of her telling Polly that he hadn't meant what he'd said, she couldn't be sure what he would do.

Now, Polly wasn't the only one to be anxious about knowing what the future held.

An hour passed and almost another. Robert had gone to bed; his work at the farm meant an early rise. Polly and Sarah were about to do the same.

As Polly lit the candles and Sarah moved to the fire, they heard the door open, footsteps in the scullery. Polly looked up sharply. Her hand came to her mouth and her eyebrows rose in silent question. Sarah picked up the poker. Pa would still be at the Scarlet Arms. So who was in the scullery?

"Pa! You gave us such a fright!" Sarah exclaimed when he stepped into the room. "We didn't think you would be back this early."

"Be that as it may, but I am back and I've got something to say, so you'd better sit down."

Sarah sat but Polly answered her pa. "If it's to be about my future then I would prefer to remain standing."

"I said 'sit'!" he barked, "and sit you will. Don't provoke me, Polly, or you'll regret it." Polly sat. He turned his back on her as he carefully filled his pipe and lit it. Sarah watched them both from her chair in the shadows. Either he has something he finds difficult to say or he is making Polly wait, she thought, and was uneasy, remembering that the only other time he had

230

smoked his pipe in the kitchen was the day when he told Polly she was to go up to the Hall. What is it to be this time? Polly's putting on a brave front; for the time being, that is. Oh, get on with it, Pa, and put us out of our misery.

John, pulling on his pipe, was soon wreathed in the pungent smoke. His expression was bleak and icy when he pointed the pipe's stem at Polly and said, "You are to be married. I have arranged it this evening."

They sat in stunned silence. Coals collapsed in the dying fire and sparks flew up the chimney.

It was some seconds before Polly found her voice. "You mean…you can't mean…?" Her face lit with a hope that she had hardly dared think about.

"Ned Tulley has agreed to take you on. He knows all about… that." He jerked his head in her direction. " You are to be married within a month. Soon as the banns are read."

Polly's look of eagerness was replaced by one of horror. "Ned Tulley! I can't marry him! It's a monstrous idea. I wouldn't marry him if… if—"

"You have no choice. In your condition, you should be grateful that anybody would want to marry you. It's a lot better than you deserve and you'll do well to remember it."

"You can't make me marry him. I'd rather die!"

"And well you might if you want to face the alternative. It's Ned Tulley or out on the streets, for I'll not have you bringing up a bastard in my house.

There's your choice."

For some minutes they all sat in silence again, each lost in his own thoughts.

John was the first to speak. "Well? What'll it be?" he challenged. But seeing the droop of Polly's shoulders and her eyes awash with tears, he didn't wait for an answer. "It'll be a proper wedding, no hole in the wall affair. There'll be folk counting on their fingers and speculatin' soon enough, so there's no sense giving them cause before time. He's calling Sunday afternoon. The two of you can step out a while. Take a turn about the village. Good thing to be seen together." He pulled ferociously on his pipe. "Sarah, see that she's rigged out for the wedding. Something for yerself too. This should do it." He threw two coins on the table and was away to his bed before either of the girls could answer him.

Sarah was the first to move. She went to the table and picked up the coins. In her hand lay two gold sovereigns.

On Sunday afternoon, Polly sat with folded arms and a scowl on her face, staring down at her boots that peeped from the folds of her blue woollen skirt. It had taken all Sarah's efforts of persuasion to get Polly to change her clothes.

"You can't go walking about the village in your everyday clothes on a Sunday. What will people think?" Sarah had asked.

"Quite frankly, I don't care what people

think. In fact, I'm past caring about anything."

If you're past caring, why are you in such high dudgeon? I should have thought you'd be pleased that Pa has found this way out. You'll be a respectable married woman with a husband who thinks the world of you."

"But Ned Tulley of all people! And what is it going to be like living with his granny? She might be spotlessly clean but she doesn't go in for any comforts. You know, yourself, there's not a picture on the wall or an ornament to be seen. All she's got are her old herbs drying from the ceiling. And what about all those bees? Horrible stinging things. She'll not get me involved with her bees."

For four days, Sarah had been exasperated by Polly's litany of complaints. One moment she had been sullen and resentful and the next had fumed and raged. By now, Sarah didn't bother to contribute to the conversation,

"And you know she's got her bed in the kitchen, now that she can't manage the stairs," Polly persisted. "Can you imagine it? Coming down to get breakfast with Granny in the corner and the smell of the piss pot under the bed."

Sarah was stung to reply. "Polly! Granny's house doesn't smell at all. You've just said, yourself, that she's spotlessly clean. I wish you wouldn't talk like that. You would never have used such an expression before. I don't like the way you have changed."

"What do you expect? A lot of things have

changed. At one time, I would never have imagined going into service and never, in a million years, would I have considered marrying Ned Tulley. I can't think why Pa picked him of all people."

"I don't suppose he was spoilt for choice. You could do a lot worse…. I hope you'll be kind to him. Poor thing. He's been casting sheep's eyes at you since he was in short trousers." And then Sarah added tartly, "I can't think why Ned agreed… in the circumstances."

Polly, with her chin in her hand, watched Sarah poke viciously at the fire. "Why are you so cross with me all the time, Sarah?" she asked. "It's me that's going through all this. Not you. I don't think I could bear it if you turned against me too."

That's typical of Polly, Sarah thought. She thinks that she is the only one affected by all this. What about me? she wanted to scream. What about my future? What about me? Nobody had considered what that is going to be like. But the temptation to say what was on her mind was removed by a knock on the door.

Ned stood there, fidgeting with a new bowler hat that he held. He had a fresh scrubbed look and evidence on his chin that he had cut himself shaving, although he looked spruce in a stiffly starched collar with a tie, and a little bunch of primroses in the lapel of his jacket. But instead of the big smile that was as much a part of him as his big hands, his open face held an anxious look. It was a look of nervousness and suppressed excitement.

Sarah felt sorry for him. She smiled warmly. "Hello, Ned. Lovely day, isn't it? I'll go and tell Polly you are here."

Shutting the door behind her, she dashed back to the kitchen. "That's Ned," she hissed. "Now, don't forget; be nice to him. It's him that's doing you a favour, not the other way round."

And before Polly could remonstrate further, she propelled her through the kitchen and out the front door.

The day was cold and the April sun shone weakly as Ned and Polly walked silently by the river. So wrapped in her thoughts, was Polly, that she didn't hear the cawing of rooks overhead, or see the squirrels darting among the oaks. She looked down at the ground as she walked and was startled when Ned eventually spoke.

"Polly. There's summat I've got to say."

"There's nothing to say. We're to be wed and that's all there is to it."

She attempted to climb the stile but he took hold of her arm. "Listen to me, Polly. Let me have me say now and get it over."

She shrugged her shoulders and looked past him to the fields of young green wheat stretching out on the other side of the river. She didn't want to look at him standing there, shifting his weight from one foot to the other and wiping his hands down the sides of his trousers as if he still wore his butcher's apron.

"I just wanted to say that I know you wouldn't have chosen me for a husband. Not in the normal run of things, like."

"Your powers of deduction do you credit." Her voice was heavy with sarcasm.

"Polly, please listen to me. I know you don't love me but I promise—"

"What do you promise?"

"I promise I'll be a good 'usband to you... and I'll be good to the nipper too. I won't ever 'old it against you... I know what it's like to be born on the wrong side of the blanket. Never allowed to forget it, was I? All through school they was allus calling after me."

For a moment he could not conceal the pain the memory evoked. It compressed his mouth and narrowed his eyes. Then, suddenly, it was replaced by a look of determination that surprised Polly.

"That won't 'appen to our child, Polly. He won't 'ave to be called names all his life. And it will be our child 'cos that's what we'll let folk in the village think. You'll 'ave to give me your word on it. I won't 'ave any of them thinking you've made a fool of me, but I'll be a good 'usband to you."

Polly looked up into his earnest face but couldn't answer him. Instead, she turned and clambered over the stile. This time he didn't stop her.

Polly wondered what it would be like to be

236

married to this giant of a man. They had known each other nearly all their lives but suddenly he was a stranger. Today, she had seen a facet of Ned's character that she would never have imagined. He had spoken of the baby. He had spoken of it as a real person, with a future and feelings, and for this alone he earned her grudging respect.

For the first time she began to consider her unborn child. Until now, nobody, not Joseph Marsden, Mrs Passmore when she'd dismissed her, Pa, nor Sarah – apart from knitting for it – had mentioned the baby. But Ned had. Ned cared.

As they approached the bridge, Ned nervously ran his finger round his collar and suggested that she might take his arm, for appearances sake of course. He looked relieved when she didn't argue. He seemed to tower above her as they strolled round the village green. Ned raised his hat to Emily Waters and ignored the banter from the young men lounging outside the Scarlet Arms.

They sat on a bench by the well and after a few minutes Ned rubbed his hand over his chin and nodding towards the butchers, said, "Do you think we could make summat of that place?" And when Polly stared at him, he added, "It'll be a nice place to bring up the nipper."

"I'm not in the mood for joking."

"But I'm not. You're looking at the new butcher of Barkwell, y'know."

Polly, suspicious that he was teasing her,

said nothing.

"George Bishop is retiring next month. He and his missus are going over to live with their daughter at Chillingford. I'm buying the business off him."

Polly saw the pride in his eyes and realised he was being serious. She listened to him telling her that it was really two cottages knocked into one. On the left was the butcher's shop with a storeroom behind and, to the right, the cottage had been extended at the back. A kitchen had been added so that the whole of the downstairs room could be used as a parlour. Above were two bedrooms.

"There's a big garden out the back where I can grow vegetables and where the nipper can play," he said.

And for the first time in weeks, Polly smiled

# CHAPTER TWENTY-ONE

Down in the village Emily set the bell on the door clanging as she scurried into the shop. Harold, looked up from wrapping a block of salt for Rosie Potter.

"What are you in such a hurry for?" he asked his wife. "You'll make yerself all hot rushing like that. I told you I could manage on my own."

Emily came behind the counter and tied an apron round her ample waist. "I know you can, Harold, but I've got something to tell…. Oh, hallo, Rosie, this'll interest you too. I've just been to Bishop's and guess what? The butcher's is changing hands."

"I'm not surprised. We knew that was going to happen. George and Alice are getting on a bit. They've been talking about it for ages," said Harold.

Rosie handed Harold the money for the salt and said, "What I want to know is who be a-taking over? And will the prices go up? Prices allus go up when shops change hands."

"I don't know about the price of meat but I do know who be a-taking over, and you'll never guess, not in a month of Sundays." Emily crossed her arms and leaned back with her head on one side, waiting for them to ask her.

Harold obliged. "Well, go on then, Em. I can see your itching to tell us."

"It's Ned Tulley no less."

"What? Young Ned! Who'd have thought…. No, I don't believe it," said Rosie.

"Go and ask Alice yerself. 'Twas her who told me not five minutes ago. What I'm asking is where's he got the money from? Alice says he's going to rent the cottage but stands to reason he's going to have to pay for the business and have money in his pocket to buy his stock."

"Happen his granny's got the money," offered Harold. "Sells her honey every year, she does, and she don't go a-spending much does she? And then there's them 'erbs she sells."

Emily pulled on her earlobe. "I reckon he might have been left it by his father."

"He ain't got no father," said Rosie.

"Stands to reason he must of done once! His ma never let on who it was at the time. I could never fathom it out but happen he was moneyed. P'raps he's always regretted not meeting his responsibilities. P'raps he's died now and left a fortune to his unclaimed son," said Emily, dramatically.

"Aw, come off it, Em," laughed Harold.

"You've been reading too many of them penny novels."

Nell Benson came in at that moment and nearly knocked a packet off the shelves in her haste. Her eyes bright with excitement, she looked the possessor of a great secret.

"Ah, Rosie! I thought I saw you come in 'ere. Have you heard? Ned Tulley's going to marry the Holland girl. The youngest; Polly."

"Where did you get that idea from?" Rosie was peeved that Nell should get hold of any news before her.

"Our Mary-Ann heard it this morning. Parson was telling his daughter about the banns to be read. Mary-Ann happened to be polishing the 'all table outside Parson's study. Can't be getting more def'nate than that, can you? She beamed with pleasure at being the bearer of such news.

Emily looked at Harold and Rosie with a knowing smile on her compressed lips. "All fits together don't it?"

"I should think," Nell continued, "that old Doctor Gilbert would turn in his grave if he knew a granddaughter of his was going to marry the likes of Ned. After all, he's never going to make anything of hisself, is he?"

"That's where yer wrong, Nell. He's taking over the butchers when the Bishops retire. And Em got that from the horse's mouth. Alice told her, just this minute, so you can't be getting more def'nate than that, can you?" It did Rosie good to feed Nell back her own words. That'll teach you to think you know it all, she thought.

"That explains why she's set her sights on him then, don't it?" Nell nodded her head, sagely. "Stands to reason, if he's going to have the shop. No wonder he was allus going up to the 'all with deliveries. He was taking things that was forgotten off the order, he told me once. That was just a load of old eyewash, if you asks me. I wasn't born yesterday. It was an excuse to see her, that's all it was. She must of turned his head with her purty ways."

"I didn't think that it was much more'n old George missing the odd thing off the order. He is getting on a bit you know," Harold ventured.

The women gave him withering looks and he retired to the back of the shop, no match for the three of them.

"Fat lot of good talking to men," Emily sniffed. "They never knows nothing."

Sarah was relieved when it looked as if Polly was going to accept the situation in which she found herself. At one time she had visualised her sister being dragged down the aisle almost kicking and screaming but strangely, Polly had come back from that first walk with Ned in a quieter and more thoughtful frame of mind.

In the days that followed she had been full of the plans she and Ned were making for the butcher's shop and the cottage where they would live. It was almost as if the only objection Polly had had to marrying Ned was the thought of living with his granny. But Sarah knew that wasn't true. It hadn't been her only objection so she wondered what had brought about the change. Surely Polly couldn't be so shallow as to be swayed by the fact that Ned was going to have his own business.

Sarah could see a ghost of the old Polly, more animated than she had been for weeks, telling her how Ned had explained the importance of being able to judge the live animals at market and know which ones would make good, tender joints of meat, and repeating Ned's description of the cottage

And so, over the weeks, Polly amused herself with grandiose plans and ways of spending the two sovereigns that Pa had given and the five from Joseph Marsden. Polly had never questioned from where Pa's two had come. A man in his position never had sovereigns to throw around when all he earned was used to feed the family. And she never asked where Ned was going to find the money to buy the butchers. She knew that they would rent the cottage and shop and that would cost six shillings a week, but Ned had to buy the butcher's block and knives and the existing stock, and have money behind him to operate.

But Sarah knew. It had been a long time since she had looked at the sovereigns in the tin trunk and wondered about their origins. But when her pa threw the two down on the kitchen table, and she later heard that Ned was buying the Bishops' business, her suspicions led her to delve down the trunk once more.

The leather pouch was considerably lighter and now more firmly tied. When she counted out the coins, sitting on Pa's bed, she found that there were thirty seven missing. She sat, holding the pouch in her hand, convinced that the money had gone to Ned. "Dear God," she said to herself, "I hope Polly never finds out that Pa has bought her a husband."

George and Alice Bishop agreed to sell Ned most of their furniture as they would only be able to take a few possessions into their daughter's already cramped house in Chillingford. So when they left the village the week before the wedding, and Ned took over the lease of the cottage it was, for the most part, furnished.

Ned spent every spare moment painting the cottage and tidying the garden for George had let things go as he advanced in age. Polly persuaded him to paper the parlour with a big, sprawling flower design and Robert went down, after work, to help him.

Four days before the wedding, Sarah and Polly took the carrier's cart along the turnpike to Chillingford, where there was a shop that sold all manner of things for the home. Some were new and others used. It was a musty shop, next to the chandlers, but Polly delighted in choosing for her new home.

There were two wicker chairs for the hearth, a brightly coloured woollen cloth for the table, copper saucepans, a kettle and jelly moulds, a chest of drawers and a pine washstand for the bedroom, paraffin lamps – one with a fancy shade that Polly couldn't resist – some rush matting and a tin bath full of a miscellany of kitchen equipment; a rolling pin, baking tins, a soup ladle and a set of three jugs.

After Polly had paid and arranged for them to be delivered, she and Sarah, arms linked, strolled down to the cobbled main street to spend the rest of the afternoon trying on the new bonnets, with wide brims flaring upwards in front – that the assistant assured them were all the rage – and choosing a new outfit for Polly.

Sarah steered her away from a cream silk gown, reminding her that whatever she bought would be her Sunday best for some time to come, and it would be as well to choose something more practical. At last, Polly picked out a claret skirt with a tight little hip-length jacket that had the fashionable full sleeves set high on the shoulder. A cream blouse with a row of tiny buttons down the front and a froth of lace at the neck, and a bonnet trimmed with ribbon completed the ensemble.

Sarah refused anything more than a soft blue skirt and some new trimming for her hat. "I don't need anything more," she said and Polly didn't press her.

The last few days went by in a whirl of

activity. They took four pots of geraniums down to the cottage, to brighten the window sills, and some dried flowers in a wreath to decorate the bedroom wall. They baked piles of jam tarts and maids-of-honour, and made jellies and junkets. The kitchen was full of the aroma of baking and boiled ham, and cluttered with trays of cakes cooling and mountains of washing up, but eventually everything was ready for the big day.

John was up before dawn on the day of the wedding to clean out the cart. Robert joined him to groom the marc before he had to hurry off to the farm for the morning's work.

The day started off cool and misty but shafts of sunshine broke through the clouds to brighten the area inside the open doorway where they worked. John watched his son, grown tall over the years, expertly picking out the horses' hooves and brushing her body from front to rear with long sure strokes.

This was the second horse they had had since John had sold the gig all that time ago. He thought back to how furious Beth had been that he hadn't consulted her when he'd sold her father's pride and joy. His eyes softened for a moment as he remembered how he had turned that passion into one of another kind. That was before any of their children were born. Children? None of them were children any more.

Perhaps it was because Polly was getting

married today that his mind kept travelling back over the years, stopping at milestones along the way. It was twenty years since he and Beth were married and nearly three since she had died. And the pain of losing her came to him as fresh as if it had been yesterday.

He wondered what she would have made of this day as he took a cloth and wiped down the plank seat of the cart; the cart that would carry his daughter to the church. And out of his life, too, for he knew in his heart that he had lost her forever.

Suddenly he felt an overwhelming need to hang on to what was left of the family and, at the same time, a sadness came with the knowledge that it was probably too late.

Robert finished brushing out the mare's mane and tail and was leaving when John stopped him. He pointed at the horse and nodded to Robert as he clapped him on the back. Robert looked startled. For a moment he searched his father's face and when he saw only approbation there, smiled broadly.

Poor bugger, thought John. It must be the first time I've ever given him any encouragement. All these years I've selfishly nursed my own disappointment, concerned with my own feelings, and not given a damn about his. He thought of the lost years he couldn't reclaim, sighed deeply and returned to the cleaning of the cart.

At seven, Sarah padded down the stairs as Polly, wiping her mouth with her handkerchief, returned from the privy.

"Are you still being sick, Polly?" she asked.

"I don't know whether it's my condition or my wedding day that makes me so."

Polly went into the scullery, drank some water and splashed her face. "Is there much rainwater in the butt? I want to wash my hair."

"I'll bring a bucket for you after breakfast and help you if you like, but we'd better get a move on. There's the salad to wash and ham to cut. We've the sandwiches to make... egg and parsley, I thought, and we have to — Why, what's the matter? Polly? Oh, please don't cry. Here, have mine." Sarah fished in her apron pocket and offered a clean handkerchief.

Polly dabbed at her eyes and blew her nose. "I don't think I can go through with this. I thought I could. It was exciting making the cottage look nice and having a new outfit and planning the wedding too. We've been so busy with everything that I've hardly had time to think, but when I do, I keep thinking about the shape I'm getting. It's not just vanity that makes me upset. It's the humiliation of knowing that everyone will know that I had to get married."

"But at least you *are* getting married," said Sarah. "There's many a girl who'd have been pleased that she's got a man to stand by her. You'll be thought none the worse on that account." And she added brightly, "Sit there. I've got something for you."

Sarah went to the cupboard and brought out a large square package. She put it on the table in front of Polly. And when she didn't move, said, "Well, go on then. Open it."

Inside the package was a patchwork quilt. Polly's eyes lit up at the sight. "Oh, Sarah, haven't you made a good job of it! It's beautiful." she opened it out, stroking the reds and blues and printed squares that made up the design.

Sarah watched her. She's no more than a child, she thought sadly. Easily distracted by something that pleases.

Polly said, suddenly, "It's lovely but I can't take this from you. I know how long it took to make. I thought you were making it for yourself. For when you get married."

Sarah turned away from Polly and busied herself with the lettuce that had to be washed. She didn't want Polly to see the desolation that she knew she couldn't hide. She managed, however, to keep the harshness from her voice when she said, "I doubt that I will ever get married."

Robert returned at midday, smelling of earth and stables. Dan had sent a message that he couldn't get away from the farm. He wouldn't be able to attend the ceremony but would try to come later.

Sarah was disappointed but watching Robert explain the reason was so funny, and when she realised what he was trying to sign, she laughed until the tears came to her eyes.

"What's he telling you? asked John.

Even he had to laugh when at last she managed to explain. "Dan's got a problem with one of his cows. It's got too much wind."

My word, Sarah thought. I've never seen Robert looking happy and acting the goat while Pa is around. And considering how Pa feels about this wedding, I'm surprised he is laughing. Wonders will never cease!

When she had dressed, Polly sat by the window in the parlour, gazing out at the garden where they would all come back for tea. A table had been set up on the daisy-speckled lawn. The whole garden was bright with summer flowers; poppies, sweet Williams, marigolds and, far against the wall, the taller lupins, foxgloves and larkspur. All the pinks and blues, mauves and oranges, together with the golden-tasselled flowers of the laburnum, formed a kaleidoscope of colour. That, and the heavy scent of roses and lavender wafting through the open window, made her stomach lurch. She closed her eyes and fought the urge to retch.

And that was as John found her. With her golden hair piled on the crown of her head and a flowered hat in her lap, she was the image of her ma. The likeness was so painful to John that the breath caught in his throat. He must have made some sound because she opened her eyes. When she saw him standing there, in the open doorway, she stood up.

Her unwavering grey eyes, that seemed huge

in her pale face, returned his stare. He ached to hold her in his arms. She looked so young and vulnerable in her grown-up clothes. He wanted to tell her how beautiful she was and how much he loved her.

But when she asked him with a childlike eagerness, "How do I look, Pa?" he could only answer gruffly.

"You'll do," he said before hurrying from the room.

They called for granny on the way. Ned had already gone on to the church. At seventy, Granny Tulley had grown frail. Her hair, white and baby-soft, was, as ever, tied in a tight little knot at the back of her head. Her liver-spotted hands now had a tremor she was unable to control. She still had, however, an active mind.

"I been a-trying to tell your pa that he'll not be a-throwing me in this 'ere cart like a sack of taters," she told the girls. "I don't disremember times he has afore now. I said I'd rather not go but telling him was no more use than putting a poultice on a wooden leg, for all the good it do."

She laughed, exposing her five remaining teeth and added with a conspiratory grin, "Still, I'm glad he took no notice 'cos I wouldn't of missed this day for all the world. My Ned's been a dark horse, paying you particular attention without me knowing, but as I said to the old bees this mornin', that's sometimes the way with a man and his maid, and it's his own business after all…. No, I wouldn't miss this day for all the tea in china and my Ned marrying a purty lass like you." She patted Polly's hand, not noticing the far off look in her eyes.

And then Granny became serious for a moment as the cart trundled over the rutted lane. "It will be a relief to see him wed and to know that nothing's expected of me any more. Maybe that's the reason the good Lord lets me live a while longer. Not that I haven't enjoyed having him. Don't put the wrong colour to what I'm saying. When the Lord took me daughter, he left me Ned to fill the gap. He's been a good lad and he's seen me all right these last few years.

"But I hope the Lord will be pleased to take me afore I get past work and become a burden to anybody." She lapsed into silence, preoccupied with her thoughts, and it was a quiet group that rode over the stone bridge into the village.

Three swifts flew round the church spire, dipping and gliding, until the flat-toned bells rang out and the wedding party emerged into the sunshine.

Jesse Caldwell poked her head in Bella's kitchen window.

"Quick, Bella. There coming out if you want to see."

Bella, still with a tea towel in her hand, followed Jesse as she scurried down the path. By God she can move when she wants to, even if she is built like a cart horse, Bella thought to herself.

Nell was standing in the lane. "Just look at that outfit she's wearing. Looks a reg'lar duchess, don't she?"

"Ooh, she do look nice," said Bella.

Jesse sniffed. "A bit set up for my taste though." They watched Ned helping Polly up into the cart.

"If you ask me, it's not only meat young Ned's been delivering," Jesse added, with a knowing wink.

"Jesse!" Bella exclaimed. By God Jesse Caldwell could come out with some things.

"Well, look at her and tell me if you don't think they has to get married."

Bella had to agree. "Happen you be right, but I can't think less of her for that. 'Tis but nature after all. Me ma allus said it was only the good girls that get caught. The others are too artful."

"Didn't I tell you that I reckoned she'd set her sights at him, 'specially once she knew he be having the business," added Nell with a satisfied smile. "That's why she's enticed him with her purty ways… and now he's got to marry her."

Jesse jerked her head towards the butchers. "Have you seen what they done with George and Alice's place? She's got him to put paper up in the parlour. Brought fancy ideas from the 'all, she has. I wouldn't of believed it if I hadn't seen it with me own eyes. Great bloomin' flowers all over the walls."

"It hasn't got birds on it, has it? Bad luck it be to have birds. Flowers is all right, but birds is unlucky. Sure to be a death in the family if you has birds."

"Rose reckons she'll be having a carpet in the butchers before you know it."

"And fancy chairs to rest me feet?"

They all laughed.

"Who's that littl'un with Sarah? I've not seen her before. She's no oil painting, is she?"

"No, but nice hair."

"She's from up the 'all. Her and Polly was thick together, Agnes says. Wouldn't be a bit surprised if she's trying to work her way in with 'em. Workhouse, she was."

"P'raps she fancies the brother."

"What? That Looney! Don't be daft, Bella. Nobody's going to take on summat like that. He's getting worse every year, I reckon. Rose was telling me, Lily's two boys was nesting a while back. Doing nobody no harm, they wasn't, and they allus leaves one egg in the nest, and he comes along, a-swinging his arms and making them awful noises, like he do. Wouldn't be a bit surprised if he has to be put away one of these days."

"Old John looks none too happy. You'd think he'd be pleased to get one of 'em off his hands."

"He's not very well, if you ask me. George says he's been off-colour for weeks. Hasn't brought his fiddle down to the Arms either, and that's not like him, is it?"

"I do like to hear him and old Patrick when they get going together. I opens the windows wide and can hear it right across the green."

Well, if he plays for his daughter's wedding, you won't hear it tonight. Look, they be going back over the bridge."

"Huh! Too stuck up to have a do at the Arms then."

"They must be going home for their teas."

"The blessing of God on ye, darling. Come here till I see you."

Polly took Patrick's outstretched hands as he smiled up at her, his old green eyes sparkling above his thinning grizzled beard.

"It makes me heart turn over, just to be looking at ye," he said as he swept her up the garden path.

John took the cart round to the side of the house and unharnessed the mare. Ned helped his granny to a seat in the shade of the laburnum and Ruth and Mary joined her.

Fanny had come. She had managed to change her afternoon off and Mrs Tatlow had lent her a pair of white gloves for the occasion.

"It were a lovely wedding weren't it?" she said, squinting at Sarah as she helped to carry the plates of food outside.

Sarah politely agreed, but privately she thought that she would be glad when it was all over.

What a picture we must have made, she thought, with Polly looking as if she was going to be sick any moment, Pa with that set look that seems to be always on his face these days, and Ned looking tired and anxious and self-conscious in his best suit and well-polished boots.

"And she had some lovely presents too. Did Miss Greenway give her them silver spoons?"

"Mmm?... Yes, she did. She's always been like an aunt to us. We've known her all our lives."

Absently, Sarah folded a cloth that had been covering the sandwiches and looked across at Ruth who was laughing at something Granny was saying.

Ruth's eyesight was failing her, although she still played the organ for the church. Her voice had been wistful when she had given the spoons to Polly saying, 'I would have liked to have embroidered a tablecloth or some such thing, for you, but I'm afraid I can't thread the needles these days. I've had to give up keeping the baby box in good order too, but Mrs Wilton has taken it over now.' Ruth had sewn baby clothes for the box that was lent out to the parish poor for as long as she could remember and it came hard to her to relinquish the responsibility.

Sarah thought how different she was to their real aunt. They hadn't seen Aunt Florrie for years, even though Pa seemed close and spent so many nights over in Chillingford. But Aunt Florrie had never taken an interest in them and she hadn't come today. She had sent over a gaudy glass vase that had prompted a pained expression from Polly. A summer cold was her excuse for not coming.

Sarah would have liked an excuse too. Her head throbbed and she would be glad to get the charade over. For that's all it was.

Pa stood with Mr McGiveney, talking about the Marquis of Salisbury and his latest reforms. They had taken off their jackets and were leaning against the gate. Both of them disliked the Conservative government and had been happier when Gladstone had been in power. In their opinion, he had been a good Liberal. If it hadn't been for him, the country labourer wouldn't have got the vote in eighty-four. A lot of good it had done them, her pa said, because the Conservatives got in in eighty-six and they hadn't done much for the working man. In his opinion, they ought to vote Gladstone back in if he stood next year.

Sarah heard her pa but she could tell by the tight line of his jaw that his heart wasn't in the conversation.

And perhaps Patrick did too because it wasn't long before he brought his penny whistle from his pocket and said, "Let us be having a bit of a tune, John. What shall it be?" and without waiting for an answer, put the whistle to his lips and started to play an Irish jig.

Mary McGiveney clapped her hands and Granny joined her in keeping time to the whirling music.

They ate. They drank Granny's coltsfoot

wine. They sang *Two Lovely Black Eyes* and *Ta-ra-ra boom-de-ay*. Ned didn't leave Polly's side. It was almost as if he thought he was dreaming and that if he looked away, or blinked his eyes, she would be gone. Polly, for her part, still had that faraway look but nobody noticed, or chose not to notice, the quietness of her manner.

At eight, John went to hitch the mare to the cart so that he could take everybody home. Robert was in the shed, feeding his animals. When he saw John he stopped what he was doing to help. They carried the harness out to where the horse stood cropping the fine turf. John backed her between the shafts of the cart and secured her there. Robert signed to his father that he would take the cart. It was a few seconds before John understood what Robert was trying to convey. When he did, he nodded, grateful that he wouldn't have to maintain his façade much longer.

Robert smiled. John looked into his face and was struck by the realisation that his son was as he remembered himself to be at that age. The same crisp dark hair and bright brown eyes. The same strong physique and a look that he could only describe as a look of eagerness for life. He had once felt that too.

And it came to him, the painful awareness, that he was looking at a replica of himself. Of all his children, the one he rejected, was the one in whom he could see himself. And he felt the weight of his guilt and the senseless waste of the irretrievable years. Would Robert ever forgive him? Or was it now too late? He sighed and, with effort, his mouth formed a tight smile as he nodded once again to his son.

Robert opened his mouth, hesitated a moment, and his eyes were bright as he formed the word. "Paa..." he said, and laughed, before he led the horse into the lane.

The goodbyes had been said. Granny and Ruth, Patrick and Mary had gone in the cart. Fanny had left earlier and Ned and Polly elected to walk down to the new home that awaited them.

"Are you not going to ride in the cart with us, Ned?" Patrick had asked and added with mock seriousness, "It will save your energy, for you'll be needing it, I'll be thinking."

Mary had rolled her eyes. "Mary, Jesus and Joseph!" she declared, "I can't be taking that man of mine anywhere, without him showing me up."

The cottage was quiet after they had disappeared down the lane. John left Sarah clearing up the kitchen and returned to the shed. He sat on the edge of an upturned wheelbarrow and rested his head in his hands.

He felt old. He was forty-five and he was tired. It wasn't only his feelings over Polly and the marriage he had arranged. That was done and now all that was left for him was to hope that they would make a go of things. Ned was not a bad fellow in many ways; it was obvious that he loved Polly.

Hadn't he said that he would marry her without the money? But John had insisted. He had persuaded him by saying that the money would enable them to have their own home and a better start to married life. And now Ned had the chance to make something of hisself. John had done his best for them; he could do no more.

No, it wasn't only Polly or Robert, or even Sarah, who claimed his concern. It was feelings about himself. He had felt unwell for weeks now. Indigestion, or a touch of biliousness, it had felt like at first. A passing indisposition best dealt with by a dose of Epsom Salts, but it had brought him no relief. He had intended to ask Granny, when he took her home, if she had something that might help.

But that could wait. He was too tired. Too weary to bother tonight. All in all, it had been quite a day.

# CHAPTER TWENTY-TWO

That year of 1891, the year that Polly and Ned were married, was a time of plenty. Fruit trees were laden with apples, pears and plums, branches bowing towards the earth in their abundance. Bees hovered over fields of purple clover and the cows in the meadows, where the tall thistles grew, chewed their cud and, daily, yielded rich creamy milk into brimming pails.

Every cottage had its store of preserves and pickles laid down on pantry shelves and every man who had worked at the Fuller's farm was happy that they had brought a good harvest home. The extra beer, the extra coins they jingled in their pockets, and the harvest dinner they had just, this evening, enjoyed, left each with the satisfaction of a job well done. And so it was with full bellies and high spirits that the women helped to clear the tables and the men rearranged the trestles and chairs to clear a space for the dancing.

Sarah stood in the farmhouse doorway with

Mrs Fuller, watching as the music struck up and everyone, excited and laughing, joined partners for the first dance. "Harvest Home! I love Harvest Home, don't you, Mrs Fuller?" she said.

"Yes I do, m'dear, but I must admit I'm not as fit as I used to be. It's bin boiling hot today and no mistake. I don't mind telling you I shall be glad when it's all over and I can get me boots off. Me feet are fair talking to me, right now."

Mrs Fuller looked across the yard to where Robert was standing next to the group of players; his pa with his fiddle under his chin, Patrick with his penny whistle and old Snowy who had been persuaded to bring out his wheezy concertina. Robert was watching Patrick's foot as he kept beat to the music and was tapping his own and clapping his hands. His face split into a wide smile and his eyes were alight with pleasure.

"God bless the boy! Just look at him. He'll be the death of me. I never knowed nobody as can enjoy hisself like what he can and he can't hear none of it neither." Mrs Fuller shook her head in wonder. "Looks like they'll be a-needing more ale at that end table. Marvellous how Walter can put it away when he's not paying for it. Where's Betsy got to? I asked her to fill those jugs ten minutes ago."

Mrs Fuller went off in search of Betsy. Sarah, catching sight of the giggling Betsy, a few minutes later, as she disappeared round the corner of the barn with Jimmy Caldwell, wondered if she should tell Mrs Fuller but decided against it. It was none of her business but she could go and give a hand. Dan had gone to see to the horses and make sure the cows were settled for the night. It would take him a good half hour so she may as well make herself useful.

The day was thickening into dusk and the dancing well under way when Joseph and his sister, Margaret, rode over the wooden bridge. They reined in their horses near the gate, dismounted and strolled into the yard.

Sarah was just coming out of the kitchen with Mrs Fuller.

"Oh my! Look who's turned up," Mrs Fuller exclaimed. "I better go over and see what they'll be a-wanting. Here, will you take this over to the far table for me, Sarah?" She thrust a jug of ale into Sarah's hands and hurried across the yard. At the same time Dan emerged from the stables, saw the newcomers and went over to greet them too.

The couple looked completely out of place in their fine riding habits and highly polished boots. The villagers had turned out in their Sunday best and had rubbed their boots to a shine you could see your face in, but they still felt at a disadvantage and their conversation became a little more subdued.

"Good evening, Mrs Fuller...Dan," Joseph said, smiling expansively as he gave a touch to his hat. "We saw you celebrating and my sister and I thought we'd drop in. Have you had a good harvest?"

"Yes, thank you, sir," Dan beamed proudly.

Mrs Fuller smiled too, her apple cheeks pink with pleasure as she gave a little bob and welcomed them. "It's good of you to come by. Can I offer you some refreshment? We've ale... or lemonade if you would prefer it, madam, and no end of food. I could cut you some roast beef or a bit of ham. Or otherwise there's some apple pie or a nice —"

"No thank you, Mrs Fuller. We haven't come to stay." Margaret said, interrupting her. At the same time her eyes raked the yard, taking in the dancers and the villagers who sat talking, laughing and drinking but in a self-conscious way.

The smile slid from Mrs Fuller's face at the rebuff. "Then if you'll excuse me. I'm meaning no disrespect but I have things to attend to in the kitchen." She gave another little bob, turned on her heel and left them.

Dan stood, awkwardly, rubbing his hands on his trousers. "Can I find you a seat?" he asked at last.

Margaret gave him the benefit of her dazzling smile. "Yes, Mr Fuller. Come and sit with me and tell me all about your farm. Tell me, how many men do you employ?" She gave Joseph a cheeky grin, as if to say it amused her to be entertained by a common farmer, and led the way across the yard. Dan, red-faced, followed her.

Sarah delivered the jug of ale to the end table and thought she would be better off in the kitchen. It's a good job Polly's not here, she thought. Polly had said she was too near her time to enjoy the festivities, although Bella Faddon was here and she was due any moment by the look of her. Sarah suspected that Polly was enjoying all the fuss and attention Ned was giving her and was playing on it. She'd got Ned jumping through hoops for her, fetching and carrying, as if she was the only woman in the world about to give birth. And, funnily enough, Ned seemed to like doing it. It was more than Polly deserved in the circumstances. He was a kind man, was Ned, and she hoped Polly appreciated it.

Sarah came out of her meditation and looking across the twirling dancers, saw Joseph watching her. He was leaning against the barn wall with his arms folded over his chest and a trace of mockery in his eyes. Yes, she decided, the best thing she could do was take herself away to the kitchen. But before she could reach the open doorway, Joseph had crossed the yard to intercept her.

"Well, well, if it isn't the doctor's grand daughter! You see, I didn't forget you." Joseph's eyes glinted with amusement.

Sarah could feel herself blushing. The last thing she wanted to do was speak to this man who had caused so much trouble for her family. How would Pa react if he saw her talking to him? Her eyes flew to where John was playing his fiddle. The lamps had been lit and in the yellow light she could see that he had noticed and by the set of his jaw he was finding it difficult to contain his anger. He was managing to continue sawing at the strings, although not so vigorously. Sarah was glad that everyone was too filled with ale to notice. John's eyes had taken on a watchful look. Sarah was at a loss to know how to handle the situation. She just wished Joseph would leave before this piece of music finished because, as sure as eggs were eggs, her pa would come striding over and cause a scene.

"What's the matter? Cat got your tongue?"

"I'm sorry. What did you say?"

"I said, would you like to dance?"

Sarah glared at him. "No thank you."

Joseph shrugged carelessly, as if it made no odds to him that she didn't care to dance. And then, catching sight of Betsy and Jimmy emerging from behind the barn, he leant forward and with his lips close to her ear, so close that she could smell the brandy on his breath, whispered, "Perhaps you would prefer to see what's behind the barn. Whatever it is, it has certainly put a twinkle in that maid's eye."

Sarah stared at him, her mouth half open in astonishment. Did he think she was a fool? She knew exactly what Betsy and Jimmy had been up to. She could hardly believe he had just said that. But at that moment, just as her mind was furiously trying to form a suitable retort, Joseph's sister appeared at his elbow.

Linking her arm through his, she looked up at him and said, "There's nothing to interest us here, Joseph. Let us go home and have a civilised meal.

I'm hungry."

Sarah's eyes widened at the remark. She couldn't believe anyone could be so rude and was glad that Mrs Fuller hadn't heard.

"Very well, my dear," he sighed. "It seems I must bid you good evening, Miss Holland. My sister must be obeyed!" He pulled a wry face and lowering his voice, added, "Until the next time, little Sarah... and I can assure you, there will be a next time."

Sarah watched them go, laughing with each other as they untied and mounted their horses, and the next moment they were disappearing down the lane at a brisk trot.

A hand grabbed her arm and pulled her round. "What did he want? What did he say to you?"

Sarah looked into John's red face. It looked screwed up and ugly in his rage. She tried to pull away from him. "You're hurting me, Pa!"

"What did he want? What did he say to you?" he repeated, shaking her arm.

"He asked me if I wanted to dance... that's all." She pulled her arm free and rubbed at it where his fingers had dug into the flesh. "It was nothing, Pa. That's all he said." She turned her head away from him, frightened that he would be able to tell by her face that it wasn't all. What he would do if he knew what else Joseph had said didn't bear thinking about.

John stared down the now empty lane,

shaking his head from side to side. His jaw worked, grinding his teeth, as he muttered to himself. "You stay clear of me and mine, Joseph Marsden. You've brought enough trouble to us. We can do without more."

"Come on, Pa. They've gone now." It was Sarah's turn to take his arm and give it a little shake. "Come on. They'll be expecting you to play."

They turned back towards the revellers; the singing and the laughter. John took up his fiddle and Sarah went in search of Dan. It had been a trivial incident but somehow the evening was spoilt and she had a nasty feeling that that wasn't the last she had seen of Joseph Marsden.


Dan dug his hand into the sack of newly-threshed corn, gladdened by the plump grains that ran through his fingers. He looked about the threshing shed, revelling in the mealy fragrance that hung on the dusty air, and gave a great sigh of pleasure.

This had been his first year of running the farm. Since the farm manager had retired, he had been solely in charge and had worked so hard. He had ploughed and scattered the seed on the raw, fresh earth. The seasons had been good to him and he had watched the spring fields of green wheat turn to summer gold, had worried over every cloud and threat of rain until the corn had ripened and the workers had come swinging down the lane on the twenty-second of August.

He would never forget the surge of

excitement as he, along with the men, had rolled up his shirtsleeves, taken up a scythe and helped to reap his first harvest. The workers spread out along one edge of the field and rhythmically their scythes cut swathes in the golden sea of corn. Dan felt the sweat soak his armpits and the kerchief at his neck and he heard the cheerful callings of the women who followed behind to bind the corn into sheaves.

Mid mornings they stopped for a breather, quaffing ale as they sat in the shade of the hawthorns that bordered the field, men in one group, sun-bonneted women in another.

The same village folk had worked the harvest for as long as Dan could remember and he had worked alongside them. As a young boy, he had followed scythes with the women and as soon as he had been big enough to wield one, he had cut the corn. But this was the very first harvest that was his own. Now he was a farmer.

Dan left the threshing shed, patted a passing cow as the herd came in for milking, and crossed the yard to the house. Before opening the door he looked across at the new yellow stacks in the rickyard and thinking that he had never seen such a splendid sight, gave another great sigh of satisfaction.

Yes. Now he was a farmer. And now he knew what he was going to do.

It was perhaps an hour later that he strolled with Sarah through the top pasture. They leaned on the gate, dark heads close together, and looked down on the clean yellow stubble of cleared fields gilded by the last rays of a lingering sun. The low farmhouse squatted in the valley beside the dairy sheds and outhouses and, behind the buildings, serene countryside stretched as far as the eye could see. The summer night was warm, scented and peaceful and a cloud of midges danced in the air.

"It's threshing better than I thought. There's a good yield this year. I must admit I was worried when those storm clouds passed over the day before we started to reap but now... well, I wouldn't mind if it rained hatchets and hammers, now it's safely gathered." He smiled down at her and she could see the pride in his eyes and was glad for him.

He cleared his throat and took her hands gently in his own. "Sarah, I know I've been lucky. This was an easy year for me. It didn't feel like it, at times, 'cos it's hard work, but I didn't have any setbacks. Another year it could be totally different. The weather can go against a man and the crop can be lost. Cattle can fall sick. In lots of ways it's a hard life but I can't imagine any other. The farm was my pa's and his pa's before him. It's not a big one, by any means, just sixty acres, but it's a good living and the only one I'm cut out for. I'm telling you this so you should know...." His voice trailed away as he searched for the right words.

"What are you trying to say, Dan?"

"I'm trying to say that I want you to share that life with me... I want you to .... Will you be my wife?"

Sarah pulled her hands away from his and turned away. She had known that one day he would propose but had hoped that it wouldn't be so soon. Although she knew that she loved him dearly, and had no doubts that those feelings were reciprocated, she cherished the foolish hope that their friendship could continue as it had been. While nothing was said, she could allow things to drift, content with the times they spent together. But she had known that this would not be enough for Dan.

A man like Dan needed to marry, have children. Now that he had declared himself, she would be obliged to urge him to seek happiness elsewhere. It would be unfair to bind him to her when she had no choice but to refuse his proposal. The thought of losing him was like a physical pain, an aching void that threatened to engulf her. While he hadn't asked she would have nothing to regret. Why? Why did he have to spoil everything? He must know how she was placed.

"I didn't think you would ask me," she said and hated herself for not keeping the reproach from her voice.

Dan misunderstood. "I would have asked you sooner only I wanted to wait until I took over the farm."

She didn't answer and Dan, baffled by her manner, grew silent. A minute passed before he said, stiffly, "Forgive me... I thought you loved me."

"I do, Dan. Believe me I do."

At this he took her by the shoulders and turned her to face him. "Then say you will marry me. I love you. You don't know how hard it has been for me to keep silent all this time. But I had to prove myself, can't you see? I would have spoken sooner but I made a vow to myself to work the land for a year before I asked you to marry me. Will you, Sarah?"

Sarah looked into his earnest face and wished she was able to say yes. Instead she found herself saying, "Don't ask me, Dan."

"Why not? What are you saying? I thought we had an understanding."

"But don't you see? Now it's impossible."

"Now? What has changed things?"

She lowered her eyes and was slow to answer him. "Dan...." she spoke carefully, choosing her words. "Your friendship has meant more to me than you can ever imagine. There have been times when I thought that if it hadn't been for you I would have gone mad. Loneliness was eating into me. We were a family until my ma died and then everything seemed to fall apart. Polly went into service and Pa was away so much. When he was there he hardly spoke. Sometimes I thought my life was almost as silent as Robert's.

"And then we became friends. I will never forget your kindness... or the love you have given me... but I can't marry you. I'm sorry, Dan, but I can't."

Dan stared in disbelief, stunned by her answer. He ran his hand through his hair and looked about him in hurt bewilderment. Walking away from her, his arm swept all he looked upon. "All this I am offering you. Is it not enough?" He came back to her. "If you love me, as you say you do, then give me one reason why you won't marry me," he demanded.

"I'll give you two," she answered in a small flat voice. My pa... and Robert."

She went on to tell him that she felt it was her duty, now that Polly was married, to remain at home to keep house for them. "And so I'm sorry, Dan. I'm sorry if I've led you to believe I was free to marry. Had you asked me a year ago... I... I don't think I have any choice."

Dan had listened to her in silence but now he gave a great shout of laughter and it was her turn to look bewildered.

"If they are the only reasons for not marrying me then we will be wed! I'll speak to your pa. When he sees how things are atween us, I'm sure he won't stand in our way. I'm not going to let you sacrifice yourself for your family. You have a life of your own to live and I want that to be with me." His eyes narrowed as he thought for a moment and then brightened. "Happen your aunt could come and take care of things."

"She would never do that. She prefers the town."

"Then your pa could go there and live with

273

her. You said, yourself, that he spends as much time under her roof as he does his own."

Hope was kindled, a little spark was lit, but as quickly extinguished.

"And what about Robert? You'd never get him there and she wouldn't want him if you did."

"I wasn't going to suggest that he goes to your aunt's. Robert belongs here. On the farm. This is where he will live. With us. Down there!" And he nodded towards the farmhouse, now pink in the setting sun and with a column of smoke rising above. "Well? What do you think?"

Sarah thought. And when she saw a glimpse of a brighter future, one for which she had dared not hope, she was filled with a deep and tearful joy that welled up like a spring from deep within her.

"Oh, Dan! Yes... yes." she whispered, her eyes gleaming.

He caught her by the waist then and swung her round until the earth spun about them. Breathless, she slid through his arms, down the length of his hard body, until her toes touched the ground. He looked down into her lovely face and they kissed, long and deeply.

It was a kiss of love and longing, hope and happiness.

# CHAPTER TWENTY-THREE

Sarah hoed the weeds from the vegetable patch in the back garden. Although her back ached she continued to push the hoe rhythmically backwards and forwards between the cabbages. John used to take care of the garden but over the months he had gradually done less and less until she and Robert were left with all the work to do between them. Robert had to fit in his chores before going to the farm as well as on his return after a long working day, so Sarah tried to do as much as she could.

Dan had wanted to come and speak to her pa at once, but she had persuaded him to wait a while.

"Let us wait for a week or so, Dan," she had suggested. "I don't think my pa is very well at the moment and our intentions, coming so soon after Polly's wedding, won't help. He's not well... I know he's not well. He's not eating properly, even when I make him his favourite meals. He hardly touches it, just pushes it round his plate. And he doesn't always eat breakfast before he goes out. I make him up his bait, as I always do, but I've no way of telling if he eats it. He could give it to the birds for all I know."

"Has he been to the doctor?"

"I think he must have. The other day I saw him take a medicine bottle, one of those blue prescription ones, out of his pocket and take a swig of whatever it was. He had his face all scrunched up, as if he was in pain, and was clutching his stomach. He didn't know I saw him. He was outside the scullery but I saw him through the open door. When I asked him if he was all right, he put on one of his smiles and said, 'Yes, of course. Why wouldn't I be? Just a bit of indigestion, that's all'. But I know it's more than that. He wouldn't have looked that way if it was only indigestion."

"That'll be why he didn't cut the east field this year."

John had had the arrangement to harvest that field in exchange for the long-straw it produced, for as long as Dan could remember. He had made the deal with Dan's father nearly twenty years earlier.

"When he came to me, this year, and said he wouldn't be cutting that field I assumed that business was not so good and he didn't need the straw. I supposed that now more and more slates are being used, there'll be less work for a thatcher. Can't beat thatch, if you ask me, but there you are. You can't stop progress. I suppose the slates don't need so much attention…. If I'd known he didn't feel up to it I would have told him he could have the straw anyway. Least I could have done after all these years."

And so Dan had agreed to wait and the week had stretched into two and then three and the situation hadn't changed.

The hoe hit a stone. Sarah bent and tossed it aside. Her thoughts turned to Polly. Perhaps she would get changed and go down to see her and the new baby. Polly had had a little girl. 'Ain't she a beauty!' the village women exclaimed. 'Unusual her having such dark hair with both of them being so fair. Must come from her grandmother,' they surmised and were satisfied.

Sarah had told John of the new arrival but he hadn't visited Polly. He merely grunted and buried his head in the *Lloyd's News*.

Sarah sighed. What are we coming to? she asked herself. Polly hasn't been near, so wrapped up is she in that new baby of hers. You'd think she'd enjoy the walk up here to give the poor mite an airing.

The last time Sarah had gone down to the shop, Polly's conversation had been a monologue of how good little Gladys was, Ned's success in the shop now that he had taken on an assistant and was buying poultry direct from the farms, and her new oil lamps and antimacassars. Not once had she asked after their pa. She had asked after Robert but, before Sarah could answer, had launched into an account of the argument Mrs Benson and Mrs

Caldwell had had right outside the shop.

Well, Polly's got her own life now, Sarah decided. She seems to be coming to terms with it and Ned treats her well. I wonder what happened to all her dreams. Perhaps they were  so different from reality that now they don't bear thinking about.

Robert seemed happy enough though. Sarah didn't see much of him, what with his work at the farm and his birds. But, strangely, the relationship between Robert and their pa had undergone a subtle change. She couldn't tell exactly what it was; a smile, perhaps, or a look exchanged. It was possible that Robert realised that Pa was not so well because whenever he was out in the shed, Robert would follow him there to see if he could help.

Sarah exchanged the hoe for a rake and was about to gather the loosened weeds together when she heard Patrick's distinctive voice in the lane as he urged the horse up the hill.

"C'mon old girl. Nearly there…. Let's be getting your master home…. Nice and easy now."

Sarah, with the rake still in her hand, ran round the side of the house as the cart stopped at the gate. Patrick was with his son and they were letting down the backboard of Pa's cart.

"We'll have to take him easy, Georgie boy," he said and then spoke into the cart. "We'll be having you in your bed in a moment, John."

"What's happened, Mr McGiveney?"

"It's your pa, Sarah. He's had an accident." Patrick turned to face her over the garden wall. "Fell

278

off the roof, over at Thurber's farm, he did. It was the old barn roof we were working on and he fell straight down onto Thurber's plough. I'll be thinking it's his leg that's broken so we'll get him into his bed and then Georgie, here, can go for the doctor."

Patrick and his son took an arm each over their shoulders and, supporting John's weight as well as they were able, carried him between them. Awkwardly, they negotiated the narrow staircase and got him to his bed.

There was a grey pallor about John's already gaunt face. He bit his lip as the pain creased his pinched features and the sweat glistened on his brow. He fell back against the pillows and Patrick gently eased his legs onto the bed. A dark red stain grew on the torn trousers.

"There now. Don't you go running round, John, until the doctor's seen you," said Patrick with mock severity. He winked at Sarah, whose concerned gaze had not left John's face. "Off you go, Georgie, and get the good doctor…and tell your mother I'll be in to see her in a while," he called to his son's retreating back. "Now, John, I'll go and unharness Peg. Put her out to graze. Is there anything else I can be doing for you?"

John grunted and shook his head, unable to speak in his pain.

The doctor came within the hour and spent considerable time alone with John. Sarah heard a cry and winced at the thought of Doctor Rudd setting the broken bone.

Too anxious to settle to any task until the doctor had gone, she fussed with the fire, plumped up the cushions and was straightening the rug on the parlour floor when she heard the doctor's heavy tread on the stairs.

"I have a bowl of hot water and some soap if you need to wash your hands," she said as she met him in the tiny hallway. "Here. In the kitchen."

On the table she had placed the enamel bowl, a clean towel and a new bar of soap. She took the kettle from the hob and added the boiling water to the cold already in the bowl. She stood, idly watching, as he washed his hands and fastidiously dried them.

She wanted to ask about her pa. Not about his leg. She wanted to ask about the medicine he took but she didn't know how to frame the words. They seldom had the need for the doctor's ministrations and she felt awed by his presence. He was a short man, rotund and pompous, with thick waving hair and bushy brows. The village folk found him brusque and unsmiling, but respected him for his expertise.

He had dried his hands and rolled down his shirtsleeves before Sarah spoke. "Doctor. May I have a word?"

"Yes, of course. What is it."

"What is wrong with my pa?"

"He has broken his leg, just below the knee.

280

I have set it and he will have to remain still to give it the best possible chance of healing."

"I don't mean his leg. There is something else wrong with him, isn't there?"

Doctor Rudd didn't answer her at once. He put on his black greatcoat and, with an unmerited concentration, fastened the buttons before he looked up. It was a thoughtful, calculating gaze that he gave her before he seemed to come to a decision.

"Sit down, Sarah."

When she had obediently seated herself at the kitchen table, he continued. "Normally, I would be disinclined to speak, even though your father has given permission for me to acquaint you of the facts. But you seem to be a sensible girl and, without doubt, it is better that you know sooner than later."

A feeling of dread settled on her.

"This accident may have been avoided, had he been eating properly. He didn't merely slip off the roof. Lack of nourishment was the cause of the vertigo that resulted in the fall. Your father came to see me about a month ago. He was suffering from pains that he described to me and I examined him. I will tell you now what I told him then."

He paused and sighed wearily, pinching the bridge of his nose with thumb and forefinger, as if it pained him to speak. Sarah swallowed to ease the lump in her throat. She sensed that her fears were about to be confirmed.

"Your father has a tumour growing in his

stomach. If he had come to me at an earlier stage in its development, perhaps something could have been done. It may have been possible to operate for its removal. It is, however, too late for that. I am afraid that there is little that can be done."

Sarah was totally unprepared, despite her fears, to absorb the doctor's words. When she did, her hand went to her mouth and she stared fixedly at him before she spoke. "My pa…. Does he know all this?"

"Oh, yes. We have had a long talk. He has been appraised of all the facts."

This was all a cruel joke. It could not be true.

"Is my pa going to die?"

"Yes, Sarah. I'm afraid he is."

Perhaps she was dreaming. Yes, this was all part of a horrible dream.

"How… how long does he have?"

"It's difficult to say. Perhaps three or, maybe, four months."

Months! Her mind was having one conversation while her tongue was having another. She needed time to assimilate this terrible news. It was in a daze that she saw the doctor pick up his bag, place his hat firmly on his head and prepare to leave.

"Allow me to suggest that you make a nice cup of tea and take it up to your father," he said with surprising gentleness. "I think he would like to talk to you."

With a promise to return in a few days, he inclined his hat politely and was gone. Sarah stood at the gate, long after the doctor's carriage had disappeared down the lane.

It was a revelation to Sarah how kind people could be. In the ensuing weeks, few days went by without a visitor to sit with John to keep him company, or to bring him some delicacy to tempt his fragile appetite. Patrick came with fish wrapped in a newspaper. Mrs Fuller sent over soups, eggs and milk puddings, thick and creamy with a crisp nutmeg skin on top. Ned frequently sent his lad up the lane with a joint of meat or a chicken and, one day, Sarah found a rabbit on the mat outside the door. She never did find out who had left it there.

The doctor brought medicine for John. It was to kill the pain, he said, and added ominously that it was as well that he didn't take too much at this stage as he would have greater need of it later on.

As soon as he was able, John clumped down the stairs on his good leg to sit for hours staring into the parlour fire. But the effort to ascend stairs was too much for him, so Robert carried up one of the parlour chairs to his bedroom and placed it by the window. There, John was able to look out across the river to the autumn-tinted hills beyond.

Florrie came. She arrived one blustery afternoon. When Sarah opened the door to Florrie's impatient knocking, she pushed past her into the parlour and, under Sarah's startled gaze, began divesting herself of her coat and gloves.

"Well? Where is he? I haven't got all day. Got to be back in the village at four if I'm to catch the carrier's cart."

It was some seconds before Sarah realised who this dry, withered old woman was, who hovered, like a black vulture, waiting for her to speak.

"He's up in his bedroom," she stammered, and added to Florrie's retreating back, "The one on the left...."

She hurriedly followed her aunt up the stairs and arrived at the bedroom door in time to see the surprise on John's face.

Florrie flapped her hand at Sarah and said in her waspish voice, "You can go and make yourself useful. Put the kettle on and make some tea... And make it strong. I can't abide weak tea. Go on then. I want to talk to your pa."

Sarah returned to the kitchen quivering with indignation. How dare she sail in here as if she owns the place, she asked herself. They didn't see her for years and she barges in without a by your leave and orders me to make tea! She shook her head in disbelief and banged the kettle on the hob.

That was the first of regular visits Florrie made. Every time it was the same. She would shut herself away with her brother, shooing Sarah away to the kitchen to make tea. After these times, John would be morosely silent for hours and Sarah questioned the benefit to her pa that his sister's visits made.

One day, Sarah, carrying the tray of tea upstairs, put her ear to the crack of the bedroom door. She hoped to overhear the muffled conversation, but the few snatches she could pick out were incomprehensible.

"Well, what shall I say?" Florrie had asked, and she made out her pa's weakening voice saying, "No. Not… to come here."

Friendship came from an unexpected source. Fanny took to visiting Sarah every week on her free afternoon. It didn't seem to matter how austere the weather became as autumn gave way to winter. She would trudge up the hill and brighten a few hours for Sarah, chatting about the happenings at Marsden Hall and once touching on her life before going to work there.

She spoke of her own father and said to Sarah, "I remember how he used to lay into me. He were a drunkard and evil when the drink was in him. In the end he abandoned us and sent me ma to an early grave,"

Sarah marvelled that Fanny was able, apparently, to speak of such things without bitterness or rancour. She liked the girl, with her big red hands and pleasant, ugly face. Fanny had an intelligent mind that would dart from one subject to another with alarming speed. If only she had been born in different circumstances, she would have been noted as an extraordinary woman, Sarah thought, and reflected that the two words 'if only' must be the saddest in the world.

If only Fanny had been born in different circumstances. If only Ma hadn't died. If only Polly hadn't got pregnant. If only Robert wasn't deaf. If only her pa was well. If only she could get out of this house for just a few hours. The list seemed endless and she felt weighed down by the unending tasks her pa's illness entailed.

By December he had taken to his bed and became weaker daily. He demanded the morphine, that Doctor Rudd prescribed, with greater frequency as his pains became more intolerable. At first, Sarah tried to persuade him to wait just a while longer but after a time she gave in, too weary to make the effort to do otherwise.

She had never imagined the day would come when she would have to do such things for her father. As his illness progressed she was called upon to do more and more. The tasks stripped him of his dignity and made her want to cry for the shame she could see he felt.

Robert did what he could, when he wasn't working on the farm, often sitting late into the night so that she may rest. One night, when Sarah peeped in, she saw that her pa was asleep and so was Robert, sitting in the parlour chair, his pa's hand held in his own.

Between father and son there had grown a

quiet acceptance, a closeness that Sarah envied. Since finding the money in the tin trunk, all that time ago, Sarah was aware that there was a secrecy about her pa that she couldn't fathom. Nothing had changed in his manner but, from that day, he had become a stranger to her since there was so much she couldn't account for; the money, the time he used to stay away from home. It was in the middle of December that part of the mystery was revealed. When she took up his medicine, he asked her to sit down as he had something to say to her.

"It's time we talked about the future," he said in his, now hoarse, whisper. "I wanted you to know that there is money for you and Robert."

"I don't want your money," she found herself saying, ungraciously. She didn't want any part of his ill-gotten horde of coins. No matter how well she wanted to think of her pa, she knew he couldn't have saved such a quantity from what he earned. Therefore, to her mind, it must have been come by dishonestly.

"It's not my money, Sarah. It never belonged to me."

Dear God, she thought. He's about to confess his sins! She made to rise not wanting to hear another word.

John saw the movement and raised a frail hand a few inches from the bedcovers. "Stay, Sarah," he pleaded. "I need to talk."

Silently, she studied his face, the sunken cheeks, the eyes dazed with pain, and was filled with compassion. She waited for him to speak and, when he did, it was as if to himself, as he travelled back slowly over the years.

"The money was your ma's.... We were married in eighteen seventy-two, a year after the government had passed a law that meant women could keep their own money. A husband wasn't automatically entitled to it after that.... When the old doctor died, he left your ma the cottage and about one hundred and twenty five pounds. I never knew the exact amount. It was all in sovereigns. He had no faith in banks and kept it in a leather bag under his bed."

He paused, his eyelids drooped a moment and, when he opened them, a fierceness had come to his watery eyes. "When we were married, she wanted me to have it but I wouldn't take a penny. I wanted to provide for her myself. Call it pride, if you like, but that's the way it was. She gave up a lot to marry me, you know. With her background and education, and her looks, she could have married anyone. But she chose me. A nobody, with nothing to call me own. She was so beautiful. Long fair hair, she had, and when she let it down, it was like a great golden cape around her shoulders and hung down past her waist.... Beautiful, she was, and she chose me."

He sighed. His eyes now took on a gentle, faraway look and a faint smile hovered about his lips as he lapsed into silence, lost in his memories. Then he remembered Sarah, sitting beside him, and turned his head towards her. He sighed again and slowly told her how her ma had insisted that he have the money and how he had buried it at the bottom of the tin trunk that now stood at the bottom of the bed. He swore that he would never touch it. It was to provide his wife with anything she needed because he knew that he would never be able to keep her in the way to which she was accustomed. But she wouldn't touch it either and in the end they agreed to keep it for the children.

He rambled on about a horse and gig, the only thing he had taken from her and spoke of the love they had shared and how much he missed her.

"And so the money is still there. In the trunk. It's for you and Robert and the cottage is in your name. Polly's had her share, although she doesn't know it. I gave it to Ned for the business. He didn't want to take it though. He said he'd marry Polly any day of the week, even if she came without a penny. And he would have, too! He's a good man, is Ned. I'm telling this so you know that I've been fair with you all, but I trust you, Sarah, not to let on to Polly 'cos she's had her pride hurt enough already…. I miss Polly. I would like to see her once again…."

His eyes closed. Sarah sat there for a long time in the darkening room, her cheeks wet with tears. She hated herself for all the years she had misjudged him and mourned the loss of those years when they had been strangers under the same roof, instead of the family they once were. It was all her fault. If she hadn't gone delving where she had no business, she would never had doubted his integrity. If only she hadn't found them. There! There were those words again; if only.

She sat with her pa while he slept and her quiet contemplation took her back to childhood when this man had seemed so huge. He had thrown her in the air; she had shrieked with excitement while he laughed his big belly-laugh. When she was little she had imagined that that laugh had been some pleasant beast who lived in his belly and its roar was the laugh she heard when her pa was happy. But now it seemed as if it had turned into a malevolent monster that growled and grew and consumed its dwelling place until all that was left was the brittle shell of a man that had once been her pa.

# CHAPTER TWENTY-FOUR

The most precious times for Sarah were the times when Robert was home and she was free to get away for a few hours. One afternoon a week and each evening after supper, she left her pa in Robert's care and got out into the fresh air. Even when it snowed and icicles, like shards of glass in the winter sunshine, hung from the evergreens, she climbed the hills. Taking great gulps of the cold air into her lungs, she hoped for a while to lose the stench of sickness that seemed permanently in her nostrils.

Some evenings, when Dan could get away, they tramped hand in hand down by the river. Muffled against the cold, they kissed by the stile and whispered their love to each other. They never spoke of the future, knowing there would be time enough eventually. It seemed wrong to speak of a life that depended on another's death. And so they spoke of love and delighted in each other's company.

Christmas came and went uncelebrated. Each time Sarah went down to the village, she called upon Polly in the little cottage next to the butcher's shop. She held the baby on her knee, exclaimed over a new tooth, admired the latest acquisition, and begged Polly to come to see their pa. Polly was adamant. She would not come.

It was a bitterly cold day in February. Patrick McGiveney had just left. He regularly came to pass an hour with his friend. He had a vast store of anecdotes and this day had been telling John about the time he had caught the largest trout the village had ever seen.

He hadn't been gone twenty minutes when Sarah was amazed to see Polly trudging up the hill with the baby, tightly bound in a shawl, clutched to her chest.

"I've come to see Pa," she announced. "You and Ned have badgered me enough to see him and I'll not have any peace from either of you till I do. Here, take Gladys for me." She thrust the baby into Sarah's arms and marched up the stairs.

She came down again fifteen minutes later. Sarah had made some tea. Polly's eyes were unnaturally bright as she sat, sipping the tea, in silence. When she had finished, she carefully placed the cup in its saucer.

"Oh, dear heaven," she cried. "I had no idea... no idea!" And her shaking shoulders were the first indication of her silent tears.

All that winter John clung to life, slipping from consciousness into unconsciousness; a time when his dreams were peopled by the dead. They came to him, accusing, taunting, chiding, reminding him of things he had long forgotten and of things he would rather forget.

Elizabeth's father, his face suffused with anger; 'scoundrel... you couldn't look after my daughter....'

And Elizabeth;'Come to bed, John....' How those startling eyes would change to softness when he made love to her. Warm summer nights, scented and peaceful, windows open to the breeze. Cold winter nights, burying under the covers, laughing as they tried to keep the quilt on the bed.

His brother, Jed, laughing; 'Go on, I dare yer.' His ma and pa....

And woven through the dreams were other faces. Sarah's; 'Time for your medicine, Pa.' And Polly's; 'Oh, Pa, Pa!' she'd cried and kissed his cheek, her own wet with tears. Florrie; 'I've a letter for you,' and Patrick's roguish grin; 'the biggest fish you ever saw.'

But Nan. Where was Nan's face? And little Jack. Where was he?

In his bemused mind he was unable to distinguish between the living and the dead.

Sarah's face again. "Time for your medicine, Pa."

By the end of February, John's ravaged body had

shrunk and his skin, paper thin, stretched over his bones; fragile containment for the soul that would not leave.

The first day of spring brought sunshine and fresh winds to billow out the washing on the lines. There was a promise of new life in the tender green leaves unfolding on the trees. But still John had not died.

At noon, Sarah took him up his medicine, the morphine that gave him some relief from the unending pain. The house was silent except for the parlour clock's incessant tick. Tick... tick.... Waiting. It seemed as if the whole house was waiting for John to die.

The sunshine, slanting through the window on the landing, captured the dust motes in the air. It fell on the plain wooden floor, strengthening the shadows lurking in the doorway. The whole house was waiting.

Sarah stood at the end of the brass bed, her hands clutching the foot rail, as she regarded her pa. My God, we're kinder to our animals, she thought. If he were a dog, we would have put him out of his misery long before now. Let the end come soon. For his sake... and for mine too because, much as I love him, I don't think I can go much longer.

John opened his eyes and saw her there. It was as if he had read her thoughts for he said, "Sarah.... Always the mother.... I'm sorry you've had all this...a man couldn't wish for a better...."

She was on her knees by his side now,

holding his hand. The tears coursed down her cheeks as she gazed at the man who had swung her, as a child, onto his shoulders and laughed his great belly-laugh; the man who had set the whole village tapping with his music.

She saw the pain leave his face. He smiled, and his soul slipped away.

All his friends came. They stood, three deep, to watch his coffin committed to the earth.

Patrick, when he heard of John's passing, closed his eyes and gave a great sigh. "Thanks be to God and our blessed Lady. It has been so long, the waiting," he said to Sarah and she knew those sentiments, simple and sincere, exactly described her feelings in the days after her pa's death. Time enough later for grieving and regrets. It was enough to experience, for a while, the relief from endless nursing and sleepless nights.

Patrick stood weeping openly and unashamedly. Reverend Greenway, now getting on in years, performed the burial rites and when it was over Patrick wiped his eyes with a big, blue handkerchief and took, from his pocket, his old penny whistle.

Such an unprecedented occurrence at one of his funerals caused the parson to knit his brows in disapproval but, nevertheless, Patrick raised the whistle to his lips and played an Irish lament.

Sarah had never heard this lonely tune before. As the plaintive notes rose, pure and clear, in the little churchyard, she was hard pressed to maintain the composure that she had, so far, managed. She dragged her eyes from the open grave and looked about her.

Polly sobbed into Ned's broad chest. He, trying to comfort, patted her shoulder with his big hand, his face for once unsmiling. Sarah was vaguely irritated by Polly's show of grief.

Next to them, Aunt Ruth stood, plump and unseeing. She was now almost blind but had insisted on attending. Her companion, Mrs Wilton – who had taken over the baby box – had guided her between the cemetery stones and now stood beside her, her hand at Ruth's elbow.

Dan had arranged the funeral and the cart, cleaned and spruced by Robert, had brought the coffin, that had lain in the parlour, down to the church. Dan, Ned, Robert and Patrick had carried it – awkwardly, as Patrick was a good head shorter than the three younger men – to its burial place next to that of Elizabeth.

They all lay in a group in the south-east corner; James Gilbert 1871, his wife for whom Sarah was named, little James Holland only five months old, Elizabeth Holland 1888, and now John Holland 1892. It seemed to Sarah that more of her family lay beneath cemetery stones than stood about them.

Florrie looked shabby in a tight black coat, that drew attention to her bony frame, and a hat with a veil that did nothing to hide the critical penetrating eyes that she fixed on Sarah and Robert. She was bristling with indignation that her brother was being buried here instead of in the churchyard of St Peter's in Chillingford where her parents and other brother had been laid to rest. Wasn't it only right he should be with his family? she had demanded, and Sarah had agreed.

"You are quite right, Auntie," she had said. "He will be buried with his family; his wife and baby son."

Robert hadn't taken his eyes off the plain wooden coffin. By the set of his jaw Sarah could see the fight he was having to control his emotions. She ached to slip her hand into his. How long ago, was it, when she had done just that at their ma's funeral? But he was now a man and she knew that she couldn't.

The villagers grouped around the chief mourners were mostly the men whose company John had shared at the Scarlet Arms. For twenty years he had entertained them with his fiddle and now they came to pay their respects to a friend and his music. They stood, solemnly, with bare heads bowed, their hats, with black crepe bands, held before them. George Potter was there, Wilfred Hopkins from the Arms, and old Albert Cooper who Sarah thought would outlast them all. Poor Harold Waters. What an agony it was for him to stand hatless in the March breeze. His hand kept straying to his head as the hair that was meant to cover his baldness was blown about. These were the folk that had come to say goodbye to her pa. She felt proud that so many had such regard for him.

But there was someone else who had come to say goodbye. Someone else who didn't join the mourners at the grave but remained on the other side of the cemetery wall. Hidden by the elm trees and a hawthorn bush, stood a woman in a brown coat. Her green eyes were filled with tears as she clutched a handkerchief to her mouth with one hand. In the other she held the chubby gloved hand of a small dark-haired boy.

# CHAPTER TWENTY-FIVE

After John's funeral Sarah faced a dilemma. Wanting to be fair, John had told her that the money was to be divided between her and Robert as Polly had, although unknowingly, had her share. But Polly, already hurt and resentful of her pa's perceived treatment of her, was going to be even more so if she thought he had left money to Sarah and Robert and not her. Polly's discovery of the true facts must be avoided. If she took it into her head that Ned had been bribed to marry her, the chances of their marriage being a success were slender.

Sarah's first instinct was to divide the money into three and say nothing. But that would mean depriving Robert of his rightful share. Perhaps she should give half to Robert and half to Polly. She wouldn't need the money if she was going to marry Dan. But on the other hand....

She puzzled over the problem for three days and at last came to a decision that, whilst not a resolution, had the merit of relieving the burden temporarily. She would discuss it with Robert. It was not going to be easy but she had to try.

So when they had eaten that evening she cleared the plates from the table and sat down opposite him. He was engrossed in his book of birds. To attract his attention she placed her hand on the open page. He looked up, saw her sign to him that she wanted to 'talk' and, marking the page with his bird's feather, laid the book to one side.

Sarah took the leather pouch out of her apron pocket. She loosened the cord that bound it and poured the gold sovereigns onto the table. They gleamed in the soft yellow light of the oil lamp and Robert's eyes widened in amazement at the sight. He stared at them for a long time. He turned questioning eyes to Sarah and she began to explain.

It was not easy. Robert could lip-read the names Ma, Pa, Polly and Sarah. She could point to the coins on the table but how was she going to sign the intricacies of the matter? After her first attempt Robert nodded but she knew that he didn't understand. She tried again and this time he merely looked puzzled. By the third attempt he was getting frustrated and Sarah began to feel the same frustration and wished she hadn't started.

She would have to find another approach, and so thinking she took some sheets of paper and a pencil from the dresser drawer. She drew figures to represent the people involved and coins and directional arrows and faces with tears. She drew

Polly and Ned getting married, the butcher's shop and faces with smiles. She made the signs he understood for secrets and, finally, the sign that asked, what shall we do?

Robert looked gravely at the pieces of paper set out in front of him. He sat there for so long that Sarah feared that he still didn't understand. And then he smiled. He took the coins and carefully divided them into three equal piles. The first, he stacked on the piece of paper that represented Sarah, the second went on the drawing of Polly, and the third on the one of himself.

He looked up and shrugged his shoulders. His expression clearly said, it's simple. What is the problem?

"I might buy some new curtains. These, the Bishops left behind, don't look right with the wallpaper. And perhaps a new dress.... Oh, I know what I'd like to do, Sarah. I'd like for Ned and me with the baby, of course, to go to the seaside for the day. Wouldn't you like to go to the seaside? We could all go together.... Eastbourne! I've always wanted to go to Eastbourne."

Sarah's answering murmur was noncommittal. Since she had given Polly the sovereigns, some forty-five minutes earlier, Polly had bounced from one idea to another; all ways of spending the money that had been hoarded for so many years.

"Perhaps Ned will have some ideas on how

301

it is to be used," Sarah ventured.

But Polly was scornful. "Ned? It's got nothing to do with Ned. It's my inheritance. It was left to me and I shall spend it as I think fit." She rearranged the pile of coins on the parlour table, her eyes gleaming with anticipation.

Ned came in at that moment whistling cheerily. But the tune died on his lips when he saw the sovereigns. "What's this then? he asked, looking from Polly to Sarah.

"Ned! Look Ned! Pa left me all this. Isn't it wonderful? Think what we could do with it." She spread the coins, then scooped them up and let them drop on the table again.

"We can't accept," he said hastily; a little too hastily to Sarah's mind.

"Good Heavens! Whatever do you mean? You don't understand. This was left to me. I can't imagine why you would say such an extraordinary thing. Of course I can accept it. It's mine. By right. Sarah has just told me so."

Polly glared at Ned and Sarah wondered what course the conversation was going to take. She hoped that Ned wouldn't say something that he would later regret.

Sarah prepared to leave. "I must go now. I didn't realise the time. Robert will be home soon, wanting to eat." She pulled on her gloves and while Polly's attention was still occupied with the coins that littered the table, she gave Ned a look that she willed him to interpret as 'It's all right, I understand. There's nothing to worry about.'

Ned did worry about it though and next day he arrived at the cottage. "I've been to see me granny and seeing as I'd walked that far I thought I might as well call in and see how you and Robert are."

"Sit down, Ned."

His huge body seemed to tower over her in the tiny room. Sarah, knowing why he had come, came straight to the point. "If you're worried about the money, Ned, please don't be. Pa explained everything to me before he died. Robert and I have decided, together, that there is nothing to be served by complicating the situation. This way Polly need never know."

"I didn't want to take the money. Your pa insisted though. He said it was the only way he could see me getting a step up in life. He didn't think that Polly would ever be content being married to a butcher's assistant." He smiled ruefully. "She wouldn't of been happy living with me granny neither, so I saw the sense in what he said. He told me the money would come to Polly in the end anyway so it didn't make no difference. It wasn't like he was paying me to marry her, was it?"

"Of course it wasn't."

"But some may think so, if it ever got out, and I can't abear to think what Polly would make of it."

He sat, nervously rubbing his big hands over his knees. Sarah had never seen him looking so anxious and miserable.

"Polly's not going to hear of it," she said firmly. "Only you and Robert and I know about it. If we don't say anything, I'm sure Robert's not going to." She smiled and he looked relieved.

"I'll pay you back. Every last penny of it. I swear I will. Not just yet, I can't, but as soon as I get on me feet. It's only right that I should."

"Don't talk such nonsense. When Dan and I are married Robert will come to the farm. The cottage will probably be sold. We'll have all we need."

He wanted to thank her but she said there was no need. "Just you get back to that wife of yours before she's spent it all on more frills and furbelows," she urged him and he laughed, glad that the weight had been lifted from his mind.

It seemed, to Sarah, that no sooner had one problem been resolved than she was faced with another.

It was the beginning of May, a day of continuous fine rain. Forced to abandon her plan to work in the garden, she decided, on a whim, to sort out her ma's tin trunk. If she laid out the tablecloths and tray cloths, bed linen, lace collars and handkerchiefs on Pa's bed, when next Polly called, she could pick out the things that took her fancy.

Sarah was to think later how fortuitous it was that she had chosen to do this task alone because half way down, between an apron and a fine-tucked nightgown, she found four letters.

On the outside of each was written the single word, 'John'. nothing else. No address. Not even a surname. She sat on the edge of the bed, turning them over in her hands, curious, yet hesitant to discover their contents. It was only six weeks since her pa's death and she was unused to the idea that now, for her, there was nothing in the trunk she may not see. No privacy to invade. The knowledge brought an overwhelming sadness.

At last, she opened one of the envelopes. Inside was a single sheet of paper torn from a cheap exercise book. It was dated the 3rd of October from an address in Chillingford.

Who had sent Pa letters from Chillingford? And so recently. It was the end of September that he had broken his leg and been confined to bed. So how had he come by a letter without her knowledge? The writing was almost childlike in its formation. She read its contents with mounting incredulity and horror.

*My dearest John,* she read. *Florrie has come to me with news of your accident. She says that you don't want me to come and see you and I am heartsore that you insist on keeping secret our friendship after all that has gone between us.*

*I kept a dinner warm for you on Thursday night. I knew something was up when you didn't come. Jack asks after you. He wants to know when you are coming again and I don't know what to tell him.*

*I hope that by the time you get this you will*

*be feeling a bit better.*

    *I send you my love. Nan.*

    Sarah opened a second, dated a week later, her eyes racing over the words, her mind in a turmoil. The third and fourth letters were dated the following two weeks and all were in the same hand.

    *Florrie brings news of you... I beg you to let me come and see you... after all that has gone between us... Jack cries for his pa... what can I tell him?... I cannot bear to think of you ailing and I not there to comfort you... the nights are lonely without you... if you value all that we have meant to each other....*

    For a long time Sarah sat with the letters scattered in her lap while the rain, now more persistent, slanted across the window panes, its gentle pattering the only sound in the otherwise silent room.

    So many questions now answered but how many more unanswered ones to take their place? The absences from home. He had been with this woman. The visits from Aunt Florrie who had wanted time alone with Pa. She had brought the letters. It must have been her. She knows what all this is about. Who was this woman? Who was this Nan who had written these letters begging to come and see her pa? And was he father to Jack? *Jack cries for his pa,* she had written. No, she couldn't believe it. It was not possible that he could have another woman, another child, and no one knowing. Why keep such a secret? He had been a widower for three years, so it was not unnatural for him to have turned to someone else.

Just when she was beginning to feel differently about her pa, just when she thought she understood him after years of misjudgement, he had become a stranger again. For days she see-sawed from one thought to another. Let sleeping dogs lie, she told herself one moment, only to be overcome with an inordinate rage that goaded her to go over to Chillingford, face her aunt and demand some explanations.

She took out her anger when she made the bread, kneading it with a vigour that caused the flour to rise in a fine white dust each time she slapped the dough down on the table. Her fury continued, unabated, when in the afternoons she sat and sewed, jabbing the needle viciously into the material and sometimes her finger.

Why was she so angry? she asked herself. She was angry because this knowledge was like an acid on her mind, corroding what good memories she cherished of her pa, and rendering her powerless to go on with her life. She wanted to look forward, with confidence, to a happy future with Dan, but all her days and the endless sleepless nights were crowded by images of her pa in the arms of another woman; images of her pa and his secret life.

Gradually the anger subsided and she got through the days, working in a moody, abstracted way, her mind constantly asking questions that demanded answers. She would have liked to talk to someone, shared this revelation with Dan or Mrs Fuller or even Aunt Ruth. Mr McGiveney was Pa's friend. He may be able to supply the answers. He and Pa had been good friends and had often worked together. Now she came to think about it, her pa had always said that he stayed over in Chillingford when he worked that way, to save coming all the way back home, but Mr McGiveney hadn't found it too far to come back to his family each evening. She had never thought of that before. Oh, how deceitful Pa had been! Yes, she would go and ask Mr McGiveney.

But she didn't go. She didn't speak to Mr McGiveney or anybody else. Her pa must have thought it very important that no one knew about this Nan woman, she reasoned, otherwise he would have let her come to visit him. Hadn't she begged him, in those letters, to let her come? But even though he was dying he had refused.

The four letters were dated at weekly intervals, the last on the twenty-fourth of October. What had happened then? Had Nan stopped writing? Aunt Florrie had continued to visit weekly until a few days before he died. And, always, she had wanted to be left alone with him.

All these thoughts weighed heavily on Sarah's mind until, finally, ten days after she had found the letters, she decided to go over to Chillingford. She knew that she wouldn't rest until she had faced the woman. There was no need to speak to Aunt Florrie because she had the address.

Church Street, Chillingford. Number twelve. She would go there and return the letters. That would be her excuse for going and while there she would ask for an explanation. That's if she found the courage.

# CHAPTER TWENTY-SIX

Sarah went on Tuesday, catching the carrier's cart from the village. The carrier was a gloomy, grumpy old man with a leathery lined face, who sat with shoulders hunched. He was not given to conversation and Sarah, sitting up beside him on the plank seat, was glad to be left alone with her thoughts. There were not many packages for the carrier to deliver and Sarah was surprised how quickly the journey passed. Before she knew it they were in Chillingford.

"Four o'clock if you want to be back," the carrier said in his doleful voice. He twitched the reins as he called to the horse and was away, disappearing into the melee of carriages and pedestrians before Sarah could answer.

She walked down to the centre of town, passed the chandlers and the second-hand store where Polly had shopped the year before, and reached the crossroads where the big stone cross stood. A cobbler sat in an open doorway, his last between his knees and his mouth full of nails as he hammered at the sole of a brown boot. Sarah asked him how she could find Church Street and he spat the nails into his hands before giving her directions.

Thanking him, she set off briskly but as the shops and wide roads gave way to narrow, meaner streets and rows of ugly terraced houses, her pace slackened and she was filled with misgivings. Perhaps it hadn't been such a good idea. She could go back now, look about the shops until it was time to catch the carrier's cart. She could send the letters back in the post.

A baker's boy whistled and wobbled on a bicycle and a harassed mother, laden with packages, dragged along a wailing child as Sarah hovered, undecided, outside a grocer's shop.

"Lost are you, dearie?" an old woman asked. "Where be you a-looking for?"

Sarah told her and somehow she knew, in that moment, that she would carry out the task she had set herself.

"Why, you're almost on Church Street already. Cut through that twitten and it's on the other side."

Sarah walked down a narrow passage with high walls. Washing hung lethargically from lines in the back yards on either side. She wrinkled her nose as the smell of cooking bloaters came wafting in the warm air. At the end of the twitten, she found herself in a dreary little cobble-stoned street lined with brick built terraced houses with front doors opening directly onto the pavement. Two little girls sat on the curb playing with a rag doll. They stared up at her as she passed. The sound of a querulous child and a mother's weary remonstrance could be heard from an open door.

Sarah found number twelve near the end of the street. White muslin curtains hung neatly in the windows and the brass knocker gleamed on the blue front door.

So this is where she lives. Sarah squared her shoulders and knocked before she could change her mind.

Nan Killock's round face paled and a smile died on her lips when she saw Sarah. "Oh dear Heaven!" she exclaimed, her hand going to her throat.

"I'm looking for someone called Nan," Sarah began uncertainly.

And Nan, scarcely concealing her agitation, said, "It's me you're looking for then. You'd better come inside."

She opened the door wide and Sarah stepped into a room that seemed to be full of washing. It hung on airing lines from the ceiling and stood in neat, ironed piles on one end of the table. On the other end lay an ironing blanket and two wicker baskets beneath the window sill were overflowing with crumpled linen. At the back of the room, a little boy sat on a rush mat playing with a set of wooden farm animals. Sarah judged him to be nearing three years old. He looked up as she entered the room and when he saw that it was a stranger, got up and ran to his mother. He held onto her skirts and timidly looked up at Sarah from dark wide-set eyes.

Nan picked him up with a rough tenderness and deposited him back on the mat. "Be a good boy and play quietly while your ma talks to the lady," she murmured and the child  obediently went back to his game.

Nan swept a pile of linen from a chair and dropped it on one of the baskets. "Excuse the mess. I get fed up with it about the place but it's a living." She had spoken cheerfully enough but Sarah could see there was a touch of anxiety underlying her words.

"You're Sarah. John's lass," she said. "I knew you was John's daughter straight away. Even if I hadn't seen you at the cemetery, I would of known you. You've got the same features. A bit finer than his, but there's no mistaking; you're John's lass all right."

Sarah watched as she folded pillowcases with a fierce energy. Whatever picture she had built in her mind of the writer of the letters she carried in her bag, it was far removed from the woman who stood before her. In her middle age, Nan was a striking woman, tall and inclined to plumpness, with a wealth or red-brown hair piled high upon her head. Green, direct eyes looked out of an open, honest face. She wore a plain grey dress, unbuttoned at the neck against the heat. The sleeves were folded up to her elbows and when she lifted a hand to push stray hair behind her ear, Sarah could see that the dress was neatly patched under the arms with a lighter grey.

The kettle sang on the hob. "Would you like a cup of tea? I was just going to make one. It wouldn't be no trouble."

"No. No thank you, Mrs...er?"

"Killick. Nancy Killick, but please call me Nan."

"I've come to return some letters to you, Mrs Killick," said Sarah, in a tight voice. "I believe that you sent them to my pa."

Nan looked up sharply. "Letters?"

"Yes, there are four of them. I found them after he died."

Nan's eyes widened in surprise and then she gave Sarah a tentative smile. "I was wondering how you came to find me. I didn't think Florrie would of spilled the beans." She took the letters from Sarah's outstretched hand and stared at them for a moment. "She brought me back all the other letters. These must be the first ones I sent him," Nan said, almost to herself. "It was careless of him to keep them... 'specially as he was the one who wanted to keep it all quiet." She tucked them behind a tin candle holder on the high mantelpiece.

For what seemed like an age they stood in awkward silence. All the questions Sarah had planned to ask had flown from her mind. From the street the high piping voices of the little girls came singing. *"Here we go round the mulberry bush,"* they sang, and a factory hooter blared.

"Sit down and let me tell you about John and me," Nan said, suddenly. She pulled a chair from the table and Sarah, wordlessly, sat.

Nan began to explain. "It started after your brother was born. John was over at—"

Sarah gasped. She couldn't help herself. "Do you mean to say that this... you and my father... this relationship has been going on for years? While my ma was alive? That is... why, that's monstrous!" Her voice throbbed with anger. In all her wild imaginings it had not occurred to her that her pa had committed adultery.

She had risen from the chair and would have run from this room that smelled of damp washing and this woman with her pleasant, friendly face who had been carrying on with her pa for years. But Nan stayed her when she said, "Go lass, if you must, but I think you will live to rue the day you didn't wait to hear the truth. You have a right to know and I think you need to understand."

Nan spoke with a quiet dignity. There was no pleading in her voice and Sarah had the impression that the worried frown that creased Nan's brow was caused by concern for her and not by any need to justify herself. She sat in stiff silence waiting for Nan to continue. Nan seated herself opposite Sarah, the table between them. She clasped her hands firmly together and, meeting Sarah's eyes squarely, she began again.

"I always loved your pa. Ever since we were young. Florrie and John, their brother, Jed, the one that died, and me. We grew up together. I knew there would never be anyone else for me and it fair broke me heart when he married your ma. Florrie said he only married her to get a step up in life, 'cos she wasn't of our class by a long chalk, but that wasn't true. He loved your ma as much as any man could love a woman." Her face clouded at the memory. "I'd just started to come to terms with life, and how I saw me own mapped out, when we met up again at Florrie's.

"When Robert was born, the doctor told John that another child would kill your ma. So they stopped being man and wife in that sense of the word. Of course, there are ways and means, if you know what I mean, but nothing's sure and he loved your ma too much to run the risk of losing her. That's when we got together."

She paused and Sarah, who had felt herself blushing at such frank conversation, found herself asking, "And my ma? Did she know? That this…."

"We was never sure." Nan sighed. "But a man needs his comforts, 'specially a man like your pa. She never said anything to him but I think she knew." Her voice hardened suddenly. "And I thought to meself, if that's the only way you can have him, Nan, then so be it. Think what you like of me but I ain't ashamed of what I done. I ain't a fast woman. There's only ever been the one man for me. I never tried to take him away from your ma. Fat chance of me doing that with him loving her and you kids the way he did."

For one or two minutes they didn't speak; Nan with her memories and Sarah mulling over all that Nan had said. Sarah bit her lip. There was a question she had to ask although she already knew the answer.

"And the child?" she flung into the silence.

"Jack? Yes. He's John's boy. Years and years we went and nothing happened. I got to thinking that I couldn't have any, which was just as well in the circumstances, and then, just after your ma died, I fell for Jack."

At his name, the child looked up and smiled. Nan caressed him with her eyes. "I never thought I'd be blessed with a child, not after all these years, but life is full of surprises, ain't it? We can't have everything we want in this world. I suppose it wouldn't be right for us. So we get sent these compensations. John's gone but I've got my Jack to remember him by."

When Sarah had first realised that her pa had taken up with another woman, she had been filled with animosity towards Nan. But as she listened, a more kindly feeling stole over her and she began to understand how things had been.

Nan had withdrawn into herself. It was almost as if she had forgotten Sarah's presence. She was so lost in her own thoughts that when Sarah spoke, she looked quite startled to see her there.

"After… after my ma passed on, it would

have been quite natural... after a period of mourning, of course... for him to have....” She broke off, uncomfortable.

“When the period of mourning was over, I was six month’s gone. How would it of looked if he had brought me home in that condition? Of course, I had high hopes that we would be wed. Not when your ma was alive, and don’t get me wrong, I never wished her dead, but of course once she’d gone ’twas only natural I should have expectations, ’specially with the little’un on the way. I thought that after a year or two, that’s what would happen. We spoke of it and I could see he wanted to but he was worried what people would say. Not for hisself, but for you and Robert and meself.

“Living in a village is a different kettle of fish to living in a town like this. Half the time, here, they don’t care if you’re dead or alive, and if there is any scandal it’s but a nine day’s wonder. In the village, he said, they’d talk about it for years and he didn’t want you to be hurt. He didn’t want you to think less of him neither. Thought the world of you, he did. Thought the world of all of you.”

She smiled and the smile was more rueful than bitter. “So we waited and first it was one thing then another. Polly got into trouble and he’d just got her sorted out and we were waiting for you to marry your farmer. Don’t look so surprised. Your pa weren’t daft, you know. He could see where the land lay. Once you was wed, he was going to come over here to live and then we’d get married. He

318

planned to bring Robert and I'd of been happy to have him too. It looked as if everything was going to turn out right for all of us. But then he got sick. I begged him to go to the doctor, and he did eventually, but the medicine he gave him didn't do him no good. I knew that 'cos he wasn't eating proper. No wonder he had that accident. Faint from not eating, he must have been, when he fell off that there roof."

Sarah saw the desolation that the painful memories had brought to Nan's eyes and it was in a softened tone that she said, "I'm sorry you weren't able to come to see him when he was ill. I think it would have been a great comfort to him."

"Well, there you go. That's life, ain't it?" Nan rose from her chair and Sarah noted the effort she made to smile bravely. Her eyes were bright with unshed tears when she asked briskly, "Now. How about that cup of tea?"

And Sarah answered, "Yes. Yes, I'd like that... Nan."

# CHAPTER TWENTY-SEVEN

That summer, Sarah discovered a freedom that hitherto she had been denied. Since leaving school she had helped her ma and then, after her death, been solely in charge of domestic arrangements. She had cared for Robert and nursed her pa. But now, with Robert at the farm all day, she was able to find time for herself. Alone, she was able to roam the downs and feel as free as Dan's flock that wandered at will, cropping the sweet, thyme-scented turf.

It was good to feel the wind blow her hair wildly about her face and bring a rosy hue to her cheeks. Even the sudden showers of rain, that sent her scurrying for shelter under the umbrella of the hawthorn's branches and leaves, could not deter her.

She climbed high, above the valley, until she could see Barkwell and the surrounding countryside spread out below her. She could see the church spire, gleaming on sunny days, as it soared above the elms. She could make out the doctor's house and the parsonage, as well as the Scarlet Arms with its gardens that sloped gently to the river and, over there, were the cottager's homes, scattered like a child's building blocks, about the green.

And all about the village were fields, golden with mustard or hazy green with young wheat rising towards the rolling downs beyond. She could see the farm and feel the thrill of knowing that one day it would be her home. And Dan. Dan, with the gentle eyes and shy ways, would be her husband. She feasted her eyes on all the varied shades of greens and golds of fields, bushes and trees, and drank in the sunshine and silence and wild beauty of the hills.

That summer, with a book under her arm and an apple in her pocket, she returned again and again to a sun-filled hollow and there, sheltered from the buffeting winds, she read all of Cowper's poems, Richardson's *Pamela*, and Trollope's *Barchester Towers,* as well as the Waverley novels.

And still she had time to lay in the fragrant, purple heather, with her hands linked behind her head, and bask in the utter quiet with the sun warm on her face and the drone of insects for company. Here, the solitude was balm for a spirit grown weary in the care of others.

And here, she was able to unravel the mixed feelings she had about her pa. She could picture him with Nan and the child in the little house in Chillingford. Indeed, she could. Quite clearly she could see him sitting in that room with the washing hanging down from the ceiling. He'd be in the chair by the fire, dangling the timid little boy, that was his son, on his knee. Or at the table, sharing a meal with Nan. And to her came the conviction, not based solely on reason but more instinctive, that he had belonged there, in some ways, far more than in his own home.

All her life she had regarded her pa as just that: a father with a duty to love and care for his family. Wasn't that what a father should do? Now, she saw him as an individual person with needs and feelings of his own, and she was filled with a melancholy that she had learnt to appreciate this fact after his death and not before.

Gradually, though, as the year advanced, she found a peace of mind. She looked forward to the day when, the mourning period over, she and Dan would be married, but for the present she revelled in her new-found freedom and was content with each hour of existence.

She visited Aunt Ruth whose face lit up with pleasure at her company. She held Sarah's hands and told her how Sarah's mother had had to wait a year to marry because she, too, had been in mourning for her own father. She told of her part as chaperone and giggled, girlishly, recalling the rumours that had spread around the village that it was she, the parson's daughter, who was meeting the handsome John Holland. She talked endlessly about the village and how it had changed since she was a girl, reliving, in her mind, her memories now that she could no longer see. Having no further use for them, she gave Sarah all her embroidery silks and materials and Sarah started another quilt.

Sitting in the shade of the apple tree in the back garden, where her ma had been used to sit, pleasant hours were passed with stitching and innocent daydreams.

Fanny made her weekly visits. One day, when they were sitting down by the river, Fanny asked Sarah if she would teach her to sign. She wanted to 'talk' to Robert. Sarah was delighted to do so especially as she had suspected, for some time, that the motivation for Fanny's visits was not herself so much as Robert.

Robert got into the habit of walking back with Fanny to the Hall at the end of her afternoon off. And it wasn't long before Fanny managed to change her free time so that it fell on the same day as Robert's.

At first Sarah thought of Fanny as another defenceless creature that Robert had taken under his wing. She watched the burgeoning friendship with amusement and then with deepening pleasure. It was wonderful to see Robert and Fanny together, smiling and talking with their fingers. It was as if they recognised in each other a solitariness, a fellow feeling, that kept them apart from others. For didn't Fanny, forced to spend her days scouring pans, have a mind that had no means of expression?

Together they roamed the countryside. Robert showed Fanny where a kestrel nested in a hollow tree, where the badgers lived and where you could watch otters slide down the bank into the river. They went to watch the hedgehogs foraging for food in the summer twilight and collected insects and worms to feed the temporary residents of Robert's cages.

They spent hours in the shed, heads together. He showed her how to lift a bird gently in both hands so that it could be held from above, very lightly, with both thumbs, and how to make a surrogate nest for fledgling birds by filling a plant pot with hay and making a hollow deep enough so that the bird wouldn't fall out.

Fanny was filled with wonder at the way Robert's birds thrived and grew and her squinty eyes shone with admiration as she watched him persuade a young cuckoo to take drops of water from the tip of his finger, or fed an injured owl with mice that he caught in the barns at the farm.

When Sarah told Dan she was teaching Fanny to sign, he insisted that she teach him too. Since Robert had started work at the farm, Dan had devised his own signs for letting Robert know what was required of him, but now Dan thought it would be good to communicate further. After all, wouldn't they all be living together as a family soon?

He encouraged his ma to learn too and she tried for a while. But she always ended in a muddle and fell about laughing. "I'll just feed him, m'dears. That be a language we both do understand," she said, and there was no doubt that, in food, she and

Robert shared a common interest.

She taught Sarah to make butter in the dairy. In there, the air was cool and the sun filtered through the tiny, high windows in yellow-green slanting rays. Sarah learnt how to skim the cream from the huge pans of milk that stood on the stone shelves, then to pour it in the churn and turn and turn it until the butter was formed. Afterwards they took the buttermilk that was drained off and made delicious scones that they ate, hot from the oven, spread with dripping butter and accompanied by brimming cups of steaming tea.

And in November, after the pigs had been killed, Sarah went over to the farm to help Mrs Fuller deal with all the meat. Whole flitches were salted down; other joints cured. Sausages were made and whole tongues pressed into pots and sealed with clarified butter. Nothing was wasted and the only parts that were eaten fresh were the shoulders and part of the forequarter, every farm worker getting a share.

At this time, the farmhouse kitchen was filled with tantalising food smells, every surface covered with pots and pans, and the atmosphere was warm with good humour and laughter. This is how life will be when I'm married, Sarah thought, and was as happy and contented as she had ever been.

Polly gave birth to another daughter at Christmas; a sister for Gladys. They called her Mabel. Such modern names, the village folk said, and exclaimed at how fair this baby was when the other was so dark.

Ned was bursting with pride for his little family and fussed around Polly. He treated her as if she was the only woman who had performed the miracle of giving birth. And Polly accepted his adoring ministrations as her due and was happy.

Ned's only sadness was that his granny was not alive to share his joy. One sunny day in August her wish not to live long enough to be a burden was fulfilled. She died, as peacefully as she had lived, sitting beside the bees she loved so much.

Ned found her there. It looked as if she was quietly snoozing. She had a gentle smile on her face and her hands lay, neatly folded, on the knitting in her lap. And the day she was taken from her cottage, to be buried in St Thomas's churchyard, the bees deserted their hive, never to return.

So the year passed, a new one began. The days flew by and as winter gave way to spring, preparations at last began for Sarah and Dan's wedding.

# CHAPTER TWENTY-EIGHT

"Just look at this." Polly flung open the door of the garden shed. "He filled four potato sacks with the packets alone. I can't tell you how many bottles and jars there are of her awful concoctions." She gave a little grimace of disgust and hitched Gladys higher on her hip.

"What are you going to do with them?" Sarah asked, idly examining the brown paper packages all neatly sewn closed with thread. If she shut her eyes and took a deep breath she could imagine she was in Granny's cottage, so strong was the smell of the mixture of herbs; comfrey and rue, camomile, myrtle and caraway.

"Heaven only knows for I don't! I suppose we'll keep them to throw away another day." Polly smiled ruefully. "Ned brought them back when he cleared out the cottage before the Caldwells moved in. He said he hadn't the heart to throw them out. Granny lived for her herbs... when she wasn't talking to her bees. I told him there was no sense in

327

keeping them if we don't know what they are for, but he insisted. So, there you are. I didn't pursue the matter. He is taking his granny's death harder than he'll own to." She shut the door and they retraced their steps up the garden path.

It was the first week in May and the garden was bright with spring flowers, the sky unusually blue for so early in the year with clouds, like locks of curly hair, drifting by.

"I'm surprised he let the cottage to Jimmy Caldwell," Sarah observed as they entered the kitchen and she gathered her belongings together, ready to leave.

Polly sat with the child on her lap. "Ned is full of surprises. At one time he wouldn't give Jimmy the time of day but I think he feels sorry for Betsy, what with them having to get married and Jimmy not holding down a job for long. I will say one thing to his credit though; he's worked hard in the garden. They've only been there a few weeks and it's looking very neat. He told Ned he is going to put up a chicken run."

The baby started to cry in its crib by the fire. Polly stretched out a foot to rock the crib gently and Sarah marvelled, not for the first time, at the ease with which Polly had slipped into motherhood.

"It was strange, the bees leaving like that," Sarah murmured. "It was almost as if they knew their keeper had gone."

"Folk say that if you don't tell the bees when somebody has died they will stop making honey. I

328

suppose Granny's bees didn't need to be told, her dying as she did. Anyway, we have jars of honey. Ned has them for sale in the shop but I've kept a couple back for you."

"That's kind of you. I'll make some honey and horehound and get Robert to take it up to the Hall for Fanny. She had a sore throat when she came last week. It must be with her still because we expected her today and she didn't come."

"She's a queer creature. I remember once asking her if she sometimes got fed up with standing at the sink day after day and do you know what she said? She said that it didn't bother her too much because most of the time she wasn't there. When I asked her where she was, she smiled that odd smile of hers and said, 'I'm in the drawing rooms listening to the gossip or on the back of an eagle soaring through the clouds'. I can't make head nor tail of half she says. I wonder where she gets her ideas. It's not books. Did you know she's never learnt to read or write? She really is extraordinary. She and Robert make a fine pair; him not saying anything and her not saying anything you can understand. How is the great romance coming along?"

Sarah smiled. "It's going very well. She brought him a jar of slugs last week. Not common garden slugs, but aristocratic ones, if you please, from the Hall gardens. A rather unusual gift for ones beloved but, I swear, he couldn't have been more delighted."

They laughed together. A few more words were exchanged and it was five o'clock when eventually Sarah said goodbye and started for home.

It was as she was crossing the green that she saw Joseph Marsden. She had just passed the covered well when she caught sight of him coming out of the Scarlet Arms. She had only seen him two or three times in the last few years. The villagers said that he spent most of his time in London now that his father had died. She had heard that he and his brother didn't get along together.

Joseph had changed from the handsome youth he had once been. A life of idleness and indulgence was beginning to have its effect, she supposed. He had grown quite bull-necked and barrel-chested. His fleshy face had the waxy pallor of someone who spent too much time drinking in smoky saloons.

Sarah couldn't help comparing him with Dan and Robert. Both were of the same height as Joseph, but they were strong, with hard muscles and clear-skinned from their work in the open air. It was a matter of wonder to her that she had ever found Joseph attractive.

He had one foot in the stirrup and was about to mount his horse when he saw Sarah. There was that bold look again. He had a way of looking at her that made her shudder.

The last time she had seen him was in January when the Hunt had met outside the inn. She had been coming from the parsonage and had stopped to admire the ladies in their tight-fitting black habits with long, flowing skirts. They sat side-saddle on their mounts, jaunty in their neat little hats. The men, immaculate in red jackets and shining black boots and the hounds weaving to and fro with their noses to the ground and tails wagging. What a splendid sight it had been.

And then she had seen Joseph Marsden. He was reaching down for a stirrup cup when he saw her. And then he winked! He had winked at her and her simple pleasure of the scene had vanished.

And just before Christmas he had come out of the Scarlet Arms with two young men who must have been guests up at the Hall. He bade her good afternoon, inclining his head as he tipped his hat with exaggerated courtesy. There had been mockery in his smile and laughter in his eyes.

No, she didn't like Joseph Marsden. He had taken a crop to Robert and abandoned Polly after taking advantage of her. She wasn't going to give him the opportunity to make sport of her again. She put her head down and hurried over the bridge.

Dusk began to shroud the valley as she took the river path home. She was so deep in thought, mulling over her conversation with Polly and thinking about Fanny and Robert, that she didn't, at first, see Joseph riding his horse in the lane.

He was keeping to a walking pace and watching her. It made her feel uncomfortable; the subtle menace of his unwavering gaze. She fixed her eyes firmly on the path ahead, refusing to let him see that she was disturbed. A few steps farther she rested her basket a moment, pulled her shawl closer about her shoulders. With the fading light it was getting cooler. She hoped that Joseph would go on but she saw, from the corner of her eye, that the horse had stopped too. For the first time she felt a stab of fear. What could she do? She could turn round and return to the village but that would avail her nothing. It would only give Joseph the satisfaction of knowing that he had frightened her. She wasn't going to give him that satisfaction. Let him play his little games. She would ignore him. He would be turning off for the Hall soon. She took a deep breath and, staring straight ahead, continued purposefully along the path.

She didn't look up towards the lane until she had passed the turning to the Hall and was nearly at Granny's cottage. The horse and its rider were gone. Sarah let out a sigh of relief and chided herself for being so silly.

Her thoughts soon turned to her wedding plans. She had bought lace from Miss Bryant's shop, before calling on Polly, and looked forward to trimming the nightgown that was part of her trousseau. She smiled as she pictured her wedding outfit that hung behind the curtain in her bedroom. It was of claret-coloured silk. The jacket fitted closely to the waist and had the fashionable leg-of-mutton sleeves. Cream braid trimmed the cuffs and hem of the skirt to match the exquisite silk blouse with its froth of lace arranged in a V shape across the bodice.

Of course, it had been wildly extravagant of her to buy such a creation but she had not been able to resist it. After all, a wedding was a very special occasion. A wedding! Her wedding. Yes, everything was going to turn out well.

"Good afternoon little Sarah."

She was startled out of her reverie and her breath caught in her throat to see Joseph lounging against the trunk of an elm. He pushed himself from the tree to stand directly in front of her, blocking her path.

"Good afternoon, sir," she answered warily. She must force herself not to show her fear. "Would you kindly stand aside and allow me to pass?"

"What's the hurry? Surely you're not in such haste that you're unable to pass the time of day with me?" He beamed amiably.

"Sir, I have neither the time nor the inclination."

His eyebrows lifted sardonically. "Such fine words! No less than I would expect from a doctor's granddaughter."

Sarah caught the amused look in his eyes and smarted with humiliation that he still remembered her silly boast. She lowered her eyes. As she looked down she saw that her boots were powdered yellow with buttercup pollen. The buttercups were early this year. Strange that she should notice a thing like that at such a time.

Perhaps it was his casual elegance that made her feel shabby.

"I will strike a bargain with you. I will stand aside and let you pass if you give me, in exchange, a kiss."

He leaned forward and lifted her chin but she jerked her head back and glared at him, her fear replaced with anger at the way his insolent eyes roved over her.

"I am not accustomed to striking such bargains. So I'll ask you again. Will you please stand aside and let me pass?"

"So you're not so accommodating as your sister. I must say she was a sight friendlier. Ah! But perhaps you, too, would like a shilling." He gave an ugly laugh and began to fish in his pocket.

Sarah clenched her fists, still glaring at him. He held out his hand, offering her the silver coin. With a sudden movement she knocked it away and it fell, out of sight, in the long grass.

Joseph peered in the direction it had fallen and when he looked up his expression was one of hurt amazement. She realised then that he was drunk.

And now it was her voice that held contempt. "I needn't tolerate this behaviour," she said. "Your manners are deplorable. If you won't let me pass, I'll return the way I came and go along the lane." She turned her back on him and began to retrace her steps.

She was congratulating herself that she had

handled the situation with dignity when, suddenly, Joseph seized her by the shoulders and spun her round. And then his lips were upon hers, bruising her with his strength. She dropped the basket. Her hands reached up towards his face. She would have scratched his eyes out if she could. Her nails raked his cheek and he flung her from him.

Gingerly, Joseph put his hand to his cheek. He looked, with astonishment, at the blood on his fingers and his face grew dark with anger.

Sarah frantically looked about her. To the right was the overgrown bank rising steeply to the lane. To the left was the river. Joseph blocked the way ahead. She could only run back the way she had come. But before she could take flight his hand came up and smashed her across the face sending her sprawling in the long grass.

"So, my little vixen. You like to play rough," he snarled. A slow smile spread over his face as he advanced towards her. "I intended to steal a kiss, that was all my intention, but you have whetted my appetite for something more."

Before she could scramble from his reach he threw himself upon her, pinioning her to the ground. She could smell the alcohol on his breath; see the white spittle at the corner of his lips as he leered down at her.

She screamed. His fist slammed into the side of her face once more. In a daze of pain she fought, ineffectually, knowing that she was no match for him. His slobbering kisses left a wet trail over her neck. He tore at her clothes and then his hand was kneading her breast, his nails digging into her flesh with a vicious cruelty. She screamed again.

He smothered her cries with his mouth, pressing so hard that she could feel the sharp pain of his teeth against her lips, already tender from his blows. She fought him, desperately, as he grabbed at her skirts and his knee tried to force her legs apart. It seemed that the more she struggled the more excited he became.

What happened next was to remain a blur in her memory forever. Joseph was hauled from her and thrown to the ground. And Robert was there; dear, gentle Robert, now crazed with rage, pumping his fists into Joseph's flaccid body.

Joseph recovered from his surprise and managed to gain his feet. He lunged at Robert, attempting to fight back, but alcohol had made him slow and he was no match for Robert's fury. He tried to protect himself from the blows but again and again Robert smashed his fist into Joseph's bloody face. Joseph, dazed by this violent assault, staggered backwards. He tripped, fell and Robert threw himself upon him.

Sarah, at last, collected her wits. Crying, "Robert! Robert enough. Enough now!" she pulled him from Joseph's inert body.

Robert was panting, his face red and the knuckles of his hands raw. For a moment he stared intently at his hands, shaking his head from side to side as if in disbelief that he had been so violent. He looked at Sarah and it was clear to see the horror etched in his face. But his expression changed to one of concern when he looked at her.

Tenderly, he wiped the tears from her bruised and swollen face. He found her shawl, wrapped it around her shoulders and crossed it in front of her to cover her naked breasts. She watched as he righted the basket. He collected the purse, the scattered packages, the two jars of honey.

Polly had given her the honey. Was that only this afternoon, when they had laughed and discussed her wedding plans? All that had just happened had taken but a few minutes. She couldn't take in what had happened. If it wasn't for the pain in her head and limbs, she could believe it was an awful nightmare and she would wake up at any moment.

Sarah slowly looked about her in the gathering dusk. Sparrows squabbled in the trees. The river gently flowed. Pale reeds whispered in the breeze. Only the flattened grasses gave any indication of the terrible thing that had happened. Everywhere was quiet. She looked down at Joseph's still body. His head was resting on a large rock.

And then the greatest fear of all possessed her. He was still. Too still. She bent down to peer closer, saw the blood that issued from the back of his head. And she knew then. She knew that Joseph Marsden was dead.

# CHAPTER TWENTY-NINE

"Jimmy! Jimmy, where are you?"

"I'm up here. What is it?"

"Come on down. I've got something to tell. I can't go a-shouting it all up the stairs."

Jimmy thumped down the stairs and appeared, blinking sleepily, in the kitchen doorway. "I hope it's summat good. I were sleeping," he grumbled and sprawled in the chair by the fire.

Betsy filled the kettle and put it on the hob. "I were coming along the lane, just now, and I saw a horse tied to a Hawthorne; 'bout halfway atween here and the Holland's place. Beautiful saddle it had on it. I was wondering what it be a-doing there when I heared voices down by the river. You'll never guess who it was."

"Go on then. Who was it?"

Joseph Marsden and Sarah Holland! I got the surprise of me life when I heard their conversation. He were asking her for a kiss and you should of heard little Miss High and Mighty." Betsy put her hands on her hips and mimicked Sarah's more refined accent. " 'I have neither the time nor the inclination,' she said. Well, to cut a long story short, he ended up trying to tumble 'er in the grass. I could of laughed out loud to see their antics if I hadn't been afeared they'd hear me. He walloped her one when she tried to scream."

"Well? Did he have his way with her?" asked Jimmy, beginning to enjoy the tale.

"That be the whole point. Summat much more interesting happened." She tied an apron round her thickening waist and smoothed the folds over the mound of her belly.

"What could be more interesting than that?"

The loony came down the hill and put a stopper to his shenanigans, that's what! He must of seen 'em from up there. He must have been collecting kindling 'cos I heared this great shout and, when I looked up, I seen him drop his bundle and come a-charging down the hill. He were waving his arms about and roaring like old Thurber's bull. He yanked Marsden off his sister and gave him such a bannicking. I've not seen the like since your brother went for George Burrows after the Jubilee celebrations. Knocked Marsden out cold, the loony did."

"Go on, he didn't! God a' mighty, I'd liked to of seen it. What happened then?"

"She did a lot of that finger talking like what they do. I don't know what it was all about, of course, but when she do finish, he climbed up the bank – I thought he was going to catch me watching so I scooted behind the bushes – and when he got to the lane he untied the horse. He slapped it on the rump and it took off down the lane. If you'd of been up 'stead of sleeping, you'd of seen it go past."

"You don't begrudge me a nap, do you? I cut all that grass today. Fair beazled I am... and I stacked all them old 'ives down the back, behind the privy. What about Marsden? I s'pose he'll have to walk back."

Betsy had begun to prepare the vegetables. She turned and wagged the paring knife at him. Her eyes gleamed with excitement. "Now we're getting to it. This is where you come into it."

"Me?"

"Yes. They went home and left him there. Marsden's still down by the river. He must be out cold. I reckon they hope that it looks like his horse threw him."

"What have I got to do with it?" Jimmy shook his head. "I'm not getting' involved. And if you take my advice, Betsy, you'll stay out of it too."

"Aw Jimmy! Don't you see? It could be to your advantage. I reckon if you went up to the 'all and told them what's happened, there could be summat in it for you. They'd have to show their gratitude, wouldn't they?"

Jimmy's eyes narrowed. "You mean, like a reward?"

"Yes. Of course, it would be best not to mention what was going on. It wouldn't reflect well."

"What am I supposed to say then?"

Betsy chopped carrots and considered. "You could say you saw the loony laying into him. After all, everyone knows he's as mad as a March hare."

"And then they'll ask me why I didn't try and stop it."

"I never thought of that…. Can't you say you was up the hill when you saw the commotion, saw the loony having a go at Marsden, but by the time you got down there, he'd gone?"

"I dunno. I reckon we ought to keep out of it."

"Jimmy Caldwell! Have your wits gone wool gathering? Have you thought what we're going to do when I leave me job? Another week or two and I won't be able to lift them milk pails. If you go up to the 'all, tell them you've run straight there for help 'cos Master Joseph have taken a fall, they're bound to be grateful. They might even give you a job. At the least it'll be a few sovereigns."

"All right…. Shall I have me tea first?"

"No, Jimmy Caldwell, you won't. You go this minute. If you hang around much longer, he'll of got up and walked home, hisself, afore you get there!"


Sarah sat in the parlour. She had sat there all morning, thoughts jostling furiously in her mind. Had she done the right thing? What else could she have done?

When she had seen Joseph lying there with

341

the blood trickling from his ear and the corner of his mouth, and the pool of it gathering, thick and sticky, in his hair, she had been filled with a numbing fear. But her first thought had been to save Robert. Joseph had fallen and hit his head on the rock. That was what had killed him. It wasn't Robert's fault. All he had done was protect her.

The thought of Joseph's brutal attack was sickening. She shuddered at the thought of his hands on her naked flesh and dreaded to think what would have happened if Robert hadn't arrived when he did. Tentatively she put up her hand to touch her swollen lip. Leaving him there seemed the only thing to do. Joseph was dead. When the horse, without its rider, arrived at the Hall, they would assume he had been thrown and look for him. There was no witness to say that it was anything other than an accident. But what would they make of his bloodied face? They would know then. No fall could have produced the injuries that Robert had inflicted in his rage.

Sarah thought of Robert. She had sent him off to the farm this morning. They must behave as normally as possible. There was nothing to connect them with Joseph's death but she was worried about Robert. In the early hours of morning, she had heard him moving about downstairs. He didn't, of course, realise the noise he was making. She had gone down to see him prowling the kitchen and he had looked at her, helplessly, aghast at what he had done. She tried to convince him that it wasn't his fault. It wasn't he who had caused Joseph's death. But all Robert did was stare miserably at her, shaking his head.

He would have gone back to the river if she hadn't stopped him. There was nothing he could do. What was done was done. No amount of wishing could make it otherwise, and now all she could do was try to protect Robert from the consequences. But her mind shrank from what those consequences might be. Her imagination conjured up disquieting pictures that filled her with a fear so terrible that it rendered her incapable of performing the simplest tasks. And so she sat in the parlour, feeling the anxious beat of her heart, aware of every breath she took, waiting with a brooding sense of unease for she knew not what.

At eleven o'clock there was a banging on the front door. Sarah heard the frantic knocking and Dan's voice calling her.

"Sarah! Sarah, are you there?"

She huddled farther into the corner of the sofa. What did he want at this time of day? At any other time she would have been delighted to see him. She longed to share her fears with him, tell him what had happened, draw strength from him, but the fewer people who knew, the better, and it wasn't fair to get him involved. She would have to pretend she wasn't there and hope that he would go away. She couldn't face anyone, not even Dan, until she had composed herself and knew what was happening.

Dan tapped on the parlour window. She could see his anxious face pressed close to the pane although he couldn't see her where she sat.

"Sarah! Sarah, if you are there, open the door," he called urgently. "It's Robert. It's about Robert."

At Robert's name Sarah ran to the door and flung it wide. "What is it? What has happened?"

Dan turned from the parlour window. When he saw the livid bruise on her cheek and her swollen mouth, he grabbed her by the arms. She winced at his grip and he let go of her. He studied her face, his own expressing shock, horror, concern.

"What has happened to your face?"

"Tell me about Robert."

"Who has done this to you, Sarah?"

"For pity's sake, Dan, tell me what's happened to Robert?"

"He's been arrested for murder. Two constables came with a warrant about an hour back. They've taken him to Chillingford." His face darkened. "Now will you tell me what's going on?"

Sarah turned on her heel and went into the kitchen. Dan followed her.

"What the hell is going on, Sarah? Robert comes into work this morning with a face as long as a wet washday and jumping at his own shadow, the constables come for him and I find you in this state!"

Sarah slumped into a chair and told him then. Dan, horrified at what he heard, grew silent.

344

She could see he was hurt that she hadn't gone straight to him.

He rubbed a hand over his chin and paced the floor, looking grubby and reeking of earth and sweat, but at this moment all she wanted was for him to take her in his arms and tell her he would take care of things.

It was as if he had read her mind because he stopped in front of her, took her in his arms and kissed the tears, still wet, on her bruised cheeks. And when he held her from him, his eyes were filled with a deep and loving kindness and his voice was gentle as he spoke.

"I'm going back home for the cart. I'll have a wash and be back within the hour. Be ready, Sarah, 'cos we're going over to Chillingford."

The inspector was a big, middle-aged man with a fleshy face and close-cropped greying hair. He had quick darting eyes, behind wire-rimmed spectacles, that roamed restlessly from Dan to Sarah and about his office and the papers on his desk as he listened to Sarah's story.

When she had finished he thanked her politely and said, "We were coming to see you anyway so you saved us a journey. The man who brought the news to the Hall...." He looked over the report in front of him. " Ah, yes. James Caldwell. He stated that he saw the deceased thrown from his horse. Of course, when we examined the body, it was evident that there were injuries that were not consistent with having been merely thrown from a horse. On questioning Caldwell he gave me a garbled account of the loo... of your brother attacking Marsden. He contradicted himself several times but when he realised that he, himself, stood in danger of being suspected of the crime, we began to get at the truth. It transpired that he hadn't even seen the body and that it was his wife who had been witness to the event." He sighed, wearily, and removed his spectacles. He polished them with a vast blue handkerchief and replaced them on his nose before continuing.

"We interviewed Mrs Caldwell and what she had to say corroborates that which you have related." He reached into the right-hand drawer of his desk and placed a small tissue-wrapped package, very precisely, in front of him. As he unwrapped it he asked, "Do you recognise this, Miss Holland?"

In the paper lay the lace she had bought for her nightgown. "Yes. Yes, it's the lace I bought yesterday. It must have fallen from my basket."

The inspector gave a satisfied nod. "The lady that has the drapers in Barkwell identified it as a purchase you made yesterday afternoon."

"You haven't wasted any time, have you?" Dan said. It was more of a statement than a question.

"We don't let the grass grow under our feet, sir, if that's what you mean. Miss Holland, I have to ask you this…." He hesitated a moment, scratching the side of his nose and choosing his words carefully. "This Caldwell chap. He referred to your brother as the loony and, I must say, we haven't been able to get anything out of him. Am I correct in assuming that he is… um… not all there?"

Sarah glared at the inspector. "My brother, Inspector, is far from being a… a fool. Robert is deaf. Has been since birth. He was never able to speak but I can assure you that he is as sane as you or me."

"So you are not of the opinion that he is dangerous?"

"Of course he isn't. Robert wouldn't hurt a fly."

"And I can vouch for that," added Dan.

"So he only acted in defence of your honour?"

"That is what I have explained. It was all a ghastly accident. Robert is no more capable of killing someone than… than jumping over the moon. The very idea is absurd." She forced a smile. "So now that everything has been made clear I would like to take my brother home."

The inspector had been looking down, rearranging the papers in neat piles before him, but now his head jerked up. "Oh no, Miss Holland. Indeed not. Charges have been made against your brother. Serious charges. Charges of murder."

"But I have explained."

"It may be my opinion that he acted in defence of your honour but, whilst I sympathise with you, there is little I can do. Lord Marsden has

347

brought charges of murder against him. He will have to remain in custody. He will have to stand trial."

The breath stopped in her chest at the inspector's words. For the last few minutes she had allowed her hopes to rise only to have them dashed again. Clutching at Dan's sleeve, she looked helplessly up at him.

"We understand that you have your job to do, Inspector, but would it be possible, at least, to let Miss Holland see her brother?"

"Yes. Yes, of course." The inspector rose from his chair. "I'll see that you are taken down there."

The keeper, who took them to the prison cells, grumbled to himself and wheezed as he led them down a flight of stone steps and through a maze of narrow, dark passages before stopping abruptly outside a heavy, oak door. He slid back a small panel that covered an even smaller opening, and peered inside. With much jangling of the bunch of keys attached to a heavy chain to his waist and a muttered, "Five minutes," he opened the door.

It swung open to reveal a tiny cell, musty and dank, for the only source of air was from a grating set high up in the wall. The only furnishings were a plank arrangement fixed to the wall and a malodorous wooden bucket in the corner.

Robert sat, miserably, with his head down and his hands hanging loosely between his knees.

When he saw Sarah and Dan standing before him he jumped to his feet. He faced Dan with reproachful eyes and signed wildly to him. He was clearly agitated and signed too quickly for Dan to understand.

Dan appealed to Sarah. "What is he saying?"

They managed to calm him down but their precious minutes passed. Sarah explained that they were not able to take him home. She tried to reassure him that everything would be all right. The police knew, now, what had happened.

Robert signed back to her. Yes, she answered. She was feeling better, the pain was less. Tenderly, he cupped her face in his hands and the tears stood in his eyes as he regarded the bruises on her face.

He asked if she would look after his birds. She said she would. And then he turned to Dan and signed that he didn't want Dan to bring Sarah to the prison again.

As they rode home, the thought gnawed at Sarah's mind that if Robert hadn't been trying to protect her this would not have happened and that, somehow, she was to blame for the fearful mess they were in. The injustice of it all filled her with a rage that threatened to suffocate her.

Dan tried to raise her spirits. It was only three weeks till the Quarter Sessions. He would come over as often as he could. He said that he would keep the horse at the farm and take care of it.

Robert had ridden into work that morning and it was still there in the meadow. He talked about the farm and the new calves that had been born, in an effort to distract her. Unable to ease her suffering he lapsed into silence and stared unhappily ahead as they rode home in the evening twilight.

When the cart stopped outside the cottage, he turned to her and said, "Sarah, come back to the farm tonight. Stay with us till it's all over." His voice grew very gentle. "I don't like you to be alone. I want to look after you."

"Thank you, Dan, but I'd rather stay here."

And then she cried. The tears that she had held back, all the way home, spilled from her eyes. Dan gathered her in his arms.

"Oh Dan! Dan, I'm so frightened."

Gently, he rocked her, making soothing sounds and stroking her hair as one might comfort a child.

He took her indoors, lit the lamps, tried to reassure her with a show of confidence he did not feel. He would have stayed but, with a man short and Betsy not turning up that morning, there were chores at the farm that couldn't be left; animals to feed and cows to be milked.

"Shall I come back later, my dear, and sit with you for a while?" he asked but she told him no, all she really needed right now was to get to bed.

# CHAPTER THIRTY

Fanny came in the morning. Sarah was surprised to see her as it wasn't her day off. She made tea and they sat at the kitchen table. Fanny was anxious for news of Robert and so Sarah told her of their trip to the courthouse.

"They are saying, up at the 'all, that Robert's not all there. That he should have been locked away in an asylum a long time ago. They didn't say it to me face 'cos they knows I'm friendly with him, but I heard them whispering. Still, I won't have to put up with them any more. Got me marching orders this morning."

"Oh no, Fanny. What ever for?"

"Old Miss Passmore sent for me this morning and told me that they preferred it if I wasn't to have anything to do with you all, in the circumstances. I told her, what I do in me own time was me own business and they couldn't stop me. Taken aback, she was. First time I've seen the old trollop flustered. She told me then that she had no alternative but to dismiss me."

"I'm so sorry. What will you do?" Sarah asked and before Fanny could answer, added, "You must stay here with me. And when it's all over, when this is all sorted out and Robert comes home, when Dan and I get married and Robert comes to the farm, then you must come too. I'll speak to Dan. They will be needing a new dairy maid now that Betsy is nearing her time. It would be wonderful, Fanny. You would have a room to yourself and good food. Mrs Fuller's such an excellent person. You'll like her and we'll all be together." Sarah's eyes lit up with the thought. It was the first positive one she had had in two days.

"Thank you, but I'm going over to Chillingford. I want to be near Robert. I think you must know that me and Robert… well, we care a lot about each other."

"But I doubt if he will see you, even if the authorities will allow you to visit. He was upset that I was there yesterday. I don't know if it was because he didn't want me to see him in such straits or if he didn't think a prison was a fit place for a female to visit. Perhaps a bit of both. Why don't you stay here, Fanny?" she urged. "Dan has said he'll go over as often as he can and he'll bring us news of Robert."

But Fanny wouldn't be persuaded. "I know you mean it kindly but I've made up me mind. Even if I can't get to see him I can stay close by. Whatever happens, I could never be happy with meself unless I did that."

Sarah thought Fanny was going to cry. She screwed up her face, the squint became more pronounced and then she looked down at her ugly hands.

"Where will you stay?"

"I don't know. I've been given me wages so I'll get by. God willing, Robert will be home soon. In the meantime I've got enough to get meself a room for a while. I'll manage."

For a while they sat in silence, both wrapped in her own thoughts. The sun streamed through the kitchen window. It seemed a mockery to their melancholy. From the hazel copse came the short chirrup of a woodcock.

Sarah suddenly had an idea and her face brightened. "I know where you can stay. I know a lady in Church Street. She would be glad to have you, especially if you tell her what has happened. She... she knows our family. I will write you a letter of introduction. It will be better than looking for rooms and it is near the courthouse."

Sarah hurried to get writing materials, glad to be doing something for her friend. She brought paper, pen and ink to the table and Fanny watched, silently, as Sarah wrote the letter, carefully blotted the wet ink and sealed it in an envelope. This she addressed, in her neat copperplate hand, to Mrs Nancy Killick, 12 Church Street, Chillingford. She read out the address to Fanny before handing it to her.

"Thank you," Fanny said and tucked it into the deep pocket of her coat. "It'll save me looking and if she can't put me up, happen she'll know of someone who will. I better be on me way soon. I left me basket under a bush at the turning. Didn't see the sense to lugging it all the way out here only to lug it back. I dare say it'll be heavy enough by the time I get to Chillingford."

"Will you have something to eat before you go?"

"No, thank you. I had a good breakfast and Cook slipped me a bite to eat for later. I only came up to say goodbye. I wanted to see how the land lies." She stood and pulled on her gloves. "I expect Robert misses his birds."

"Oh, the birds! The birds!" Sarah exclaimed and her hand flew to her mouth. She had forgotten Robert's birds out in the shed.

They hurried outside and flung the door open. There were six cages but only four were occupied; a blue jay with an injured leg, a wood pigeon with an oddly twisted wing and two young sparrows.

The sparrows lay on the floors of their cages. They were dead.

"Oh, dear heaven!" Sarah looked helplessly at Fanny. "With all that has happened, I didn't give it a thought. Oh, the pity, the pity of it all! The senseless waste…."

They cleaned the cages, fed the surviving birds with a chopped apple and the acorns and grain

Robert kept in jars on the shelf. Sarah went to fetch fresh water and when she returned she saw that Fanny had disposed of the dead birds.

Fanny stared intently at the injured jay and it seemed as if she was talking to herself when she murmured, "We're all like little birds in cages."

Sarah was puzzled. She waited for Fanny to continue and when she didn't, asked, "What do you mean?"

"It seems that all of us do live in a cage 'cept we can't see it. Sometimes we makes it for ourselves and sometimes it's other people who does the job for us. Sometimes we're born with it. A cage can protect us from the world, but more often than not, it prevents us from living proper lives."

"I've never thought of things in that way. You think everyone has this invisible cage?"

"Yes."

"What do you see as mine?"

"Your duty to your family. It's what's stopped you from having a life of your own."

"And yours, Fanny? What is your cage? Was it Marsden Hall?"

"No. No, mine was the cage of poverty. Me and me ma before me."

"And Robert's is his deafness."

"Yes. He was born into one, a cage of silence, weren't he? Now he's in another cage... but this one ain't invisible." She gave a little moan.

"You sound as if there is no hope for any of us."

Fanny looked at her bleakly. "No. No, Sarah, there isn't."

"So what is left? What can we do?"

Fanny was silent for a long time. She had the glazed look about her that people have when their body is in one place and their mind is miles away. It was a look so far off and distant that Sarah wondered where she was.

And then Fanny said, in a strange dead voice, "Nothing, Sarah. Nothing at all."

"Have mercy upon us miserable sinners," the parson prayed that Sunday.

It was open to interpretation as to who was the sinner and who was sinned against. The village was divided. It buzzed with the news. Never had anything been discussed so avidly and so heatedly.

In the taproom of the Scarlet Arms, men nodded and drew on their pipes. They pointed the bitten stems at their neighbours to emphasize a point. "Right's right and wrong's no man's right," they said.

"It don't matter what the provocation, if he killed a man then he must pay the price."

"But how do we know he killed him? It could be a verdic' of accidental death if young Marsden died from cracking his head on that rock."

"Whatever the ins and outs of it the poor bugger don't stand a chance. You can't go lifting a hand to the gentry and get away with it."

"When all's said and done, one of they is

dead and he'll swing for it right enough."

"Hope for his sake he don't get tried on a Friday. Hangman's day that is. Allus gets stiffer sentence on a Friday."

"You can't get a stiffer sentence than hanging!"

On Thursday morning Joseph Marsden was buried on the south side of the cemetery, in the Marsden's private plot that was separated by iron railings from the other graves. Here, great stone angels and cherubim, with dimpled hands and small pursed lips, guarded generations of Mardens who had gone before.

The huge black hearse, draped in black velvet and embellished with black ostrich plumes, came swaying over the bridge and round the green. It was drawn by four coal-black horses and driven by the undertaker's men, their faces suitably melancholy and their top hats decked with long black streamers. Behind, came the mourners' carriages, each pulled by a black horse. In the first, the dowager with her son, Samuel, sat weeping into a black edged handkerchief. There were black parasols and black feather boas. Everything black.

Along the greensward, the villagers stood in silence, watching the funeral procession as the church bell tolled. The men stood bare-headed while the women held on to their children, hushing them when they made to cry. The dead were the dead, whoever they were, and the dead were to be respected.

Most of the blinds in the cottages and shops had been pulled down, except for those of the McGiveneys, the butcher's and Miss Bryant's drapery shop. In a rare moment of defiance, Miss Bryant decided not to acknowledge the passing of such a wicked person, even though he be gentry. It was a fine state of affairs when an innocent girl couldn't walk home without being molested and, while she didn't hold with brawling, he had got what he deserved. God's justice was swift and sure, but she trembled at the thought of that poor boy – and he was but a boy – arrested for murder when all he had sought to do was defend his sister. It had been an accident, of that she was sure, and while such injustice prevailed, she felt that it behoved her to make her protest.

Later, the women gathered in Emily's store. Bella, Jessie and Nell were there. They huddled together in the cramped space in front of the counter, their eyes alive with the excitement, each wearing about her an air of pious horror.

Bella's youngest tugged at her ma's skirt. "Did you see how many carriages there was, Ma? There was eleven carriages behind the hearse."

"Now what did I tell you? You mustn't go a-counting the number of carriages at a funeral. 'Tis unlucky if you do. And when I take you to see the grave later, don't you be a-pointing at it else your finger will rot and fall off."

Emily leaned over the counter. "It were a

fine turnout weren't it? More carriages than when the old lord died."

Mary McGiveney, examining the pudding basins in the far corner, wanted no part of it. You couldn't go anywhere in the village this past week without bumping into groups of villagers with their heads together gossiping. On the green, old men sat and speculated, and round the well women put down their pails and spouted their opinions, pecking at the air like a lot of old hens.

Patrick had told her it was the same in the Scarlet Arms. They didn't seem capable of talking about anything else. "'Tis a pity, entirely, that ye don't have anything better to do," he'd told them and had come home early, which showed how upset he'd been. "And I hope, Mary, my love, you'll not be listening to such tittle-tattle," he said to her.

"The Lord save us, this blessed day, Patrick McGiveney, if ye don't know me better than that. It's never been my way to desert people in misfortune," she had answered, "and I'll not be starting now."

No. She wanted no part of the conversation that was now taking place.

"I allus did think he were a danger. That boy should have been put away years ago. Look how he carried on when my boys were a-nesting. They wasn't doing no harm and they allus leave one egg in the nest. And that time down by the river with their catapults, he were as mad as a bull. Took Tommy's catapult, he did, and flung it in the water.

I don't s'pose they'd have hit them old ducks anyway."

"I don't think he's a loony. I think he had a grudge 'gainst Marsden. Creating all that fuss when the shoot were on and I can remember that time, one Christmas, when he must of upset Marsden, 'cos Marsden took a whip to him and young Sarah flew off the 'andle about it. He were but a lad then but I remember him a-shaking his fist at Marsden before he run off. No, you ain't a-goin' to tell me he's a loony. I think he's as sane as you and me. Depend upon it; he meant to do him in, all right."

"Well, I've got a bit of a tell. It's something Betsy told me," said Jessie Caldwell. She enjoyed the fact that her own daughter-in-law had seen it with her own eyes and felt that the connection gave her a standing above the other women. She paused for effect and gave a sly smile. "I'm not one to tell tales out of school but has it ever crossed your minds that Polly's oldest girl might not be Ned's?"

"When Gladys is dark and they both be fair…."

"I allus thought there was something queer there."

"What are you getting at?"

"Betsy let drop that when she heard Marsden talking, he said summat to Sarah 'bout not being friendly, not like her little sister. You know me; full of the milk of human kindness, I am. Wouldn't think ill of no one but I couldn't help thinking. That girl worked up at the 'all, didn't she? Left sudden like and next thing we know, she's going to wed young Ned. We allus knew he had a soft spot for her but she never seemed to take a fancy to him, did she?" She gave them a meaningful look and added, "Not till she had a bun in the oven and Ned suddenly had the where-with-all to buy George Bishop's little business."

For a moment nobody spoke. All that could be heard was the old clock, on the wall behind the counter, clicking past the hour. The women were digesting this new piece of information.

"So you reckon the little'un is Joseph Marsden's by-blow?"

"And he paid her off to keep it hushed up? Scandilus!"

"And he paid Ned to marry her? Bribed him?"

"It's allus been a wonder to me where he got his money from."

"So her brother did have a grudge 'gainst Marsden. After bringing down one sister, no wonder he killed him when he caught him trying to tumble the — "

Emily turned pale and caught hold of Nell's arm. She and the others followed Emily's alarmed gaze. With dismay they caught sight of Polly's horrified expression before she turned and ran from the store.

Mary McGiveney sent the china clattering as she banged down the basin she had intended to buy. She encompassed them all in her furious glare.

"Have you no pity?" she cried, "They've had enough the day without having to put up with the likes of ye at the end of it!"

She flounced out of the shop. But the damage had been done.

By that evening the news had spread. Ruth's keen ears. at the parsonage, heard the cook and the maidservant talking about it. She sent them about their work with harsh words.

For the first time in her life she began to doubt her belief in the inherent goodness in people. In her room she knelt to pray. She trembled with rage at the senseless gossip that she heard and, heedless of the coir matting that dug into her plump knees, and the silent tears that spilled from her sightless old eyes, she prayed for Robert and Sarah and Polly.

And she prayed for the villagers. "Dear God," she prayed, "send them some wisdom, for You must know, they have their share of ignorance already!

# CHAPTER THIRTY-ONE

"I shall never be able to hold my head up in the village again. How can I face them? We will have to move. Oh, the shame, the shame of it all!" Polly repeated the words on a groan and prowled the kitchen. "I've been bought and sold. That's all it amounts to. Pa bribed Ned with a butcher's block, a pile of hares and some lamb chops! Oh, the ignominy of it all!"

Sarah had listened to Polly's ranting for the best part of a half hour. She had heard how Polly had stormed into the butcher's shop and dragged Ned into the storeroom at the back. "Where did you get the money from for the shop?" she had demanded. Ned had looked confused and evasive at first, but Polly persisted and at last he told her. Now she was demanding answers from Sarah. "Why didn't you tell me?" she had asked and Sarah had tried to explain.

"What a fool I have been. It didn't occur to

me to ask him where he got the money from. I assumed that his granny had helped him. How will I be able to endure the looks and whispers of those old crones down there? It really is too bad. Robert has got us into a fearful mess. He had no right to bring such dishonour to the family, dragging us through the mud in this way."

Sarah had been scarcely listening. She had been absently rubbing the plate that she held, but at Robert's name she was stung to reply.

"Enough! That'll do! Have you no compassion, Polly? Robert is at this very moment awaiting trial. Heaven only knows how he must feel, locked up in that tiny cell without a blanket to cover him at night. He must be frightened to death, poor boy, not knowing what is happening. Bringing dishonour to the family? If he hadn't been protecting my honour this wouldn't have happened." She paused for a moment and then added, harshly, "And all you can do is snivel because you had a father who loved you enough to want what was best for you, even though you had blotted your copy book. Or have you forgotten?"

Polly shrugged. "Huh! Is that all you can say? The pot calls the kettle black. It is you, I think, that has no compassion. It's all right for you, living out here. You don't have to face all the knowing smiles and false sympathy, all the sniggers as soon as your back is turned. No. you can live here in splendid isolation and let others bear the brunt."

Her voice choked on a sob. Sarah studied

her sister. Could Polly really be so self-centred? Could she really think that she was the only one affected? Sarah was more hurt than angry that Polly should accuse her of indifference.

"I'm sorry that you should feel like that," she said, and her voice was quiet in contrast to Polly's shrill cries. "I never imagined you would believe me to be so indifferent to the sufferings of others. I've explained to you what happened and if Ned and I are guilty of keeping it from you then we are also guilty of loving you enough to care about your feelings. You are behaving exactly as we thought you would and it is for this very reason that we have kept quiet.

"You have a husband who thinks the world of you. He took you on when you were carrying another man's child and you have much to be thankful for. Go home to him, Polly. He's probably as miserable at this moment as you are. Go home and leave me to my own worries."

She didn't wait for Polly to answer but went into the scullery to continue the washing up that Polly's visit had interrupted. When she returned to the kitchen Polly had gone.

The days were long. Dan came every evening to sit with Sarah. She spoke of her pa, how she had misjudged him. And of Polly. How can a family live together, year in and year out, and not really know each other? she asked him. How can you love someone and still be prepared to think the worst of them, as she had of her pa and Polly had of Ned? Dan didn't have the answers. She didn't expect him to.

And when the fire was reduced to glowing embers, Dan had kissed her and she had waved to him from the open doorway, there were the nights to face. Nights of sleeplessness when she would stare wide-eyed into the darkness and be filled with doubts and recriminations. Had she been wrong to speak to Polly as she had? Was it her fault that Robert was in prison? And after the endless nights, when the grey mingled with red in the morning clouds, another endless day would begin.

Assiduously, she looked after the two birds in the shed. It seemed terribly important that they should not only survive but flourish. In some way she felt that, as long as they were well, everything would be all right; just as she had felt sure, as a child, that if she could cross the parlour carpet without stepping on a rose, or climb the stairs without a single one creaking, that the sun would shine for the Sunday School outing or she would do well in her next spelling test.

The day that she found the woodpigeon dead in the bottom of its cage she was filled with a grief that was so deep it physically hurt. She had hovered on the brink of despair for days and the bird's demise was enough to push her over the edge. It was the darkest, deepest thing she had ever experienced. She lost interest in what she ate and spent hours sitting motionless, staring fixedly out over the river, losing all count of time.

There was no past, no future, only an endless despair that was overwhelming at times and seemed more than could be endured.

Dan tried to console her. "It was but a bird," he said. "It would probably have died anyway."

But she would not be comforted.

Again, he implored her to come to stay at the farm but she was adamant. She must stay at home. Dan had never felt so helpless. He could only visit the prison as often as possible and bring her news of Robert.

"He is well," he told her. What he didn't say was that Robert had withdrawn into himself. It was hard to get his attention; hard to tempt him to eat the delicacies his ma kept baking.

When Robert looked at Dan it was with eyes in which life seemed to have been extinguished. Dan was haunted by those lightless eyes that spoke eloquently of the desolation that Robert must feel, and Dan was filled with a rage at the stupidity of it all.

This was the devil's own muddle, he thought, and wondered how it would all end.

Of course, it was Dan who brought the news. He stood in the lane a full five minutes before he could bring himself to walk up the path and knock on the door.

Sarah stood in the doorway, shadows beneath her eyes like great bruises, and her fingers plucking at the buttons of her blouse. Silently she searched his face and what she saw there caused a sharp intake of breath and for her to bring her hand to her mouth.

"It's bad news," she said, her voice flat but her eyes begging him to say it wasn't so. Turning, she went into the kitchen and sank onto a chair by the fire.

Dan followed, hesitating a moment in the doorway, his arm resting on the doorframe as he ducked his head. What was he going to say? How was he going to tell her?

She sat very still, her eyes never leaving his face. "Tell me, Dan. What's happened? Have they set the date back for the trial? Poor Robert. I can't bear to think of him locked up in that terrible place. He'll go mad. I know he will. A person like Robert needs to be out on the downs, breathing the fresh air…. How much longer can it be? Oh, Dan, don't keep me guessing. The reality can't be worse than what I may imagine."

At last Dan spoke. "I'd give anything not to have to be the one to bear such news…. There is no way to break it gently. Sarah… oh Sarah, Robert is dead!"

She stared at him, uncomprehending. Haltingly, he told her, the words dragged from him, his eyes shining with the tears he dare not shed. He told her how he had gone to the prison that morning, had taken a pie that his ma had made, and how the prison governor had taken him aside. And he had heard how they had discovered Robert's body that morning, hanging from the bars of the high grating. He had killed himself.

Dan wanted to tell Sarah that Robert was unlikely to have escaped the hangman's noose and, even if he had, then being locked up in an institution for the criminally insane would have been a living death. He wanted to give her some word of comfort but he knew that anything he said, at this moment, would be inadequate. They would just be words. Empty words.

He saw the anguish in her face and heard her utter a cry such as he would long remember. Gently, he drew her into his arms and held her while her cries shook her body; great heaving sobs that would not stop.

Dan cried too; for the gentle boy who lived in a silent world and had loved all the wild creatures of the earth, and for a cruel world that had allowed such a thing to happen.

How long they stood that way, he could not tell, but twilight had fallen when he drew her down onto a seat by the fire. There they sat, gazing on the glowing embers in the darkening room, both lost in thought, until he remembered and reached into his pocket to pull out a blue book. It was the book of birds that Ruth had given Robert so many years ago; the book that he had treasured and had been his constant companion.

Awkwardly, Dan held it out to her and she took it from him. A feather marked a place. Always,

Robert had used a feather to mark a page. Slowly, Sarah opened the book and looked at the page that was marked.

For a while she stared at the illustration and then she understood. Robert had left her a sign of explanation. It was a sign far more than a thousand words, had he been able to speak.

It was the picture of a magpie.

Also by
Bunny Mitchell

## The Farthing Mark

It was a hot summer, the summer of 1886, when Hannah first saw the man. She had been in the front garden and happened to look up to the summit of the downs just as he came into view. Nearing midday, the sun was high in the sky. She had to lift her hand to shield her eyes so that she could see more clearly, but something compelled her to watch the man's progress.

At first it wasn't apparent how tall he was because he was bent over the burden on his cart, but as he began the slow descent, he leant back, digging his heels into the dusty chalk track in his effort to prevent the weight of the cart running away with him. And then she could see that he was a tall man, uncommonly tall, in stiff Sunday clothes and a hard felt hat obscuring the upper part of his face so that the only part visible was a square chin and a wide mouth set in a grim line.

A small girl trailed in his shadow, dragging along a smaller boy. A solemn girl of six or seven, who kept craning her head upwards to dart uncertain eyes at the man, like a young dog trying to judge its master's mood and hoping to understand what was expected of it. She, too, was in her Sunday best: a blue cotton dress covered by a spotless white apron. On her feet she wore black button boots, coated with a fine film of dust, and her bright golden hair was tied back from her face with a blue ribbon. The little boy sucked his thumb.

Every so often the man stopped to adjust his load, unhurriedly and with great care, as if the cart contained his most treasured possession. He stroked the box and patted it two or three times before resuming his journey.

Hannah, curious, watched him as he came into the lane that led past her cottage and into the village. She was still standing at the gate as he passed by. He neither paused nor greeted her but continued on, staring straight ahead as if he hadn't seen her. The small boy, still sucking his thumb, fingers hooked over his nose, twisted his head to look back at her with round and innocent eyes.

Hannah saw, then, what was on the cart. It was a plain wooden box made of new wood, partly covered by a cloth of worn linen. She wished now that she hadn't been standing there and lowered her eyes.

She hadn't realised that the man was taking a coffin to the graveyard.

Coming Soon
(Also by Bunny Mitchell)

# Blind Bargain

The sun rested on the broad hillside where the slopes lay deep in summer grass. Now and then a blackbird called but otherwise there was nothing to disturb her solitude.

Lily had grown plump and comfortable in her old age, content to stay at home and pass the time sitting in the sunshine. Normally one day resembled another, but today she had received a letter.

A breeze rustled the paper as it lay in her lap. She picked it up, turned it over and folded it before slipping it in her pocket. It had come from France. Hector had written it; the spidery letters evidence of the shaking that plagued him these days.

So Charles had gone. Lily was glad that the end had been quick and without pain. And she was glad that he had found a peace and a quiet contentment living with Hector all these years.

He had been a truly remarkable man. And he had been kind. She had thought that when she first met him and he had never given her any cause to change her opinion. Lily smiled to herself as she remembered. He had opened up her eyes and mind and greatly influenced her creative efforts, but it had been his kindness that had enabled her to rise above the pain of delusion. She had lived a life of deception and self-deception but never once, in the ensuing years, had she regretted the time she had spent with Charles.

There were moments, though, when she had wondered about Edward. Had he really loved her? At one time she would have said yes but perhaps it had been wishful thinking and his love had only existed in her imagination. He had remarried as soon as his divorce from Eleanor had come through; an American heiress by all accounts, if the gossip was true. If she had had any doubts about her decision not to accompany him to America, they had been dispelled as soon as she heard that news.

But it had all happened so long ago. She wouldn't be thinking about it now, raking over old ground, if it hadn't been for the letter. Now her mind was travelling back to when it all began.

It seemed in that year, in the year that she had loved Edward, carried his child and married Charles, that she had lost the joy of her childhood, and when Charles had left for France, coming back had been a kind of pilgrimage.

Nobody had wanted the Big house after her father had died. Josh and Mary had their own established home, poor Freddie had died in the Great War, the others were scattered elsewhere and even Violet had surprised them all, taking off, the way she did, to join the suffragists in London. And so Lily had come back to live in Pimberton with just Hilda to look after her. Father's workshop had been cleared out, the hoary old cobwebs swept away, and Josh had enlarged the little casement windows to let in more light so that she could paint.

And how she had painted! She had been obsessed with painting children, trying to capture the innocence in their bright lively faces. She realised now that it was a search for something pure and beautiful. A panacea for her wounded feelings. A balm for her soul.

So long ago! The years since had been kind to her. Now that she was old she slept a lot and lived on her memories. So often, these days, they were the memories of childhood. It seemed as if she had come full circle and she wondered if that was the way with all mankind; to travel back down the years to where it all began.

When she closed her eyes she could see the ghosts of children in the ephemeral mists that played over the meadow, hear their laughter in the trees, their shrieks in the call of a magpie as it darted from bough to bough.

And today, perhaps because of the letter and the memories it had stirred, as she dozed she heard her mother's voice speaking to her over the years. 'One day you'll understand' she had said, that time when Lily had come running home; running home after the discovery of Charles's secret passions. What was it she was meant to understand?

She understood that it was possible to will herself into contentment, to accept the difference between what she had expected and what she discovered, what she had hoped for and what she got. But she didn't understand why some were destined to lead a life of unhappiness because of other men's bigotry. No, she didn't understand any more now than she did then.

Even the perspective of time had been unable to supply the answers.